Praise for

CHUCK PALAHNIUK

"Maybe our generation has found its Don DeLillo."
—Bret Easton Ellis

SURVIVOR

"Palahniuk is one of the freshest, most intriguing voices to appear in a long time. He rearranges Vonnegut's sly humor, DeLillo's mordant social analysis and Pynchon's antic surrealism (or is it R. Crumb's?) into a gleaming puzzle palace all his own. . . . *Survivor* is a turbo-charged, deliciously manic satire of contemporary American life."
—*Newsday*

"Convoluted, maniacally comic, partaking deeply of the America that streams toward us in the dead of the night from the cable channels—that place of outrageous expectation, slavish idolatry, fanatic consumerism, and mind-stopping banality."
—*Esquire*

FIGHT CLUB

"A volatile, brilliantly creepy satire."
—*The Washington Post*

"*Fight Club* is hot. It's great. Even I can't write that well."
—Thom Jones

"*Fight Club* is a powerful, dark, original novel. This is a memorable debut by an important new writer."
—Robert Stone

CHUCK PALAHNIUK

SURVIVOR

Chuck Palahniuk's novels are the best-selling *Lullaby* and *Fight Club* (which was made into a film by director David Fincher), *Diary*, *Invisible Monsters*, and *Choke*. He is also the author of *Fugitives and Refugees* and *Stranger Than Fiction*. He lives in the Pacific Northwest.

SURVIVOR

SURVIVOR

A NOVEL

CHUCK
PALAHNIUK

ANCHOR BOOKS
A DIVISION OF RANDOM HOUSE, INC.
NEW YORK

FIRST ANCHOR BOOKS EDITION, FEBRUARY 2000

Copyright © 1999 by Chuck Palahniuk

Library of Congress Cataloging in Publication Data
Palahniuk, Chuck.
Survivor : a novel / Chuck Palahniuk. — 1st Anchor Books ed.
p. cm.
ISBN 0-385-49872-1 (pbk.)
1. Autobiography—Authorship—Fiction. 2. Suicide victims—
Fiction. 3. Cults—Fiction. I. Title.
PS3566.A4554 S87 2000
813'54—dc21 99-053228

Book design by Chris Welch

www.anchorbooks.com

Printed in the United States of America
79B8

For Mike Keefe and Mike Smith

For Shawn Grant and Heidi Weeden and Matt Palahniuk

The agent in this book is not Edward Hibbert, who represents my work with all his humor, energy, and skill.

No one in this book is as clever as my editor, Gerry Howard.

No one anywhere is as relentless and helpful as Lois Rosenthal.

This book would not exist without the Tuesday Night Writers' Workshop at Suzy's house.

Who has pages, tonight?

SURVIVOR

47

Testing, testing. One, two, three.
Testing, testing. One, two, three.

Maybe this is working. I don't know. If you can even hear me, I don't know.

But if you can hear me, listen. And if you're listening, then what you've found is the story of everything that went wrong. This is what you'd call the flight recorder of Flight 2039. The black box, people call it, even though it's orange, and on the inside is a loop of wire that's the permanent record of all that's left. What you've found is the story of what happened.

And go ahead.

You can heat this wire to white-hot, and it will still tell you the exact same story.

Testing, testing. One, two, three.

And if you're listening, you should know right off the bat the passengers are at home, safe. The passengers, they did what you'd call their deplaning in the New Hebrides Islands. Then, after it was just him and me back in the air, the pilot parachuted out over somewhere. Some kind of water. What you'd call an ocean.

I'm going to keep saying it, but it's true. I'm not a murderer.

And I'm alone up here.

The Flying Dutchman.

And if you're listening to this, you should know that I'm alone in the cockpit of Flight 2039 with a whole crowd of those little child-sized bottles of mostly dead vodka and gin lined up on the place you sit at against the front windows, the instrument panel. In the cabin, the little trays of everybody's Chicken Kiev or Beef Stroganoff entrées are half eaten with the air conditioner cleaning up any left-over food smell. Magazines are still open to where people were reading. With all the seats empty, you could pretend everyone's just gone to the bathroom. Out of the plastic stereo headsets you can hear a little hum of prerecorded music.

Up here above the weather, it's just me in a Boeing 747-400 time capsule with two hundred leftover chocolate cake desserts and an upstairs piano bar which I can just walk up to on the spiral staircase and mix myself another little drink.

God forbid I should bore you with all the details, but I'm on autopilot up here until we run out of gas. Flame out, the pilot calls it. One engine at a time, each engine will flame out, he said. He wanted me to know just what to expect. Then he went on to bore me with a lot of details about jet engines, the venturi effect, increasing lift by increasing camber with the flaps, and how after all four engines flame out the plane will turn into a 450,000-pound glider. Then since the autopilot will have it trimmed out to fly in a straight line, the glider will begin what the pilot calls a controlled descent.

That kind of a descent, I tell him, would be nice for a change. You just don't know what I've been through this past year.

Under his parachute, the pilot still had on his nothing special blah-colored uniform that looked designed by an engineer. Except for this, he was really helpful. More helpful than I'd be with someone holding a pistol to my head and asking about how much fuel was left and how far would it get us. He told me how I could get the plane back up to cruising altitude after he'd parachuted out over the ocean. And he told me all about the flight recorder.

The four engines are numbered one through four, left to right.

The last part of the controlled descent will be a nosedive into the ground. This he calls the *terminal phase* of the descent, where you're going thirty-two feet per second straight at the ground. This he calls *terminal velocity,* the speed where objects of equal mass all travel at the same speed. Then he slows everything down with a lot of details about Newtonian physics and the Tower of Pisa.

He says, "Don't quote me on any of this. It's been a long time since I've been tested."

He says the APU, the Auxiliary Power Unit, will keep generating electricity right up to the moment the plane hits the ground.

You'll have air-conditioning and stereo music, he says, for as long as you can feel anything.

The last time I felt anything, I tell him, was a ways back. About a year ago. Top priority for me is getting him off this plane so I can finally set down my gun.

I've clenched this gun so long I've lost all feeling.

What you forget when you're planning a hijack by yourself is somewhere along the line, you might need to neglect your hostages just long enough so you can use the bathroom.

Before we touched down in Port Vila, I was running all over the cabin with my gun, trying to get the passengers and crew fed. Did they need a fresh drink? Who needed a pillow? Which did they prefer, I was asking everybody, the chicken or the beef? Was that decaf or regular?

Food service is the only skill where I really excel. The problem was all this meal service and rushing around had to be one-handed, of course, since I had to keep ahold of the gun.

When we were on the ground and the passengers and crew were deplaning, I stood at the forward cabin door and said, I'm sorry. I apologize for any inconvenience. Please have a safe and enjoyable trip and thank you for flying Blah-Blah Airlines.

When it was just the pilot and me left on board, we took off again.

The pilot, just before he jumps, he tells me how when each engine fails, an alarm will announce Flame Out in Engine Number One or Three or whichever, over and over. After all the engines are gone, the only way to keep flying will be to keep the nose up. You just pull back on the steering wheel. The yoke, he calls it. To move what he calls the elevators in the tail. You'll lose speed, but keep altitude. It will look like you have a choice, speed or height, but either way you're still going to nose-dive into the ground.

That's enough, I tell him, I'm not getting what you'd call a pilot's license. I just need to use the toilet like nobody's business. I just want him out that door.

Then we slow to 175 knots. Not to bore you with the details, but we drop to under 10,000 feet and pull open the forward cabin door. Then the pilot's gone, and even before I shut the cabin door, I stand at the edge of the doorway and take a leak after him.

Nothing in my life has ever felt that good.

If Sir Isaac Newton was right, this wouldn't be a problem for the pilot on his way down.

So now I'm flying west on autopilot at mach 0.83 or 455 miles per hour, true airspeed, and at this speed and latitude the sun is stuck in one place all the time. Time is stopped. I'm flying above the clouds at a cruising altitude of 39,000 feet, over the Pacific Ocean, flying toward disaster, toward Australia, toward the end of my life story, straight line southwest until all four engines flame out.

Testing, testing. One, two, three.

One more time, you're listening to the flight recorder of Flight 2039.

And at this altitude, listen, and at this speed, with the plane empty, the pilot says there are six or maybe seven hours of fuel left.

So I'll try to make this quick.

The flight recorder will record my every word in the cockpit. And my story won't get bashed into a zillion bloody shreds and then burned with a thousand tons of burning jet. And after the plane wrecks, people will hunt down the flight recorder. And my story will survive.

Testing, testing. One, two, three.

It was just before the pilot jumped, with the cabin door pulled inside and the military ships shadowing us, with the invisible radar tracking us, in the open doorway with the engines shrieking and the air howling past, the pilot stood there in his parachute and yelled, "So why do you want to die so bad?"

And I yelled back for him to be sure and listen to the tape.

"Then remember," he yelled. "You have only a few hours. And remember," he yelled, "you don't know exactly when the fuel will run out. There's always the chance you could die right in the middle of your life story."

And I yelled, So what else is new?

And, Tell me something I don't know.

And the pilot jumped. I took a leak, then I pushed the cabin door back into place. In the cockpit, I push the throttle forward and pull the yoke back until we fly high enough. All that's left to do is press the button and the autopilot takes charge. That brings us back to right here.

So if you're listening to this, the indestructible black box of Flight 2039, you can go look and see where this plane ended its terminal descent and what's left. You'll know I'm not a pilot after you see the mess and the crater. If you're listening to this, you know that I'm dead.

And I have a few hours to tell my story here.

So I figure there's maybe a chance I'll get this story right.

Testing, testing. One, two, three.

The sky is blue and righteous in every direction. The sun is total and burning and just right there in front. We're on top of the clouds, and this is a beautiful day forever.

So let's us take it from the top. Let me start at the start.

Flight 2039, here's what really happened. Take one.

And.

Just for the record, how I feel right now is very terrific.

And.

I've already wasted ten minutes.

And.

Action.

46

The way I live, it's hard enough to bread a veal cutlet. Some nights it's different; it's fish or chicken. But the minute my one hand is covered in raw egg and the other's holding the meat someone is going to call me in trouble.

This is almost every night of my life now.

Tonight, a girl calls me from inside a pounding dance club. Her only words I can make out are "behind."

She says, "asshole."

She says what could be "muffin" or "nothing." The fact of the matter is you can't begin to fill in the blanks so I'm in the kitchen, alone and yelling to be heard over the dance mix wherever. She sounds young and worn out, so I ask if she'll trust me. Is she tired of hurting? I ask if there's only one way to end her pain, will she do it?

My goldfish is swimming around all excited inside the fishbowl on the fridge so I reach up and drop a Valium in its water.

I'm yelling at this girl: has she had enough?

I'm yelling: I'm not going to stand here and listen to her complain.

To stand here and try to fix her life is just a big waste of time. People don't want their lives fixed. Nobody wants their problems solved. Their dramas. Their distractions. Their stories resolved. Their messes cleaned up. Because what would they have left? Just the big scary unknown.

Most people who call me already know what they want. Some want to die but are just looking for my permission. Some want to die and just need a little encouragement. A little push. Someone bent on suicide won't have much sense of humor left. One wrong word, and they're an obituary the next week. Most of the calls I get, I'm only half listening anyway. Most of the people, I decide who lives and who dies just by the tone of their voice.

This is getting nowhere with the girl at the dance club so I tell her, Kill yourself.

She's saying, "What?"

Kill yourself.

She's saying, "What?"

Try barbiturates and alcohol with your head inside a dry cleaning bag.

She says, "What?"

You cannot bread a veal cutlet and do a good job with only one hand so I tell her, now or never. Pull the trigger or don't. I'm with her right now. She's not going to die alone, but I don't have all night.

What sounds like part of the dance mix is her starting to cry really hard. So I hang up.

On top of breading a veal cutlet, these people want me to straighten their whole life out.

The phone in my one hand, I'm trying to get bread crumbs to stick with my other. Nothing should be this hard. You flop the cutlet in raw egg. Then you shake it dry, then crumbs. The problem with the cutlet is I can't get the crumbs right. Some places, the cutlet is bare. The crumbs are so thick in other places you can't tell what's inside.

It used to be this was a lot of fun. People just call you on the verge of suicide. Women would call. Here I am just alone with my goldfish, alone in my dirty kitchen breading a pork chop or whatnot, wearing just my boxers, hearing somebody's prayer. Dishing out guidance and punishment.

A guy will call. After I'm fast asleep, it happens. These calls will come all night if I don't unplug the phone. Some loser will call tonight just after the bars close to say he's sitting cross-legged on the floor in his apartment. He can't sleep without having these terrible nightmares. In his dreams, he sees planes full of people crash. It's so real and then no one will help him. He can't sleep. He can't get help. He tells me he's got a rifle tucked up under his chin and he wants me to give him one good reason not to pull the trigger.

He can't live with knowing the future and not being able to save anyone.

These victims, they call. These chronic sufferers. They call. They break up my own little tedium. It's better than television.

I tell him, Go ahead. I'm only half awake. It's three in the morning, and I have to work tomorrow. I tell him, Hurry before I fall back asleep, pull the trigger.

I tell him this isn't such a beautiful world that he has to stay in it and suffer. This isn't much of a world at all.

My job is most of the time I work for a housecleaning service. Full-time drudge. Part-time god.

Past experience tells me to hold the phone a ways from my ear when I hear the little click of the trigger. There's the blast, just a burst of static, and somewhere a receiver clunks to the floor. I'm the last person to talk to him, and I'm back asleep before the ringing in my ear starts to fade.

There's the obituary to look for the next week, six column inches about nothing that really mattered. You need the obituary, otherwise you're not sure if it happened or if it was just a dream.

I don't expect you to understand.

It's a different kind of entertainment. It's a rush, having that kind of control. The guy with the shotgun was named Trevor Hollis in his obituary, and finding out he was a real person feels wonderful. It's murder, but it's not, depending on how much credit you take. I can't even say doing crisis intervention was my own idea.

The truth is this is a terrible world, and I ended his suffering.

The idea came by accident when a newspaper did a feature about a real crisis hotline. The phone number in the paper was mine by mistake. It was a typo. Nobody read the correction they ran the next day, and people just started calling me day and night with their problems.

Please don't think I'm here to save lives. To be or not to be, I don't labor the decision. And don't think I'm above talking to women this way. Vulnerable women. Emotional cripples.

McDonald's almost hired me one time, and I only applied for the job to meet younger girls. Black girls, Hispanic, white, and Chinese girls, it says right on the job application how McDonald's hires different races and ethnic backgrounds. It's girls, girls, girls, buffet-style. Also on the application McDonald's says if you have any of the following diseases:

Hepatitis A

Salmonella

Shigella

Staphylococcus

Giardia

or Campylobacter, then you may not work there. This is more of a guarantee than you get meeting girls on the street. You can't be too careful. At least at McDonald's she's gone on the record saying she's clean. Plus, there's a very good chance she's going to be young. Pimple young. Giggling young. Silly young and as stupid as me.

Eighteen-, nineteen-, twenty-year-old girls, I only want to talk to them. Community college girls. High school seniors. Emancipated minors.

It's the same with these suicide girls calling me up. Most of them are so young. Crying with their hair wet down in the rain at a public telephone, they call me to the rescue. Curled in a ball alone in bed for days, they call me. Messiah. They call me. Savior. They sniff and choke and tell me what I ask for in every little detail.

It's so perfect some nights to hear them in the dark. The girl will just trust me. The phone in my one hand, I can imagine my other hand is her.

It's not that I want to get married. I admire guys who can commit to a tattoo.

After the newspaper got the phone number right, the calls started to peter out. The loads of people who called me at first, they were all dead or pissed off at me. No new people were calling. They wouldn't hire me at McDonald's, so I made a bunch of big sticky labels.

The labels had to stand out. You need the stickers to be easy to read at night and by somebody crying on drugs or drunk. The stickers I use are just black on white with the black letters saying:

Give Yourself, Your Life, Just One More Chance. Call Me for Help. Then my phone number.

My second choice was:

If You're a Young Sexually Irresponsible Girl with a Drinking Problem, Get the Help You Need. Call—and then my phone number.

Take my word for it. Don't make this second kind of sticker. With this kind of sticker, someone from the police will pay you a visit. Just from your phone number, they can use a reverse directory and put your name on a list as a probable felon. Forever after that you'll hear the little click . . . click . . . click . . . of a wiretap behind every telephone call you ever make.

Take my word for it.

If you use the first kind of sticker, you'll get people calling to confess sins, complain, ask advice, seek approval.

The girls you meet are never very far from their worst-case scenario. A harem of women will be clutching their telephones on the brink and asking you to call back, please, call back. Please.

Call me a sexual predator, but when I think of predators I think of lions, tigers, big cats, sharks. This isn't so much a predator versus prey relationship. This isn't a scavenger, a vulture, or a laughing hyena versus a carcass. This isn't a parasite versus a host.

We're all miserable together.

It's the opposite of a victimless crime.

What's most important is you need to put the stickers in public telephones. Try inside dirty phone booths near bridges over deep water. Put them next to taverns where people with no place to go get thrown out at closing time.

In no time at all, you'll be in business.

You'll need one of those speakerphones where it sounds like you're calling from deep inside somewhere. Then people will call in crisis and hear you flush the toilet. They'll hear the roar of the blender and know how you couldn't care less.

These days, what I need is one of those cordless telephone headsets. A kind of Walkman of human misery. Live or die. Sex or death. This way, you can make hands-free life-and-death decisions every hour when people call to talk about their one terrible crime. You give out penance. You sentence people. You give guys on the edge the phone numbers of girls in the same position.

The same as most prayers, the bulk of what you hear is complaints and demands. Help me. Hear me. Lead me. Forgive me.

The phone is ringing again already. The thin little coating of crumbs on the veal cutlet is almost impossible for me to get right, and on the phone is a new girl, crying. I ask right away if she'll trust me. I ask if she'll tell me everything.

My goldfish and me, both of us are just here swimming in one place.

The cutlet looks dug out of a cat box.

To calm this girl down, to get her to listen, I tell her the story about my fish. This is fish number six hundred and forty-one in a lifetime of goldfish. My parents bought me the first one to teach me about loving and caring for another living breathing creature of God. Six hundred and forty fish later, the only thing I know is everything you love will die. The first time you meet that someone special, you can count on them one day being dead and in the ground.

45

The night before I left home, my big brother told me everything he knew about the outside world.

In the outside world, he said, women had the power to change the color of their hair. And their eyes. And their lips.

We were on the back porch in just the light from the kitchen window. My brother, Adam, was cutting my hair the way he cut wheat, gathering handfuls of it and cutting it with a straight razor at about the halfway point. He'd pinch my chin between his thumb and forefinger and force me to look at him straight on, his brown eyes darting back and forth between each of my sideburns.

To get my sideburns even, he'd cut one, then the other, then the first, over and over until both sideburns were gone.

My seven little brothers were sitting along the edges of the porch, watching the darkness for all the evils Adam described.

In the outside world, he said, people kept birds inside their houses. He'd seen it.

Adam had been outside the church district colony just one time, when he and his wife had to register their marriage to make it legal with the government.

In the outside world, he said, people were visited in their houses by spirits they called television.

Spirits spoke to people through what they called the radio.

People used what they called a telephone because they hated being close together and they were too scared of being alone.

He went on cutting my hair, not for style as much as he was pruning it the way he'd prune a tree. Around us on the porch boards, the hair piled up, not so much cut as harvested.

In the church district colony, we hung bags of cut hair in the orchard to scare away deer. Adam told me the rule about not wasting anything is one of the blessings you give up when you leave the church colony. The hardest blessing you give up is silence.

In the outside world, he told me, there was no real silence. Not the fake silence you get when you plug your ears so you hear nothing but your heart, but real out-of-doors silence.

The week they were married, he and Biddy Gleason rode in a bus from the church district colony, escorted by a church elder. The whole trip, the bus was loud inside. The automobiles on the road with them were roaring. People in the outside world said something stupid with their every breath, and when they didn't talk their radios filled the gap with the copied voices of people singing the same songs over and over.

Adam said the other blessing you have to give up in the outside world is darkness. You can close your eyes, and sit in a cupboard, but that's not the same thing. The darkness at night in the church district colony is complete. The stars are thick above us in this kind of darkness. You can see how the moon is rough with mountain ranges and etched with rivers and smoothed with oceans.

On a night without the moon or stars you can't see a thing, but you can imagine anything.

At least that's how I remember.

My mother was inside the kitchen ironing and folding the clothes I'd be allowed to take with me. My father was I don't know where. I'd never see either of them again.

It's funny, but people always ask if she was crying. They ask if my father cried and threw his arms around me before I left. And people are always amazed when I say no. Nobody cried or hugged.

Nobody cried or hugged when we sold a pig either. Nobody cried and hugged before they killed a chicken or picked an apple.

Nobody lay awake at night wondering if the wheat they'd raised was truly happy and fulfilled being made into bread.

My brother was just cutting my hair. My mother was just done ironing and she'd sat down to sew. She was pregnant. I remember she was always pregnant, and my sisters were all around her with their skirts spread on the kitchen benches or on the floor, all of them sewing.

People always ask if I was scared or excited or what.

According to church doctrine only the firstborn son, Adam, would ever marry and grow old in the church district. When we turned seventeen the rest of us, me and my seven brothers and five sisters, would all go out for work. My father lives here because he was the firstborn son in his family. My mother lives here because the church elders chose her for my father.

People are always so disappointed if I tell them the truth, that none of us lived in oppressed turmoil. None of us resented the church. We just lived. None of us were tortured by feelings very much.

That was the complete depth of our faith. Call it shallow or deep. There was nothing that could scare us. That's how people raised in the church district colony believed. Whatever happened in the world was a decree from God. A task to be completed. Any crying or joy just got in the way of your being useful. Any emotion was decadent. Anticipation or regret was a silly extra. A luxury.

That was the definition of our faith. Nothing was to be known. Anything was to be expected.

In the outside world, Adam said it was a bargain with the devil that powered automobiles and carried airplanes across the sky. Evil flowed through electric wires to make people lazy. People put their dishes back in the cupboard dirty, and the cupboard washed them. Water in pipes carried away their garbage and shit so that it was someone else's problem. Adam pinched my chin with his thumb and forefinger and leaned down to look me straight in the face, and said how in the outside world, people looked in mirrors.

Right in front of him on the bus, he said, people had mirrors and everyone was busy seeing how they looked. It was shameful.

I remember that was the last haircut I got for a long long time, but I don't really remember why. My head was a bristling field of straw with just the short hairs that were left.

In the outside world, Adam said, all the counting was done inside machines.

All the food was fed to people by waitresses.

The one time he left the colony, my brother and his wife and the church elder who escorted them stayed overnight in a hotel in downtown Robinsville, Nebraska. They didn't any of them sleep. The next day the bus brought them home for the rest of their lives.

A hotel, he told me, was a big house where a lot of people lived and ate and slept, but no one knew each other. He said that described most families in the outside world.

Churches in the outside world, my brother told me, were just the local stores that sold people lies made up in the distant factories of giant religions.

He said a lot more I don't remember.

That haircut was sixteen years ago.

My father had sired Adam and me and all fourteen of his children by the time he was the age I am now.

I was seventeen years old the night I left home.

The way my father looked the last time I saw him is the way I look now.

Looking at Adam was as good as looking in a mirror. He was my big brother by just three minutes and thirty seconds, but in the Creedish church district there was no such thing as twins.

That last night I ever saw Adam Branson, I remember thinking my big brother was a very kind and a very wise man.

That's how stupid I was.

44

P art of my job is to preview the menu for a dinner party
tonight. This means taking a bus from the house where
I work to another big house, and asking some strange cook
what they expect everybody to eat. Who I work for doesn't
like surprises, so part of my job is telling my employers
ahead of time if tonight they'll be asked to eat something
difficult like a lobster or an artichoke. If there's anything
threatening on the menu, I have to teach them how to eat
it right.

This is what I do for a living.

The house where I clean, the man and woman who live

here are never around. That's just the kind of jobs they have. The only details I know about them are from cleaning what they own. All I can figure out is from picking up after them. Cleaning up their little messes, day after day. Rewinding their videotapes:

Full Service Anal Escorts

The giant breasts of Letha Weapons. The adventures of little Sinderella.

By the time my bus drops me off here, the people who I work for are gone to work downtown. By the time they drive home, I'm back downtown in my housing voucher studio apartment that used to be just a tiny hotel room until somebody crowded in a stove and a fridge to raise the rent. The bathroom's still out in the hall.

The only way I ever talk to my employers is by speakerphone. This is just a plastic box sitting on their kitchen counter and yelling at me to get more done.

Ezekiel, Chapter Nineteen, Verse Seven:

"And he knew their desolate palaces . . ." something, something, something. You can't keep the whole Bible balanced in your head. You wouldn't have room to remember your name.

The house I've been cleaning the last six years is about what you'd expect, big, and it's in a real tony part of town. This is compared to where I live. All the studio apartments in my neighborhood are the same as a warm toilet seat. Somebody was there just a second before you and somebody will be there the minute you get up.

The part of town where I go to work every morning, there are paintings on the walls. Behind the front door, there are rooms and rooms nobody ever goes into. Kitchens where nobody cooks. Bathrooms that never get dirty. The money they leave out to test me, will I take it, the money is never less than a fifty-dollar bill, dropped behind the dresser as if by accident. The clothes they own look designed by an architect.

Next to the speakerphone is a fat daily planner book they keep full of things for me to get done. They want me to account for my next ten years, task by task. Their way, everything in your life turns into an item on a list. Something to accomplish. You get to see how your life looks flattened out.

The shortest distance between two points is a time line, a schedule, a map of your time, the itinerary for the rest of your life.

Nothing shows you the straight line from here to death like a list.

"I want to be able to look at your planner," the speakerphone yells at me, "and know exactly where I can find you at four o'clock on this day five years from now. I want you to be that exact."

Seeing it down in black and white, somehow you're always disappointed in your life expectancy. How little you'll really get done. The résumé of your future.

It's two o'clock Saturday afternoon so according to my daily planner, I'm about to boil five lobsters for them to practice eating. That's how much money they make.

The only way I can afford to eat veal is when I smuggle it home on the bus sitting in my lap.

The secret to boiling a lobster is simple. First you fill a kettle with cold water and a pinch of salt. You can use equal parts of water and vermouth or vodka. You can add some seaweed to the water for a stronger flavor. These are the basics they teach in Home Economics.

Most everything else I know is from the messes these people leave behind.

Just ask me how to get bloodstains out of a fur coat.

No, really, go ahead.

Ask me.

The secret is cornmeal and brushing the fur the wrong way. The tricky part is keeping your mouth shut.

To get blood off of piano keys, polish them with talcum powder or powdered milk.

This isn't the most marketable job skill, but to get bloodstains out of wallpaper, put on a paste of cornstarch and cold water. This will work just as well to get blood out of a mattress or a davenport. The trick is to forget how fast these things can happen. Suicides. Accidents. Crimes of passion.

Just concentrate on the stain until your memory is completely erased. Practice really does make perfect. If you could call it that.

Ignore how it feels when the only real talent you have is for hiding the truth. You have a God-given knack for committing a terrible sin. It's your calling. You have a natural gift for denial. A blessing.

If you could call it that.

Even after sixteen years of cleaning people's houses, I want to think the world is getting better and better, but really I know it's not. You want there to be some improvement in people, but there won't be. And you want to think there's something you can get done.

Cleaning this same house every day, all that gets better is my skill at denying what's wrong.

God forbid I should ever meet who I work for in person.

Please don't get the idea I don't like my employers. The caseworker has gotten me lots worse postings. I don't hate them. I don't love them, but I don't hate them. I've worked for lots worse.

Just ask me how to get urine stains out of drapes and a tablecloth.

Ask me what's the fastest way to hide bullet holes in a living-room wall. The answer is toothpaste. For larger calibers, mix a paste of equal parts starch and salt.

Call me the voice of experience.

Five lobsters is how many I figure they'll take to learn the tricky details of getting the back open. The carapace, I figure. Inside's the brain or the heart you're supposed to be hunting for. The trick is to put the lobsters in the water and then turn up the heat. The secret is to go slow. Allow at least thirty minutes for the water to reach a hundred degrees. This way, the lobsters are supposed to die a painless death.

My daily planner tells me to keep busy, polishing the copper the best way, with half a lemon dipped in salt.

These lobsters we have to practice with are called Jumbos since they're around three pounds apiece. Lobsters under a pound are called Chickens. Lobsters missing a claw are called Culls. The ones I take out of the refrigerator packed in wet seaweed will need to boil about half an hour. This is more stuff you learn in Home Economics.

Of the two large forward claws, the larger claw lined with what look like molars is called the Crusher. The smaller claw lined with incisors is called the Cutter. The smaller side legs are called the Walking Legs. On the underside of the tail are five rows of small fins called Swimmerets. More Home Economics. If the front row of swimmerets is soft and feathery, the lobster is female. If the front row is hard and rough, the lobster is male.

If the lobster is female, look for a bony heart-shaped hollow between the two rear walking legs. This is where the female will still be carrying live sperm if she's had sex within the past two years.

The speakerphone rings while I'm setting the lobsters, three male and two female, no sperm, in the pot on the stove.

The speakerphone rings as I turn up the heat just another notch.

The speakerphone rings while I wash my hands.

The speakerphone rings while I go pour myself a cup of coffee and mix in cream and sugar.

The speakerphone rings while I take a handful of seaweed from the lobster bag and sprinkle it in on top of the lobsters in the pot. One lobster lifts a crusher claw for a stay of execution. Crusher claws and cutter claws, they're all rubber-banded.

The speakerphone rings while I go wash and dry my hands again.

The speakerphone rings, and I answer it.

Gaston House, I say.

"Gaston *Residence!*" the speakerphone yells at me. "Say it, Gaston *Residence! Say it the way we told you how!"

What they teach you in Home Economics is it's correct to call a house a *residence* only in printing and engraving. We've gone over this a million times.

I drink a little coffee and fiddle with the heat under the lobsters. The speakerphone keeps yelling, "Is anyone there? Hello? Have we been cut off?"

This couple I work for, at one party they were the only guests who didn't know to lift the doily with the finger bowl. Since then, they've been addicted to learning etiquette. They still say it's pointless, it's useless, but they're terrified of not knowing every little ritual.

The speakerphone keeps yelling, "Answer me! Damn it! Tell me about the party tonight! What kind of food are we going up against? We've been worried sick all day!"

I look in the cabinet over the stove for the lobster gear, the nutcrackers and nutpicks and bibs.

Thanks to my lessons, these people know all three acceptable ways to place your dessert silver. It's my doing that they can drink iced tea the right way with the long spoon still in the glass. This is tricky, but you have to hold the spoon handle between your index and middle fingers, against the edge of the glass opposite your mouth. Be careful to not poke your eye out. Not a lot of people know this way. You see people taking the wet spoon out and looking for a place to set it and not wreck the tablecloth. Or worse, they just put it anywhere and leave a wet tea stain.

When the speakerphone goes silent, then and only then do I start.

I ask the speakerphone, Are you listening?

I tell the speakerphone, Picture a dinner plate.

Tonight, I say, the spinach soufflé will be at the one-o'clock position. The beets thing will be at four o'clock. A meat thing with slivered almonds was going to be on the other half of the plate in the nine-o'clock position. To eat it, the guests would have to use a knife. And there are going to be bones in the meat.

This is the best posting I've ever had, no kids, no cats, no-wax floors, so I don't want to botch it. If I didn't care, I'd start telling who I work for to do any monkey business I could imagine. Like: You eat the sorbet by licking it out of the bowl, dog-dish fashion.

Or: Pick up the lamb chop with your teeth and shake your head vigorously, side to side.

And what's terrible is they'd probably do this. It's because I've never steered them wrong, they trust me.

Except for teaching them etiquette, my toughest challenge is living down to their expectations.

Ask me how to repair stab holes in nightgowns, tuxedos, and hats. My secret is a little clear nail polish on the inside of the puncture.

Nobody teaches you all the job skills you need in Home Economics, but over enough time, you pick them up. In the church district where I grew up, they teach you the way to make candles dripless is soak them in strong salt water. Store candles in the freezer until ready to use. That's their kind of household hint. Light candles with a strand of raw spaghetti. Sixteen years I've been cleaning for people in their homes, and never has anybody asked me to walk around with a piece of spaghetti on fire in my hand.

No matter what they stress in Home Economics, it's just not a priority in the outside world.

For example, no one teaches you that green-tinted moisturizer will help hide red, slapped skin. And any gentleman who's ever been backhanded by a lady with her diamond ring should know a styptic pencil will stop the bleeding. Close the gash with a dab of Super Glue and you can be photographed at a movie premier, smiling and without stitches or a scar.

Always keep a red washcloth around for wiping up blood, and you'll never have a stain to presoak.

My daily planner tells me I'm sharpening a butcher knife.

About the dinner tonight, I keep briefing who I work for about what to expect.

The important part is not to panic. Yes, there's going to be a lobster they'll have to deal with.

There's going to be a single saltcellar. A game course will be served after the roast. The game is going to be squab. It's a kind of bird, and if there's anything more complicated to eat than a lobster, it's a squab. All those little bones you have to dismantle, everybody dressed up for their dissection. Another wine will come after the aperitif, the sherry with the soup course, the white wine with the lobster, the red with the roast, another red wine with the greasy ordeal of the squab. By this time, the table will be spotted with everybody's piddling island archipelagoes of dressings and sauces and wine sprayed across the white tablecloth.

This is how my job goes. Even in a good posting, nobody wants to know where the male guest of honor is supposed to sit.

That exquisite dinner your teachers in Home Economics talked about, the pause with fresh flowers and demitasse after a perfect day of poise and elegant living, well, nobody gives a rat's ass about that.

Tonight, at some moment between the soup course and the roast, everybody at the table will get to mutilate a big dead lobster. Thirty-four captains of industry, thirty-four successful monsters, thirty-four acclaimed savages in black tie will pretend they know how to eat.

And after the lobster, the footmen will present hot finger bowls with floating slices of lemon, and these thirty-four botched autopsies will end with garlic and butter up to the elbow of every sleeve and every smiling greasy face will look up from sucking out meat from some cavity in the thorax.

After seventeen years of working in private houses every day, the things I know the most about are slapped faces, creamed corn, black eyes, wrenched shoulders, beaten eggs, kicked shins, scratched corneas, chopped onions, bites of all sorts, nicotine stains, sexual lubricants, knocked-out teeth, split lips, whipped cream, twisted arms, vaginal tears, deviled ham, cigarette burns, crushed pineapple, hernias, terminated pregnancies, pet stains, shredded coconut, gouged eyes, sprains, and stretch marks.

The ladies who you work for, after they sob for hours on end, make them use blue or mauve eyeliner to make their bloodshot eyes look whiter. The next time someone socks a tooth out of her husband's mouth, save the tooth in a glass of milk until he can see the dentist. In the meantime, mix zinc oxide and oil of cloves into a white paste. Rinse the empty socket and pack it with the paste for a quick and easy filling that hardens lickety-split.

For tear stains in a pillow case, treat them the same way you would a perspiration stain. Dissolve five aspirin in water and daub the stain until it's gone. Even if there's a mascara stain, the problem's solved.

If you could call it solved.

Whether you clean a stain, a fish, a house, you want to think you're making the world a better place, but really you're just letting things get worse. You think maybe if you just work harder and faster, you can hold off the chaos, but then one day you're changing a patio lightbulb with a five-year life span and you realize how you'll only be changing this light maybe ten more times before you'll be dead.

Time is running out. There isn't the kind of energy you used to have. You start to slow down.

You start to give in.

This year there's hair on my back, and my nose keeps getting bigger. How my face looks every morning is more and more what you'd call a mug.

After working in these rich houses, I know the best way to get blood out of the trunk of a car is not to ask any questions.

The speakerphone is saying, "Hello?"

The best way to keep a good job is just do what they want.

The speakerphone is saying, "Hello?"

To get lipstick out of a collar, rub in a little white vinegar.

For stubborn protein-based stains, like semen, try rinsing with cold salt water, then wash as usual.

This is valuable on-the-job training. Feel free to take notes.

To pick up broken glass from that jimmied bedroom window or smashed highball, you can blot up even the tiniest shards with a slice of bread.

Stop me if you already know all this.

The speakerphone is saying, "Hello?"

Been there. Done that.

What else they teach you in Home Economics is the correct way to respond to a wedding invitation. How to address the Pope. The right way to monogram silver. In the Creedish church school, they teach how the world can be a perfect elegant little stage play of perfect manners where you're the director. The teachers, they paint a picture of dinner parties where everyone will already know how to eat a lobster.

Then it's not.

Then all you can do is get lost in the tiny details of every day doing the same tasks over and over.

There's the fireplace to clean.

There's the lawn to mow.

Turn all the bottles in the wine cellar.

There's the lawn to mow, again.

There's the silver to polish.

Repeat.

Still, just one time, I'd like to prove I know something better. I can do more than just cover up. The world can be a lot better than we settle for. All you have to do is ask.

No, really, go ahead. Ask me.

How do you eat an artichoke?

How do you eat asparagus?

Ask me.

How do you eat a lobster?

The lobsters in the pot look dead enough so I lift one out. I tell the speakerphone, First, twist off each of the big front claws.

The other lobsters I'll put in the refrigerator for them to practice taking apart. To the speakerphone I say, Take notes.

I crack the claws and eat the meat inside.

Then bend the lobster backward until its tail snaps away from its body. Snap off the tip of the tail, the Telson, and use a seafood fork to push out the tail meat. Remove the intestinal vein that runs the length of the tail. If the vein is clear, the lobster hasn't eaten anything for a while. A thick dark vein is fresh and still full of dung.

I eat the tail meat.

The seafood fork, I tell the speakerphone with my mouth full, the seafood fork is the little baby fork with three prongs.

Next, you unhinge the back shell, the carapace, from the body, and eat the green digestive gland called the Tomalley. Eat the copper-based blood that congeals into white gunk. Eat the coral-colored immature egg masses.

I eat them all.

Lobsters have what you'd call an "open" circulatory system where the blood just sloshes around inside their cavities, bathing the different organs.

The lungs are spongy and tough, but you can eat them, I tell the speakerphone and lick my fingers. The stomach is the tough sack of what look like teeth just behind the head. Don't eat the stomach.

I dig around inside the body. I suck the little meat out of each walking leg. I bite off the tiny gill bailers. I bypass the ganglia of the brain.

I stop.

What I find is impossible.

The speakerphone is yelling, "Okay, now what? Was that everything? What's there left to eat?"

This can't be happening because according to my daily planner, it's almost three o'clock. I'm supposed to be outside digging up the garden. At four, I'll rearrange the flower beds. At five-thirty, I'll pull up the salvia and replace them with dutch iris, roses, snapdragons, ferns, ground cover.

The speakerphone is yelling, "What is happening there? Answer me! What's gone wrong?"

I check my schedule, and it says I'm happy. I'm productive. I work hard. It's all right down here in black and white. I'm getting things done.

The speakerphone yells, "What do we do next?"

Today is just one of those days the sun comes out to really humiliate you.

The speakerphone yells, "What's there left to do?"

I ignore the speakerphone because there's nothing left to do. Almost nothing's left.

And maybe this is just a trick of the light, but I've eaten almost the whole lobster before I notice the heart beat.

43

According to my daily planner, I'm trying to keep my balance. I'm up at the top of a ladder with my arms full of fake flowers: roses, daisies, delphiniums, stock. I'm trying to keep from falling, my toes curled up tight in my shoes. I'm collecting another polyester bouquet, an obituary from last week all folded up in my shirt pocket.

The man I killed last week is around here somewhere. What's left of him. The one with the shotgun under his chin, sitting alone in his empty apartment, asking over the phone for me to give him just one good reason not to pull the trigger, I'm sure enough going to find him. Trevor Hollis.

Gone But Not Forgotten.

Resting in Peace.

Called from This Life.

Or he's going to find me. That's what I always hope.

Up at the top of a ladder, I must be twenty, twenty-five, thirty feet above the gallery floor while I pretend to catalog another artificial flower, my glasses pinching at the end of my nose. My pen leaves words in my notebook. Specimen Number 786, I'm writing, is a red rose around a hundred years old.

What I hope is everybody else here is dead.

Part of my job is I have to arrange fresh flowers around the house where I work. I have to pick flowers out of the garden I'm supposed to tend.

What you need to understand is I'm not a ghoul.

The petals and calyx (sepals) of the rose are red celluloid. First created in 1863, celluloid is the oldest and least stable form of plastic. I'm writing in my notebook, the leaves of the rose are green-tinted celluloid.

I stop writing and look over my glasses. Down at the end of the gallery and so far away she's just a tiny black outline against a huge stained-glass window is somebody. The stained glass is a picture of somewhere, Sodom or Jericho or the Temple of Solomon being destroyed by fire in the Old Testament, silent and blazing. Twisted feathers of orange and red flame twist around falling blocks of stone, pillars, friezes, and out of this walks a figure in a little black dress getting bigger as she gets close.

And what I hope is she's dead. My secret wish is right now to be romancing this dead girl. A dead girl. Any dead girl. I'm not what you'd call choosy.

The lie I tell people is I'm doing research into the evolution of artificial flowers during the Industrial Revolution. All this is supposed to be my thesis for Nature and Design 456. Why I'm so old is I'm a graduate student.

The girl has long red hair that women only have these days if it's part of some orthodox religion. From up so high on my ladder, the thin bendable little arms and legs of the girl make me look again and again and wonder if someday I could be a pedophile.

Although not the oldest specimen in my study, this rose I pretend to examine is the most fragile. The female sex organ, the Pistil, including the Stigma, the Style, and the Ovary, are cast jet. The male sex organs, the Stamen, include a wire Filament topped with a tiny glass Anther.

Part of my job is I have to grow fresh flowers in the garden, but I can't. I can't grow a weed.

The lie I tell myself is I'm here to gather flowers, fresh ones for inside the house. I steal the fake flowers for sticking out in the garden. The people I work for only look at their garden from inside so I stick the bare dirt full of fake greenery, ferns or needlepoint ivy, then I stick in fake seasonal flowers. The landscaping is beautiful as long as you don't look too close.

The flowers look so lifelike. So natural. So peaceful.

The best place to find bulbs for forcing is in the Dumpster behind the mausoleum. Thrown away are plastic pots of dormant bulbs, hyacinths and tulips, tiger and stargazer lilies, daffodils and crocus ready to take home and bring back to life.

Specimen Number 786, I write, occurs in the vase of Crypt 2387, in the highest tier of Crypts, in the lesser south gallery, on the seventh floor of the Serenity wing. This location, I write, thirty feet above the floor of the gallery, might account for the almost perfect condition of this rose, found on one of the oldest crypts in one of the original wings of the Columbia Memorial Mausoleum.

Then I steal the rose.

What I tell people who see me here is another story.

The official version for why I'm here is this mausoleum provides the best examples of artificial flowers dating back into the mid nineteenth century. Each of the six main wings, the Serenity wing, the

Contentment wing, the Eternity, Tranquillity, Harmony, and New Hope wings, is five to eighteen stories tall. The concrete honeycomb of every wall is nine feet thick so it can accommodate even the longest casket inserted lengthwise. Air doesn't circulate in the miles of galleries. Visitors seldom visit. Their typical visit is short. The average year-round temperature and humidity are low and constant.

The oldest specimens derive from the culture of Victorian flower language. Based on the 1840 classic *Le langage des fleurs* by Madame de la Tour, purple lilacs meant death. White lilacs, the genus *Syringa,* meant the first discovery of love.

The geranium meant gentility.

The buttercup, childishness.

Because most artificial flowers were made to decorate hats, a mausoleum provides the best specimens that still exist.

That's what I tell people. My official version of the truth.

During the day, if people see me with my notebook and my pen, most times I'm at the top of a ladder swiping some bunch of fake pansies left at a crypt high in the wall. It's for a college class is what I cup my hand around my mouth and whisper down to them.

I'm conducting a study.

Sometimes I'll be here late at night. This is after everyone's gone. Then I'll be walking around alone after midnight and my dream is that some night around the next corner will be an open crypt in the wall and near it will be a desiccated cadaver, the skin wilted on its face and its dress suit stiff and blotched with the fluids dripping and leaked out of its body. I'll come across this carcass in some dim gallery, silent except for the buzz of a single fluorescent tube flashing strobes of lightning in the last few moments before it will leave me in the dark, forever, with this dead monster.

The cadaver eyes should be collapsed into dark sockets, and I want it to stumble blind and clutching the cold marble walls with smears of rotted paste that expose the bones inside each hand. The tired mouth of it hanging open, the lost nose of it just two dark holes, the loose shirt of it resting low on the exposed collarbones.

I'll be looking for names I know from the obituaries. Carved here forever are the names of people who took my advice.

Go ahead. Kill yourself.

Beloved Son. Gentle Daughter. Devoted Friend.

Pull the trigger.

Exalted soul.

Here I am. It's payback time. I dare you to.

Come and get me.

I want to be chased by flesh-eating zombies.

I want to be walking past the marble slab covering a crypt and hear something scratching and struggling inside. At night, I flatten my ear cold against the marble and wait. This is why I'm really here.

Specimen Number 786, I write in my notebook, has a main stem of green cotton-covered 30-gauge millinery wire. Each leaf stem appears to be 20-gauge.

Not that I'm crazy or anything, I just want some proof that death isn't the end. Even if crazed zombies grabbed me in some dark hall one night, even if they tore me apart, at least that wouldn't be the absolute end. There would be some comfort in that.

It would prove some kind of life after death, and I would die happy. So I wait. So I watch. I listen. I put my ear to each cold crypt. I write, No activity within Crypt 7896.

No activity within Crypt 7897.

No activity within Crypt 7898.

I write, Specimen Number 45 is a white Bakelite rose. The oldest synthetic plastic, Bakelite was invented in 1907 when a chemist heated a mixture of phenol and formaldehyde. In the language of Victorian flower culture, a white rose means silence.

The day I meet the girl is the best day to document new flowers. It's the day after Memorial Day weekend when the crowds are gone for another year. It's with everyone gone that I first see this girl I hope will be dead.

The day after Memorial Day, the janitor comes along with a rolling garbage bin and collects all the fresh flowers. The lowest grade of fresh flowers is what florists call "Funeral Grade."

The janitor and I have crossed paths, but we've never spoken. Him in his blue coveralls, he caught me one time with my ear to a crypt. The circle of his flashlight spotlighting me there, even that time he only looked the other way. With the heel of one shoe in my hand, I was knocking and saying, Hello. In Morse code I was asking, could anybody hear me?

The problem with Funeral Grade flowers is they only look good for one day. A day later, they start to rot. Then with flowers hanging from the bronze vase attached to each crypt, hanging there dark and withered, dripping their stink water on the marble floor and furry with mold, it's too easy to imagine what's happening to the beloved sealed inside.

The day after Memorial Day, the janitor throws them out. The wilting flowers.

Left behind is a new crop of fake peonies, dark magenta and soaked with dye to make their silk almost black. This year there are artificially perfumed sprays of plastic orchids. The long poly-silk vines of blue and white huge morning glories are worth the trouble to steal.

The oldest old specimens include flowers made of chiffon, organza, velvet, velveteen georgette, crepe de chine, and wide satin ribbon. Heaped in my arms are snapdragons, sweet peas, and salvia. Hollyhocks, four-o'clocks, and forget-me-nots. Fake and beautiful but stiff and scratchy, this year the new flowers are spritzed with clear droplets of polystyrene plastic dew.

This year, this girl is here a day late with a nothing-special assortment of polyester tulips and anemone, the classic Victorian flower of sorrow and death, of sickness and desertion, and watching her from my ladder, at the far end of the west gallery, on the sixth floor of Contentment, making notes in my little field guide, is me.

The flower in front of me is Specimen 237, a postwar rayon

chrysanthemum, postwar because there wasn't silk enough or rayon or wire enough to make flowers during World War Two. Wartime flowers are crepe paper or rice paper, and even in the constant dry fifty degrees of the Columbia Memorial Mausoleum, these flowers have all crumbled to dust.

In front of me is Crypt Number 678, Trevor Hollis, age twenty-four, survived by his mother and father and his sister. Much Beloved. Loving Son. In Loving Remembrance. My latest victim. I've found him.

Crypt Number 678 is in a tier high up in the gallery wall. The only way to get a closer look is with a stepladder or a casket lift, and even from the top of a stepladder, two steps higher than is safe, I can see something is different about the girl. It's something European. Something malnourished. It isn't the daily recommended allowance of food and sunshine that make you beautiful by any North American standard. There's something waxy about how her arms and legs come out of her dress looking raw and white. You could see her living behind barbed wire. And coming up inside me is the desperate hope that maybe she's dead. This is how I feel watching old movies at home where vampires and zombies come back from the grave, hungry for human flesh. Inside me is the same desperate hope I have watching the ravenous undead and thinking, Oh please, oh please, oh please.

The craving inside of me is to be clutched at by some dead girl. To put my ear to her chest and be hearing nothing. Even getting munched on by zombies beats the idea that I'm only flesh and blood, skin and bone. Demon or angel or evil spirit, I just need something to show itself. Ghoulie or ghosty or long-legged beastie, I just want my hand held.

From up here in the sixth tier of crypts, her black dress looks ironed to a high gloss. The thin white arms and legs of her look covered tight in a newer low-quality kind of human skin. Even from up high, her face looks mass-produced.

Song of Solomon, Chapter Seven, Verse One:

"How beautiful are thy feet with shoes, O prince's daughter! the joints of thy thighs are like jewels. . . ."

Even with the sun on everything outside, everything inside is still cold to the touch. The light is through stained glass. The smell is rain soaked into the walls made of cement. The feel of everything is polished marble. The sound is somewhere, the drip of old rain sliding along rebar, the drip of rain through the cracked skylights, the drip of rain inside unsold crypts.

Rolled airy shapes of collected dust and dander and hair wander around the floor. Ghost turds, people call those.

The girl looks up and has to see me, and then she's coming soundless in her black felt kind of shoes across the marble floor.

You can get lost easy enough here. Hallways run into hallways at odd angles. Finding the right crypt takes a map. Galleries open into galleries in telescope vistas so long the carved sofa or the marble statue at the far end could be something you'd never imagine. The repeating pastel soft shades of marble are so after you're lost you don't panic.

The girl walks up to the ladder, and I'm trapped at the top, halfway between her at my feet and the heaven of angels painted on the ceiling. The wall of polished marble crypts reflects me full-length among the epitaphs.

This Stone Erected in the Honor.

Erected on This Spot.

Erected in Loving Tribute.

I am all of the above.

My cold fingers feel crabbed around my pen. Specimen Number 98 is a pink camellia of china silk. The absolute pink proves the cultivated silk was boiled in soapy water to remove all sericin. The primary stem is a wire cast in green polypropylene typical of shrubs of the period. A camellia is supposed to mean unmatched excellence.

The girl's plain round mask of a face looks up at me from the foot of the ladder. How to tell if she's alive or a ghost, I don't know. There's too much of her dress for me to see any rise and fall of her chest. The air is too warm for her breathing to show.

Song of Solomon, Chapter Seven, Verse Two:

"Thy navel is like a round goblet which wanteth not liquor: thy belly is like an heap of wheat set about with lilies."

The Bible collapses sex and food a lot.

Here with Specimen Number 136, little conch shells painted pink to look like rosebuds, and Specimen Number 78, the Bakelite daffodil, I want to be hugged in her cold, dead arms and told that life has no absolute end. My life is not some Funeral Grade bit of compost that will rot tomorrow and be outlived by my name in an obituary.

The feeling in those miles of marble walls with people sealed inside, you get the sense we're in a crowded building dense with thousands of people, but at the same time, we're alone. A year could pass between her asking a question and my answer.

My breath fogs the carved dates that bracket the short life of Trevor Hollis. The epitaph reads:

> To the World He Was a Loser,
> But to Me He Was the World.

Trevor Hollis, do your worst. I dare you, come and seek your revenge.

Her head thrown back, the girl smiles up at me standing above her. Against the gray of everything stone, her red hair blazes, and up at me, she says, "You brought flowers."

My arms shift and some flowers, violas, daisies, dahlias, float down around her.

She catches a hydrangea and says, "Nobody's been here to visit since the funeral."

Song of Solomon, Chapter Seven, Verse Three:

"Thy two breasts are like two young roes that are twins."

Her mouth with its too-thin red-red lips looks cut open with a knife. She says, "Hi. I'm Fertility."

She hands the flower up and holds it in the air as if I'm not impossibly out of her reach, and she asks, "So, how did you know my brother, Trevor?"

H er name was Fertility Hollis. That's her full name, no kidding, and she's what I really want to share about the next day with my caseworker.

It's part of my terms of observation, I have to meet with my caseworker for one hour, once a week. In exchange, I keep getting housing vouchers. The program makes me eligible for subsidized housing. Free government cheese, powdered milk, honey, and butter. Free job placement. These are just a few of the perks you get in the Federal Survivor Retention Program. My doggy little apartment and surplus cheese. My doggy little job with all the veal I can smuggle home on the bus. You get just enough to make ends meet.

You don't get anything really choice, you don't get handicapped parking, but once a week for one hour, you get a caseworker. Every Tuesday, mine drives up to the house where I'm working in her plain-colored government pool car with her professional compassion and case history folders and her mileage log for keeping track of the miles between each client visit. This week, she has twenty-four clients. Last week, she had twenty-six.

Every Tuesday she comes to listen.

Every week, I ask her how many survivors are left, nationwide.

She's in the kitchen scarfing daiquiris and tortilla chips. Her shoes are kicked off and her canvas tote bag full of client files is on the kitchen table between us while she takes out a clipboard and flips through the client weekly status forms to put mine on top. She wipes her fingertip down a column of numbers, and says, "One hundred and fifty-seven survivors. Nationwide."

She starts filling in the date and checks her watch for the time to write on my weekly check-in form. She turns her clipboard around for me to read and hands it over for my signature at the bottom. This is to prove she was here. That we talked. We shared. She handed me a pen. We opened our hearts. Hear me, heal me, save me, believe me. It's not her fault if after she leaves I cut my throat.

While I'm signing the form she asks, "Did you know the woman down the street who worked in the big gray-and-tan house?"

No. Yeah. Okay, I know who she's talking about.

"Big woman. Long blond hair in a braid. A real Brunhild," the caseworker says. "Well, she checked out two nights ago. She hung herself with an extension cord." The caseworker looks at her fingernails, first with her fingers curled into her palms, then with her fingers spread wide. She goes back into her big tote bag and gets a bottle of bright red fingernail polish. "Well," she says. "Good riddance. I never liked her."

I hand the clipboard back and ask, Anybody else?

"A gardener," she says. She starts shaking the little bottle of bright red with a long white top next to her ear. With her other hand, she flips through the forms to find one. She holds the clipboard up for me to see this week's check-in form for Client Number 134, stamped with the big red word RELEASED. Then the date.

The stamp is something left over from an inpatient hospital program. In some other program RELEASED used to mean a client was set free. Now it means a client is dead. Nobody wanted to special-order a stamp that said DEAD. The caseworker told me this a few years ago when the suicides started back up again. Ashes to ashes. Dust to dust. This is how things get recycled.

"This guy drank some kind of herbicide," she says. Her hands twist the bottle between them. They twist. They twist until her knuckles look white. She says, "These people will do anything to make me look incompetent."

She knocks the bottle on the edge of the table and tries to twist it open again. "Here," she says and hands it across the table to me. "Open this for me, will you?"

I open the bottle, no problem, and hand it back.

"So did you know these two?" she says.

Well, no. I didn't know them. I knew who they were, but I don't remember them from before. I didn't know them from growing up, but over the past few years I'd seen them around the neighborhood. They still wore the old regulation church clothes. The man wore the suspenders, the baggy pants, the long-sleeved shirt with the collar buttoned on even the hottest day of summer. The woman wore the blah-colored smock of a dress I remember church women had to wear. On her head, she still wore the bonnet. The man always wore the wide-brimmed hat, straw in summer, black felt in winter.

Yeah. Okay. I saw them around. They were hard to miss.

"When you saw them," the caseworker says as she's sliding the little paintbrush, red on red, down the length of each nail, "were you upset? Did seeing people from your old church ever make you sad? Did you cry? Seeing people the way they used to dress when you were part of the church, did it maybe make you angry?"

The speakerphone rings.

"Does it make you remember your parents?"

The speakerphone rings.

"Does it make you angry about what happened to your family?"

The speakerphone rings.

"Do you ever remember what it was like before the suicides?"

The speakerphone rings.

The caseworker says, "Are you going to answer that?"

In a minute. First I have to check my daily planner. I hold the fat book up for her to see the list of everything I'm supposed to get done today. The people I work for try to call and trip me up. God forbid I should be inside to answer the phone if right this minute I'm supposed to be outside cleaning the pool.

The speakerphone rings.

According to my daily planner book, I'm supposed to be steaming the drapes in the blue guest room. Whatever that means.

The caseworker's crunching tortilla chips so I wave at her to quiet down.

The speakerphone rings, and I answer it.

The speakerphone yells, "What can you tell us about tonight's banquet?"

Relax, I say. It's a no-brainer. Salmon with no bones. Some kind of bite-sized carrots. Braised endive.

"What's that?"

It's a burned leaf, I say. You eat it with the little fork farthest to the left. Tines down. You already know braised endive. I know you know braised endive. You had it last year at a Christmas party. You love braised endive. Eat just three bites, I tell the speakerphone. I promise you'll love it.

The speakerphone asks, "Could you get the stains out of the fireplace mantel?"

According to my daily planner book, I'm not supposed to do that task until tomorrow.

"Oh," the speakerphone says. "We forgot."

Yeah. Right. You forgot.

Sleazes.

You could call me a gentleman's gentleman but you'd be wrong on both counts.

"Anything else we should know about?"

It's Mother's Day.

"Oh, shit. Fuck. Damn!" the speakerphone says. "Have you gone ahead and sent something? Are we covered?"

Of course. I sent each of their mothers a beautiful flower arrangement, and the florist will bill their account.

"What did you say in the card?"

I said:

To My Dearest Mother Whom I Cherish and Always Remember. A Loving Son/Daughter Has Never Had a Mother Who Loved Him/Her More. With My Deepest Love. Then the applicable signature.

Then P.S.: A dried flower is just as lovely as a fresh one.

"Sounds good. That should hold them for another year," the speakerphone says. "Remember to water all the plants in the sunporch. It's written in the planner book."

Then they hang up. They never have to remind me to do anything. They just have to have the last word.

No sweat off my back.

The caseworker is fanning her fresh red nails back and forth in front of her mouth and blowing them dry. Between long exhales, she asks, "Your family?"

She blows her nails.

She asks, "Your own mother?"

She blows her nails.

"Do you remember your mother?"

She blows her nails.

"Do you think she felt anything?"

She blows her nails.

"I mean, when she killed herself?"

Matthew, Chapter Twenty-four, Verse Thirteen:

"But he that shall endure to the end, the same shall be saved."

According to my daily planner, I should be cleaning the air conditioner filter. I should be dusting the green living room. There's the brass doorknobs to polish. There's all the old newspapers to recycle.

The hour is almost up, and what I never got to talk about was Fertility Hollis. How we met at the mausoleum. We walked around for an hour, and she told me about different twentieth-century art movements and how they depicted Jesus crucified. In the oldest wing of the mausoleum, the wing called Contentment, Jesus is gaunt and romantic with a woman's huge wet eyes and long eyelashes. In the wing built in the 1930s, Jesus is a Social Realist with huge superhero muscles. In the forties, in the Serenity wing, Jesus becomes an abstract assembly of planes and cubes. The fifties Jesus is polished fruitwood, a Danish Modern skeleton. The sixties Jesus is pegged together out of driftwood.

There's no seventies wing, and in the eighties wing, there's no Jesus, just the same secular green polished marble and brass you'd find in a department store.

Fertility talked about art and we wandered through Contentment, Serenity, Peace, Joy, Salvation, Rapture, and Enchantment.

She told me her name was Fertility Hollis.

I told her to call me Tender Branson. That's as close as I have to a real name name.

Every week from now on, she's going to visit her brother's crypt. That's where she promised to be next Wednesday.

The caseworker asks, "It's been ten years. Why don't you ever want to open up and share any feelings about your dead family?"

I'm sorry, I tell her, but I really need to get back to work. I tell her our hour is up.

Before it's too late, before we get too close to my plane crash, I need to explain about my name. Tender Branson. It's not really a name. It's more of a rank. It's the same as somebody in another culture naming a child Lieutenant Smith or Bishop Jones. Or Governor Brown. Or Doctor Moore. Sheriff Peterson.

The only names in Creedish culture were family names. The family name came from the husband. A family name was the way to claim property. The family name was a label.

My family name is Branson.

My rank is Tender Branson. It's the lowest rank.

The caseworker asked one time if the family name wasn't a kind of endorsement or a curse when sons and daughters were contracted for work in the outside world.

Since the suicides, people in the outside world have the same lurid picture of Creedish culture that my brother, Adam, had of them.

In the outside world, my brother told me, people were as reckless as animals and fornicated with strangers on the street.

These days, people in the outside world will ask me if certain family names brought higher prices. Did some family names bring lower labor contract prices?

These people usually go on to ask if some Creedish fathers would impregnate their daughters to increase cash flow. They'll ask if the Creedish children who weren't allowed to marry were castrated, meaning was I. They'll ask if Creedish sons masturbated or went with farm animals or sodomized each other, meaning do I.

Did I. Was I.

Strangers will ask me to my face if I'm a virgin.

I don't know. I forget. Or the entire issue is none of your business.

For the record, my brother Adam Branson was my older brother by three minutes and thirty seconds, but by Creedish standards it could've been years.

Since Creedish doctrine didn't recognize a second-place finisher.

In every family, the firstborn son was named Adam, and it was Adam Branson who would inherit our land in the church district colony.

All sons after Adam were named Tender. In the Branson family that makes me one of at least eight Tender Bransons my parents released to be labor missionaries.

All daughters, the first through the last, were named Biddy.

Tenders are workers who tend.

Biddies do your bidding.

It's a good guess that both words are slang, nicknames for longer traditional names, but I don't know what.

I know that if the church elders chose a Biddy Branson to marry the Adam of another family, her first name, really her rank, changed to Author.

When she married Adam Maxton, Biddy Branson would become Author Maxton.

The parents of that Adam Maxton were also called Adam and Author Maxton, until their just-married son and his wife had a child. After that, you addressed both members of the older couple as Elder Maxton.

Most couples, by the time her firstborn son had his first child, the female Elder Maxton would be dead from having child after child after child.

Almost all the church elders were men. A man could become a church elder by the time he was thirty-five if he was quick enough.

It wasn't complicated.

It was nothing compared to the outside world and its ranking system of parents and grandparents and great-grandparents, aunts and uncles, nieces and nephews, all of them with their own first names.

In Creedish culture, your name told everybody just where you belonged. Tender or Biddy. Adam or Author. Or Elder. Your name told you just how your life would go.

People ask if I'm ever mad that I lost the right to own property and raise a family just because my brother was three and a half minutes ahead of me. And I've learned to tell them yes. That's what people in the outside world want to hear. But it's not true. I've never been mad.

This would be the same as getting angry over the idea that if you had been born with longer fingers you might be a concert violinist.

It's the same as wishing that your parents had been taller, thin-

ner, stronger, happy. There are details in the past you have no control over.

The truth is, Adam was born first. And maybe Adam envied me
because I would get to go out and see the outside world. While I
was packing to leave, Adam was getting married to a Biddy Gleason
he'd hardly met.

It was the body of church elders who kept elaborate charts of
who'd married which biddy from which family so that what people
in the outside world call "cousins" never married. Every generation
as the Adams started turning seventeen, the church elders met to
assign them wives as far from their family history as possible. Every
generation, there was a season of marriages. There were almost
forty families in the church district colony, and every generation
almost every family would have at-home weddings and parties. For
a tender or a biddy, a wedding season was something you'd watch
only from around the edges.

If you were a biddy, it was something you might dream of happening to you.

If you were a tender, you didn't dream.

40

Tonight, the calls come the same as every night. Outside's a full moon. People are ready to die for their bad grades in school. Their family upsets. Their boyfriend problems. Their doggy little jobs. This is while I'm trying to butterfly a couple of stolen lamb chops.

People are calling long-distance with the operator asking if I'll accept the charges for a collect cry for attention from John Doe.

Tonight I'm trying out a new way to eat salmon *en croûte,* a sexy new turn of the wrist, a little flourish for the people who I work for to wow the other guests at their next dinner party. A little parlor trick. Here's the etiquette equivalent of ballroom dancing. I'm working up a showy little routine for getting creamed onions into your mouth. I've just about perfected a fail-safe technique for mopping up extra saged cream when the phone rings, again.

A guy's calling to say he's failing Algebra II.

Just as a point of practice, I say, Kill yourself.

A woman calls and says her kids won't behave.

Without missing a beat, I tell her, Kill yourself.

A man calls to say his car won't start.

Kill yourself.

A woman calls to ask what time the late movie starts.

Kill yourself.

She asks, "Isn't this 555-1327? Is this the Moorehouse CinePlex?"

I say, Kill yourself. Kill yourself. Kill yourself.

A girl calls and asks, "Does it hurt very much to die?"

Well, sweetheart, I tell her, yes, but it hurts a lot more to keep living.

"I was just wondering," she says. "Last week, my brother killed himself."

This has to be Fertility Hollis. I ask, how old was her brother? I make my voice sound deeper, different enough I hope so she won't know me.

"Twenty-four," she says, not crying or anything. She doesn't even sound all that sad.

Her voice makes me think of her mouth makes me think of her breath makes me think of her breasts.

I Corinthians, Chapter Six, Verse Eighteen:

"Flee fornication. . . . he that committeth fornication sinneth against his own body."

In my new, deeper voice, I ask her to talk about what she's feeling.

"Timing-wise," she says, "I can't decide. Spring term is almost over, and I'm really hating my job. My lease on my apartment is almost run out. The tags on my car expire next week. If I'm ever going to do it, this just seems like a good time to kill myself."

There are a lot of good reasons to live, I tell her, and hope she won't ask for a list. I ask, isn't there someone who shares her grief over her brother? Maybe an old friend of her brother's who can help support her in this tragedy?

"Not really."

I ask, nobody else goes to her brother's grave?

"Nope."

I ask, not one person? Nobody else puts flowers on the grave? Not a single old friend?

"Nope."

It's clear I made a big impression.

"No," she says. "Wait. There is this one pretty weird guy."

Great. I'm weird.

I ask, how does she mean, weird?

"You remember those cult people who all killed themselves?" she says. "It was about seven or eight years ago. Their whole town they started, they all went to church and drank poison, and the FBI found them all holding hands on the floor, dead. This guy remind-ed me of that. It wasn't so much his dorky clothes, but his hair was cut like he did it himself with his eyes closed."

It was ten years ago, and all I want to do is hang up.

II Chronicles, Chapter Twenty-one, Verse Nineteen:

". . . his bowels fell out . . ."

"Hello," she says. "Anybody still here?"

Yeah, I say. What else?

"Nothing else," she says. "He was just at my brother's crypt with a big bunch of flowers."

You see, I say. That's just the kind of loving person she needs to run to in this crisis.

"I don't think so," she says.

Is she married, I ask.

"No."

Is she seeing anybody?

"No."

Then get to know this guy, I tell her. Let your mutual loss bring the two of you together. This could be a big breakthrough in romance for her.

"I don't think so," she says. "First of all, you didn't see this guy. I mean, I always wondered if my brother might be a homosexual, and this weird guy with all the flowers just confirms all my suspicions. Besides, he wasn't that attractive."

Lamentations, Chapter Two, Verse Eleven:

". . . my bowels are troubled, my liver is poured upon the earth . . ."

I say, Maybe if he got a better haircut. You could help him out. Give him a makeover.

"I don't think so," she says. "This guy is pretty intensively ugly. He has his terrible haircut with these long sideburns that come down almost to his mouth. It's not like when guys use a little topiary facial hair the way women use makeup, you know, to hide the fact they have a double chin or they don't have any cheekbones. This guy just doesn't have any good features to work with. That and he's queer."

I Corinthians, Chapter Eleven, Verse Fourteen:

"Doth not even nature itself teach you, that if a man have long hair it is a shame unto him?"

I say, she has no proof he's a sodomite.

"What kind of proof do you need?"

I say, ask him. Isn't she supposed to see him again?

"Well," she says, "I told him I'd meet him at the crypt next week, but I don't know. I didn't mean it. I pretty much just said that just to get away from him. He was just so needy and pathetic. He followed me all over the mausoleum for an hour."

But she still has to meet him, I say. She promised. Think of poor dead Trevor, her brother. What would Trevor think of her ditching his one remaining friend?

She asks, "How did you know his name?"

Whose name?

"My brother, Trevor. You said his name."

She must've said it first, I say. Just a minute ago she said it. Trevor. Twenty-four. Killed himself last week. Homosexual. Maybe. Had a secret lover who desperately needs her shoulder to cry on.

"You caught all that? You're a good listener," she says. "I'm impressed. What do you look like?"

Ugly, I say. Hideous. Ugly hair. Ugly past. She wouldn't like the looks of me at all.

I ask about her brother's friend, maybe lover, widower, is she going to meet him next week like she promised?

"I don't know," she says. "Maybe. I'll meet the dork next week if you'll do something for me right now."

Just remember, I tell her. You have the chance to make a big difference in someone's loneliness. Here's a perfect chance to bring love and supportive nurturing support to a man who needs your love desperately.

"Fuck love," she says, her voice dropping lower to meet mine. "Say something to get me off."

I don't know what she means.

"You know what I mean," she says.

Genesis, Chapter Three, Verse Twelve:

". . . The woman whom thou gavest to be with me, she gave me of the tree, and I did eat."

Listen, I say. I'm not alone here. All around me are caring nurturing volunteers giving their time.

"Do it," she says. "Lick my tits."

I say she's taking advantage of my naturally caring nurturing nature. I tell her I'll have to hang up now.

She says, "Put your mouth all over me."

I say, I'm hanging up now.

"Harder," she says. "Do it harder. Oh, harder, do me harder," she laughs and says. "Lick me. Lick me. Lick me. Lick. Me."

I say, I'm hanging up now. But I don't.

Fertility's saying, "You know you want me. Tell me what you want me to do. You know you want to. Make me do something terrible."

And before I can even take myself out, Fertility Hollis screams a ragged howling porn goddess orgasm scream.

And I hang up.

I Timothy, Chapter Five, Verse Fifteen:

"For some are already turned aside after Satan."

How I feel is cheap and used, dirty and humiliated. Dirty and tricked and thrown away.

Then the phone rings. It's her. This has to be her so I don't pick up.

All night long the phone rings, and I sit here feeling cheated and don't dare answer.

39

About ten years ago I had my first one-on-one session with my caseworker, who's a real person with a name and an office but I don't want to get her in trouble. She has her own set of problems. She has a degree in social work. She's thirty-five years old and can't keep a boyfriend. Ten years ago she was twenty-five and just out of college and she was swamped with collecting the clients assigned to her as part of the federal government's brand-new Survivor Retention Program.

What happened was a policeman came to the front door of the house where I worked back then. Ten years ago, I was twenty-three years old, and this was still my first posting because I still worked really hard. I didn't know any better. The yards around the house were always wet dark green and clipped so smooth they rolled out soft and perfect as a green mink coat. Nothing inside the house ever looked depreciated. When you're twenty-three, you think you can keep up this level of performance forever.

A ways back from the policeman at the front door were two more police and the caseworker standing in the driveway by a police car.

You can't understand how good my work felt up to the moment I opened that door. My whole life growing up, I'd been working toward this, toward baptism and getting placed in a job cleaning houses in the wicked outside world.

When the people I worked for had sent the church a donation for my first month's work, I was beaming. I really believed I was helping create Heaven on Earth.

No matter how people stared at me, I wore the mandatory church costume everywhere, the hat, the baggy trousers with no pockets. The long-sleeved white shirt. No matter how hot it got, I wore the brown coat if I went out in public, no matter what silly things people said to me.

"How come you can wear shirts with buttons?" somebody at the hardware store would want to know.

Because I'm not Amish.

"Do you have to wear special secret undergarments?"

I think they were talking about Mormons.

"Isn't it against your religion to live outside your colony?"

That sounds more like the Mennonites.

"I've never met a Hutterite before."

You still haven't.

It felt good to stand out from the world, just mysterious and pious. You weren't a lantern under any basket. You stood out right-eous as a sore thumb. You were the one holy man to keep God from crushing all of the Sodom and Gomorrah seething around you in the Valley Plaza Shopping Center.

You were everyone's savior, whether they knew it or not. On a sweltering day in your heavy blah-colored wool, you were a martyr burning at the stake.

It felt even more wonderful to meet someone dressed the same as you. The brown pants or the brown dress, we all wore the same lumpy brown potato shoes. The two of you would come together in a quiet little pocket of conversation. There were so few things we were allowed to say to each other in the outside world. You could only say three or four things so you wanted to start slow and not hurry a word. Shopping was the only reason you were allowed out in public, and this was only if you were trusted with money.

If you met someone from the church district colony, you could say:

May you be of complete service in your lifetime.

You could say:

Praise and glory to the Lord for this day through which we labor.

You could say:

May our efforts bring all those around us to Heaven.

And you could say:

May you die with all your work complete.

That was the limit.

You'd see someone else looking righteous and hot in their church district costume, and you'd run through this little handful of conversation in your head. The two of you would rush together and you weren't allowed to touch. No hugging. No handshaking. You would say one approved bit. She would say one. The two of you would go back and forth until each of you had said two lines. You kept your heads bowed, and you each went back to your task.

Those were just the smallest parts of the smallest part of all the rules you had to remember. Growing up inside the church district colony, half your studies were about church doctrine and rules. Half were about service. Service included gardening, etiquette, fabric care, cleaning, carpentry, sewing, animals, arithmetic, getting out stains, and tolerance.

Rules for the outside world included you had to write weekly letters of confession back to the elders in the church district. You had to refrain from eating candy. Drinking and smoking were forbidden. Present a clean and orderly appearance at all times. You could not indulge in broadcast forms of entertainment. You could not participate in sexual relations.

Luke, Chapter Twenty, Verse Thirty-five:

"But they which shall be accounted worthy . . . neither marry, nor are given in marriage."

Elders of the Creedish church made celibacy sound as easy as choosing not to play baseball.

Just say no.

The other rules just went on and on. God forbid you should ever dance. Or eat refined sugar. Or sing. But the most important rule to remember was always:

If the members of the church district colony felt summoned by God, rejoice. When the apocalypse was imminent, celebrate, and all Creedish must deliver themselves unto God, amen.

And you had to follow.

It didn't matter how far away. It didn't matter how long you'd been working outside the district colony. Since listening to broadcast communication was a no-no, it might take years for all church members to find out about the Deliverance. Church doctrine named it that. The Deliverance. The flight to Egypt. The flight out of Egypt. People are all the time running from one place to another in the Bible.

You might not find out for years, but the moment you found out, you had to find a gun, drink some poison, drown, hang, slash, or jump.

You had to deliver yourself to Heaven.

This is why there were three police and the caseworker here to collect me.

The policeman said, "This isn't going to be easy for you to hear," and I knew I'd been left behind.

It was the apocalypse, the Deliverance, and despite all my work and all the money I'd earned toward our plan, Heaven on Earth just wasn't going to happen.

Before I could think, the caseworker stepped forward and said, "We know what you've been programmed to do at this point. We're prepared to hold you for observation to prevent that."

Back when the church district colony first decreed the Deliverance, there were around fifteen hundred church district members scattered all over the country in job postings. A week later, there would be six hundred. A year later, four hundred.

Since then, even a couple of caseworkers have killed themselves.

The government found me and most of the other survivors by our letters of confession we sent back to the church district colony every month. We didn't know we were writing and sending our wages to church elders who were already dead and in Heaven. We couldn't know that caseworkers were reading our tally every month of how many times we swore or had unpure thoughts. Now there was nothing I could tell the caseworker that she didn't already know.

Ten years have passed, and you never see surviving church members together. The survivors who see each other now, there's nothing left between us except embarrassment and disgust. We've failed in our ultimate sacrament. Our shame is for ourselves. Our disgust is for each other. The survivors who still wear church costume do it to brag about their pain. Sackcloth and ashes. They couldn't save themselves. They were weak. The rules are all gone, and it doesn't matter. We're all going overnight express delivery straight to Hell.

And I was weak.

So I took the trip downtown in the back of a police car, and sitting beside me, the caseworker said, "You were the innocent victim of a terrible oppressive cult, but we're here to help you get back on your feet."

The minutes were already taking me farther and farther away from what I should've done.

The caseworker said, "I understand you have a problem with masturbation. Would you like to talk about it?"

Every minute made it harder to do what I'd promised at my baptism. Shoot, cut, choke, bleed, or jump.

The world was passing by so fast outside the car my eyes went goofy.

The caseworker said, "Your life has been a miserable nightmare up to now, but you're going to be okay. Are you hearing me? Be patient, and you'll be just fine."

This was almost ten years ago, and I'm still waiting.

The easy thing to do was give her the benefit of the doubt.

Jump ahead ten years, and not much has changed. Ten years of therapy, and I'm still in about the same place. This probably isn't something we should celebrate.

We're still together. Today's our weekly session number five hundred and something, and today we're in the blue guest bathroom. This is different from the green, white, yellow, or lavender guest bathrooms. This is how much money these people make. The caseworker's sitting on the edge of the bathtub with her bare feet soaking in a few inches of warm water. Her shoes are on the closed lid of the toilet with her martini glass of grenadine, crushed ice, superfine sugar, and white rum. After every couple of questions she leans over with the ballpoint pen still in her hand and pinches the stem of the glass, holding the pen and glass crossed chop-stick style.

Her latest boyfriend is out of the picture, she told me.

God forbid she should offer to help clean.

She takes a drink. She puts the glass back while I answer. She writes on the yellow legal pad rested on her knees, asks another question, takes another drink. Her face looks paved under a layer of makeup.

Larry, Barry, Jerry, Terry, Gary, all her lost boyfriends run together. She says her lists of lost clients and lost boyfriends are running neck and neck.

This week, she says, we've hit a new low, one hundred and thirty-two survivors, nationwide, but the suicide rate is leveling off.

According to my daily planner, I'm scrubbing the grout between the six-sided little blue tiles on the floor. This is more than a trillion miles of grout. Laid end to end, just the grout in this bathroom would stretch to the moon and back, ten times, and all of it's shitty with black mildew. The ammonia I dip a toothbrush in and scrub with, the way it smells mixed with her cigarette smoke, makes me tired and my heart pound.

And maybe I'm a little out of my head. The ammonia. The smoke. Fertility Hollis keeps calling me at home. I don't dare answer the phone, but I know for sure it's her.

"Have any strangers approached you, lately?" the caseworker asks.

She asks, "Have you gotten any phone calls you'd describe as threatening?"

The way the caseworker keeps asking me stuff with half her mouth clamped around her cigarette looks the way a dog would sit there drinking a pink martini and snarling at you. A cigarette, a sip, a question; breathing, drinking, and asking, she demonstrates all the basic applications for the human mouth.

She never used to smoke but more and more she tells me she can't stand the idea of living to a ripe old age.

"Maybe if just one little part of my life was working out," she tells a new cigarette in her hand before she lights up. Then something invisible somewhere starts to beep and beep and beep until she presses on her watch to stop it. She twists to reach her tote bag on the floor beside the toilet and gets a plastic bottle.

"Imipramine," she says. "Sorry I can't offer you one."

Early on, the retention program tried to baby-sit all the survivors by giving them medication, Xanax, Prozac, Valium, imipramine. The plan crashed because too many clients tried to hoard their weekly prescriptions for three weeks, six weeks, eight weeks, depending on their body weight, and then downed their stash with a scotch chaser.

Even if the medication didn't work for the clients, it's been great for the caseworkers.

"Have you noticed anyone following you," the caseworker asks, "anyone with a gun or a knife, at night or when you walk home from your bus stop?"

I scrub the cracks between the tiles from black to brown to white and ask, why is she asking me these things?

"No reason," she says.

No, I say, I'm not threatened.

"I tried to call you on the phone this week, and there was never any answer," she says. "What's up?"

I tell her nothing's up.

The real truth I'm not answering the phone is I don't want to talk to Fertility Hollis until I can see her in person. Over the phone, she sounded so turned on sexwise I can't risk it. Here I am competing with myself. I don't want her falling in love with me as a voice on the phone while at the same time she's trying to ditch me as a real person. It's best if she never talks to me on the phone ever again. The living, breathing creepy geeky ugly me can't stand up to her fantasy, so I have a plan, a terrible plan, to make her hate me and at the same time fall in love with me. The plan is to unseduce her. Unattract her.

"When you're not in your apartment," the caseworker asks, "does anyone else have access to the food you eat?"

Tomorrow is my next afternoon with Fertility Hollis at the mortuary, if she shows up. Then the first part of my plan will get off the ground.

The caseworker asks, "Have you gotten any threatening or unexplained mail?"

She asks, "Are you even listening to me?"

I ask, so what's with all these questions? I say I'm going to drink this bottle of ammonia if she won't tell me what's going on.

The caseworker checks her watch. She taps the point of her pen on her tablet, and makes me wait for her to take a puff on her cigarette and blow out the smoke.

If she really wants to help me, I tell her and I hand her a toothbrush, then she needs to start scrubbing.

She puts down her drink and takes the toothbrush. She rubs back and forth over an inch of grout on the tiled wall beside her. She stops and looks, scrubs some more. She takes another look.

"Oh my gosh," she says. "This is working. Look how clean it gets underneath." With her feet still soaking in a few inches of bathwater, the caseworker moves around to reach the wall better and scrubs some more. "God, I forgot how good it feels to get something accomplished."

She doesn't notice, but I've stopped. I sit back on my heels and watch her really attack the mildew.

"Listen to me," she says, scrubbing in different directions to follow the grout around each little blue tile.

"None of this might be true," she says, "but it's for your own good. Things could be getting a tiny bit dangerous for you."

She isn't supposed to tell me, but some of the survivor suicides are looking a little suspect. Most of the suicides look fine. The majority are just normal run-of-the-mill everyday garden-variety suicides, she says, but in between are a few strange cases. In one case, a right-handed man shot himself with his left hand. In another case, a woman hung herself with a bathrobe tie, but one of her arms was dislocated and both her wrists were bruised.

"These weren't the only cases," the caseworker says, still scrubbing. "But there's a pattern."

At first, nobody in the program paid much attention, she says. Suicides are just suicides, especially in this population. Client suicides come in clusters. Stampedes. One or two will trigger as many as twenty. Lemmings.

The yellow legal pad on her lap slips to the floor, and she says, "Suicide is very contagious."

The pattern of these new false suicides shows they're more likely to occur when a cluster of natural suicides has ended.

I ask, what does she mean, *false* suicides?

I sneak her martini, and it has a weird mouthwash taste.

"Murders," the caseworker says. "Someone is maybe killing survivors and making it look like suicide."

When a cluster of real suicides dwindles out, the murders appear to happen to get the ball rolling again. After two or three murders that look like suicide, then suicide looks very fresh and attractive again and another dozen survivors get caught up in the trend and check out.

"It's easy to imagine a killer, just one person or a hit squad of church members out to make sure you all get to Heaven together," the caseworker says. "It sounds silly and paranoid, but it makes perfect sense."

The Deliverance.

So why is she asking me all these questions?

"Because fewer and fewer survivors are killing themselves these days," she says. "The natural trend of normal suicides is winding down. Whoever's doing this is going to kill again to get the suicide rate back up. The pattern of murders is spread all over the country," she says. She scrubs with her toothbrush. She dips it in the jar of ammonia. With her cigarette smoking in her one hand, she scrubs more. She says, "Except for the time they happen, there's no real pattern. It's men. It's women. Young. Old. You need to be careful because you could be next."

The only new person I've met in months is Fertility Hollis.

I ask the caseworker, her being a woman and all, How do women want a man to look? What does she look for in a sex partner?

She's leaving behind a crooked trail of clean white grout.

"The other thing to remember," the caseworker says, "is this might all have a natural explanation. It might be that nobody's going to kill you. You might have absolutely nothing at all to be terrified about."

P art of my job is gardening, so I spray everything with twice the recommended strength of poison, weeds and real plants alike. Then I straighten the beds of artificial salvia and hollyhocks. The look I'm after this season is a fake cottage garden. Last year, I did artificial French parterres. Before that was a Japanese garden of all plastic plants. All I have to do is yank all the flowers. Sort them, and stick them all back in the ground in a new pattern. Maintenance is a snap. Dull flowers get a little touch-up with red or yellow spray paint.

A shot of clear lacquer or hair spray stops silk flowers from fraying at the edge.

The fake yarrow and plastic nasturtiums need the dust hosed off them. The plastic roses wired onto the poisoned dead skeletons of the original rose bushes need a shot of smell.

Some kind of blue-colored birds are walking around the lawn as if they're looking for a lost contact lens.

For the roses, I empty the poison out of the sprayer and fill it with three gallons of water and half a bottle of Eternity by Calvin Klein. I spray the fake Shasta daisies with watered-down vanilla from the kitchen. The artificial asters get White Shoulders. For most of the other plants, I use aerosol cans of floral room freshener. The artificial lemon thyme I spray with Lemon Pledge furniture polish.

Part of my strategy for courting Fertility Hollis is to look ugly on purpose, and my getting dirty is a start. Looking a little rough around the edges. Still, it's hard to get dirty gardening when you never really touch the ground, but my clothes smell from the poison, and my nose is a little sunburned. With the wire stem of a plastic calla lily, I chop up a handful of the hard dead soil, and I rub it in my hair. I wedge the dirt in under my fingernails.

God forbid I should try and look good for Fertility. The worst strategy I could pursue is self-improvement. It would be a big mistake to dress up, make my best effort, comb my hair, maybe even borrow some swell clothes from the man I work for, something all-cotton and pastel shirtwise, brush my teeth, put on what they call deodorant and walk into the Columbia Memorial Mausoleum for my big second date still looking ugly, but showing signs I really tried to look good.

So here I am. This is as good as it gets. Take it or leave it.

As if I don't care what she thinks.

Looking good is not part of the big plan. My plan is to look like untapped potential. The look I'm going for is natural. Real. The look

I'm after is, raw material. Not desperate and needy, but ripe with potential. Not hungry. Sure, I want to look like I'm worth the effort. Washed but not ironed. Clean but not polished. Confident but humble.

Honest is how I want to look. The truth doesn't glitter and shine.

Here's passive aggression in action.

My idea is to make ugly work in my favor. Establish a low baseline for contrast with my later on. Before and After. The frog and the prince.

It's two on Wednesday afternoon. According to my daily planner, I'm rotating the oriental rug in the pink drawing room so it won't get a wear pattern. You have to move all the furniture to another room, including the piano. Roll the rug. Roll the carpet pad. Vacuum. Mop the floor. The rug is twelve feet by sixteen feet. Then turn the pad and unroll it. Turn and unroll the carpet. Drag all the furniture back.

According to my daily planner book, this shouldn't take me more than half an hour.

Instead, I just fluff the traffic patterns in the carpet and untie the strand of fringe the people I work for tied in a knot. I tie another strand on the opposite end of the rug so the whole thing looks rotated. I move all the furniture a little and put ice in the little divots left in the carpet. As the ice melts, the matted divots will fluff back up.

I scuff the shine off my shoes. At the makeup mirror of the woman I work for, I put her mascara up inside each nostril until my nose hair looks thick and full. Then I catch a bus.

Another part of the Survivor Retention Program is you get a free bus pass every month. Stamped on the back of the pass it says: Property of the Department of Human Resources.

Nontransferable.

The whole way to the mausoleum, I'm telling myself I don't give a shit if Fertility shows up or not.

A lot of half-gone church district prayers recite themselves in my mind. My head is just a mishmash of old prayers and responses.

> *May I be of complete and utmost service.*
> *Let my every task be my grace.*
> *In my every labor lies my salvation.*
> *Let my effort not be wasted.*
> *Through my works may I save the world.*

Really I'm thinking, oh please, oh please, oh please, be there this afternoon Fertility Hollis.

Inside the mausoleum front doors, there's the usual cheap reproductions of real beautiful music to make you feel not so alone. It's the same ten songs only with just the music and no singing. They don't play it except for certain days. Some of the old galleries in the Sincerity and New Hope wings never have the music. You don't hear it anywhere unless you really listen.

It's music as wallpaper, utilitarian, music as Prozac or Xanax to control how you feel. Music as aerosol room freshener.

I walk through the Serenity wing and don't see Fertility. I go through Faith, Joy, and Tranquillity, and she's not here. I swipe some plastic roses off some dead person's crypt so I won't show up empty-handed.

I'm heading into hatred, anger, fear, and resignation, and there, standing at Crypt 678 in Contentment, is Fertility Hollis with her red hair. She waits until I've been walked up next to her for two hundred and forty seconds before she turns and says hi.

She can't be the same person who was screaming her orgasm at me over the phone.

I say, Hi.

In her hands is a bunch of fake orange blossoms, nice enough but nothing I'd bother to steal. Her dress today is the same kind of brocade they make curtains out of, patterned white on a white background. It looks stiff and flame-retardant. Stain-repellent. Wrinkle-resistant. Mother-of-the-bride modest in her pleated skirt with long sleeves, she says, "Do you miss him, too?"

Everything about her looks martyr-proofed.

I ask, Miss who?

"Trevor," she says. She's barefoot on the stone floor.

Yeah right, Trevor, I tell myself. My secret sodomite lover. I forgot.

I say, Yeah. I miss him, too.

Her hair looks gathered in a field and piled on her head to dry. "Did he ever tell you about the cruise he took me on?"

No.

"It was completely illegal."

She looks from Crypt Number 678 to up at the ceiling where the music comes down from the little speakers next to the painted-on clouds and angels.

"First, he made me take dancing lessons with him. We learned all the ballroom dances they call the Cha-Cha and the Fox-trot. The Rumba and the Swing. The Waltz. The Waltz was easy."

The angels play their music above us for a minute, telling her something, and Fertility Hollis listens.

"Here," she says and turns to me. She takes my flowers and hers and puts them against the wall. She asks, "You can waltz, right?"

Wrong.

"I can't believe you could know Trevor and not know how to waltz," she says and shakes her head.

In her head, there's a picture of Trevor and me dancing together. Laughing together. Having anal sex. This is the handicap I'm up against, this and the idea I killed her brother.

She says, "Open your arms."

And I do.

She comes in face-to-face close with me and cups one hand on the back of my neck. Her other hand grabs my hand and pulls it out far away from us. She says, "Take your other hand and put it against my bra."

So I do.

"On my back!" she says, and twists away from me. "Put your hand on my bra where it crosses my spine."

So I do.

For our feet, she shows me how to step forward with my left foot, then my right foot, then bring my feet together while she does this all in the opposite direction.

"It's called a Box Step," she says. "Now listen to the music."

She counts, "One, two, three."

The music goes, One. Two. Three.

We count over and over, and step each time we count and we're dancing. The flowers in all the crypts up and down the walls lean out over us. The marble smooths under our feet. We're dancing. The light is through stained-glass windows. The statues are carved in their niches. The music comes out the speakers weak and echoes off the stone until it's moving back and forth in drafts and currents, notes and chords around us. And we're dancing.

"What I remember about the cruise," Fertility says, and her arm is curved to rest against the whole length of my arm. "I remember the faces of the last passengers as their lifeboats were lowered past the ballroom windows. Their orange canvas life vests sort of framed their heads, so their heads looked cut off and put on orange pillows, and they just stared with big wide-open fish eyes at Trevor and me still inside the ship's ballroom while the ship was starting to sink."

She was on a sinking boat?

"A ship," Fertility says. "It was called the *Ocean Excursion*. Try to say *that* three times fast."

And it was sinking?

"It was beautiful," she says. "The travel agent said not to come crying back to her. It was an old French Line ship, the travel agent warned us, only now it was sold to some outfit in South America. It was very art deco. It was trashed. It was the Chrysler Building floating sideways in the ocean and cruising up and down the Atlantic coast of South America full of lower-middle-class people from Argentina and their wives and kids. Argentineans. All the light fixtures on the walls were pink glass shaped into gigantic marquise-cut diamond shapes. Everything on the ship was in this pink diamond light and the carpets had big stains and worn-out spots."

We're dancing in place, and then we start to turn.

The one, two, three, box step of it. The forward and back of the hesitation step. The lift of the heel in a perfect bit of Cuban step-two-three, I turn with Fertility Hollis bent inside the hug of my arm. We turn again and again, we turn again, turn again, turn again.

And Fertility says how the lifeboats were gone. All the lifeboats were gone, and the ship trailed its empty lifeboat rigging in the relaxed Caribbean evening. The lifeboats rowed off into the sunset, the crowd in their orange life vests starting to wail and scam for their jewelry and prescriptions. People were doing that sign of the cross thing.

Fertility and I one, two, three; waltz, two, three, across the marble gallery.

In her story, Fertility and Trevor waltzed across the tilting mahogany parquet, the Versailles Ballroom tilting as the bow sank and the stern pointed the four-leaf clovers of each cloverleaf propeller into the evening air. A flock of little gilt ballroom chairs hurried past them and collected under a statue of that Greek moon goddess, Diana. The gold brocade curtains hung crooked across each window. They were the last passengers aboard the SS *Ocean Excursion*.

The steam was still up because the pink chandeliers—"Just like regular chandeliers," Fertility says, "but on an ocean liner they hang rigid as icicles"—the chandeliers in the Versailles Ballroom sparkled, and the public address system still filled the ship with a crackling music, one after another of elevator waltzes melting into each other as Trevor and Fertility turned, turned, turned.

As Fertility and I turn, turn, and step in place, then slide toe to toe across the mausoleum floor.

Belowdecks, the Caribbean was rising in the Trianon Dining Room, floating the edges of a hundred linen tablecloths.

The ship was drifting with all engines dead.

The warm blue water was spread out flat to the horizon in every direction.

Under even a little water, the checkerboard floor of mahogany and walnut parquet looked lost and out of reach. Here was one last look at the continent of Atlantis, with salt water rising around the statues and the marble pillars as Trevor and Fertility waltzed past the legend of a lost civilization, gold-painted carvings and carved French palace tables. Sea level rose diagonal against life-sized paintings of queens wearing crowns as the ship tilted and vases spilled flowers: roses and orchids and stalks of ginger into the water where bottles of champagne bobbed and Trevor and Fertility splashed past.

The metal skeleton of the ship, the bulkheads behind the lining of paneling and tapestries, shuddered and groaned.

I ask, was she going to drown herself?

"Don't be stupid," Fertility says with her head against my chest, breathing the poison smell all over me. "Trevor was never wrong. That was his whole problem."

Never wrong about what?

Trevor Hollis had dreams, she told me. He'd dream a plane was going to crash. Trevor would tell the airline, and no one would believe him. Then the plane would crash and the FBI would bring him in for questioning. It was always easier to believe he was a terrorist than a psychic. The dreams got so he couldn't sleep. He didn't dare read a newspaper or watch television or he'd see the report of some two hundred people dying in a plane crash he knew would happen, but couldn't stop.

He couldn't save anybody.

"Our mom killed herself because she had the same kind of dreams," Fertility says. "Suicide is an old family tradition for us."

Still dancing, I tell myself, At least we have something in common.

"He knew the ship was only going to sink about halfway. Some valve or something was going to fail and water would fill the engine rooms and some of the big public rooms on the lower decks," Fertility says. "He knew from his dreams that we'd have hours with the whole ship to ourselves. We'd have all that food and wine. Then someone would come along to rescue us."

Still dancing, I ask, Is that why he killed himself?

The music is my only answer for a minute.

"You can't imagine how beautiful it all was, the flooded ballrooms with pianos under water and all the needlepoint furniture floating around," Fertility says against my chest. "It was my nicest memory, ever."

We dance past statues of saints in somebody else's religion. To me they're just rock shaped into glorified nobodies.

"The Atlantic water was so clear. It was pouring down the grand staircase," she says. "We just took off our shoes and kept dancing."

Still dancing, counting one to three, I ask, does she have the same kind of dreams?

"A little bit," she says. "Not very much. More and more all the time. More than I want to."

I ask, so is she going to kill herself the same as her brother?

"No," Fertility says. She lifts her head and smiles at me.

We dance, one, two, three.

She says, "No way would I shoot myself. I'd probably take pills."

At home is my stash of government-issue antidepressants, hypnotics, mood equalizers, sedatives, MAO inhibitors in the candy dish beside my goldfish on my fridge.

We dance, one, two, three.

She says, "Just kidding."

We dance.

She puts her head back on my chest and says, "It all depends on how terrible my dreams get."

37

It's that night I start answering the phone again. This is after I'm so horny I have to go downtown and hunt for something to steal. This isn't so much for the cash as to get off. It's okay. The caseworker says it's okay. It's a sexual release, she tells me. It's perfectly natural. You find what you want. You stalk it. You grab it and make it your own. After you've had it, you throw it away.

It was the caseworker who got me started shoplifting in the first place.

The caseworker called me a textbook example of klepto-mania. She cited studies. My stealing, she said, was to prevent anybody from stealing my penis (Fenichel, 1945). Stealing was an impulse I couldn't control (Goldman, 1991). I stole because of a mood disorder (McElroy et al., 1991). It didn't matter what: shoes, masking tape, a tennis racket.

The only trouble is now even stealing doesn't give me the old feeling of wow.

Maybe this is because I've met Fertility.

Or maybe I've met Fertility because I'm getting bored with my sex life of crime.

Lately, I'm not even shoplifting, not in the classic, formal sense. Instead of stealing merchandise, I'll walk around downtown until I find a cash register receipt someone's just dropped.

You take the receipt into the store it's from. You pretend to shop until you find an item on the receipt. You take the item around the store for a while, then you use the receipt to return the item for cash. Of course this works best in big stores. It works best with itemized receipts. Don't use receipts that are old or dirty. Don't use the same receipt twice. Try to vary the stores you scam.

This is to real shoplifting what masturbation is to sex.

And of course, stores know all about this scam.

Other good scams include shopping with a big cup of soda you can drop small items into. Another way is to buy a cheap can of paint, then loosen the lid and drop something expensive inside. The metal of the can blocks the x-rays from the security system.

This afternoon, instead of finding a receipt, I just walk around trying to figure out the next part of my plan to grab Fertility and make her my own. Have her. Throw her away, maybe. I have to take advantage of her terrible dreams. Our dancing together has to be a tool I can use.

Fertility and I danced most of the afternoon. As the music changed, she taught me the basic Cha-Cha, the Cha-Cha crossover step, and the female under-arm Cha-Cha turn. She showed me the basic Fox-trot.

She told me what she did for a living was terrible. It was worse than anything I could imagine.

And when I asked, What?

She laughed.

Walking around downtown, I find a register receipt for a color television. This should feel like I've found a winning lottery ticket, but I put the receipt in a trash can.

Maybe what I liked most about dancing is the rules. In the world where anything goes, here are solid arbitrary rules. The Fox-trot is two slow steps and two fast. The Cha-Cha is two slow and three fast. The choreography, the discipline, isn't up for debate.

These are good old-fashioned rules. How to dance the Box Step isn't going to change every week.

To the caseworker, when we started together ten years ago I wasn't a crook. Originally, I was an obsessive-compulsive disorder. She'd just got her degree and still had all her textbooks to prove it. Obsessive-compulsives, she told me, would either check on things or clean them (Rachman & Hodgson, 1980). According to her, I was the second kind.

Really, I just liked to clean, but all my life I've been trained to obey. All I did was try and make her lousy diagnosis look right. The caseworker told me the symptoms, and I did my best to manifest them and then let her cure me.

After being obsessive-compulsive, I was a posttraumatic stress disorder.

Then I was an agoraphobic.

I was a panic disorder.

My feet are walking down the sidewalk in the one slow, two fast steps of a waltz. My head is counting one, two, three. Wherever you look among the pigeons there are big-ticket receipts all over the sidewalk. Walking around downtown, I pick up another receipt. This one's good for a hundred seventy-three dollars cash. Then I throw it away.

For about three months after I first met the caseworker, I was a dissociative identity disorder because I wouldn't tell the caseworker about my childhood.

Then I was a schizotypal personality disorder because I didn't want to join her weekly therapy group.

Then because she thought it would make a good case study, I had Koro Syndrome, where you're convinced your penis is getting smaller and smaller and when it disappears, you'll die (Fabian, 1991; Tseng et al., 1992).

Then she switched me to have Dhat Syndrome, where you're in crisis over the belief you're losing all your sperm when you have wet dreams or take a leak (Chadda & Ahuja, 1990). This is based on an old Hindu belief that it takes forty drops of blood to create a drop of bone marrow and forty drops of marrow to create a drop of sperm (Akhtar, 1988). She said it was no wonder I was so tired all the time.

Sperm makes me think of sex makes me think of punishment makes me think of death makes me think of Fertility Hollis. We did what the caseworker called Free Association.

Every session we had, she diagnosed me with another problem she thought I might have, and she gave me a book so I could study the symptoms. By the next week, I had whatever the problem was down pat.

One week, pyromaniac. One week, gender identity disorder.

She told me I was an exhibitionist so the next week, I mooned her.

She told me I was attention-deficient so I kept changing the subject. I was claustrophobic so we had to meet outside on the patio.

Walking around downtown, my feet switch to the two slow, three fast, two slow steps of a Cha-Cha. In my head is the same ten songs we listened to all afternoon. I pass up another receipt, as legal tender as a five-dollar bill on the sidewalk, and I Cha-Cha right past it.

The book the caseworker gave me was called the *Diagnostic and Statistical Manual of Mental Disorders*. We called it the DSM for short. She gave me a lot of her old textbooks to read, and inside were color photographs of models getting paid to look happy by holding naked babies overhead or walking hand in hand on a beach at sunset. For pictures of misery, models were getting paid to needle illegal drugs into their arms or slump alone at a table with a drink. It got so the caseworker could throw the DSM on the floor and whatever page it fell open to, that was how I'd try to look for the week.

We were happy enough this way. For a while. She felt she was making progress every week. I had a script to tell me how to act. It wasn't boring, and she gave me too many fake problems for me to stress about anything real. Every Tuesday, the caseworker would give me her diagnosis, and that was my new assignment.

Our first year together, there wasn't enough free time for me to consider suicide.

We did the Stanford-Binet to figure out how old my brain was. We did the Wechsler. We did the Minnesota Multiphasic Personality Inventory. The Millon Clinical Multiaxial Inventory. The Beck Depression Inventory.

The caseworker found out everything about me except for the truth.

I just didn't want to be fixed.

Whatever my real problems might be, I didn't want them cured. None of the little secrets inside me wanted to be found and explained away. By myths. By my childhood. By chemistry. My fear was, what would be left? So none of my real grudges and dreads ever came out into the light of day. I didn't want to resolve any angst. I'd never talk about my dead family. Express my grief, she called it. Resolve it. Leave it behind.

The caseworker cured me of a hundred syndromes, none of them real, and then declared me sane. She was so happy and proud.

She sent me out into the light of day, cured. You are healed. Go forth. Walk. A miracle of modern psychology.

Arise.

Dr. Frankenstein and her monster.

It was pretty heady stuff when you're twenty-five years old.

The only side effect is now I tend to steal. My intro to kleptomania felt too good to leave behind. Until tonight.

Walking around downtown today, ten years later, I pick up another receipt. I throw it away. After ten years of stowing away my problems so the caseworker couldn't monkey around with them, all I have to do is dance the Cha-Cha with some girl and even my chronic stealing is gone. My one real psychosis I denied the caseworker is cured by a stranger.

That's all we did was dance. Fertility talked about her brother and how the FBI had his phone tapped so every time she talked to him she could hear the click . . . click . . . click . . . of a government tape recorder in the background. Even before Trevor killed himself, she knew he would. It was in her first dream of the future. Fertility and I danced some more. Then she had to leave. Then she promised, next week, next Wednesday, same time, same place, she'd be there.

Tonight, streetlight to streetlight, I walk the Fox-trot. In my mind, I hear the waltz. The memory of Fertility Hollis is in my arms and resting against my chest. This is how I get home. Upstairs, the phone is already ringing off the hook. Maybe it's schizoids, paranoids, pedophiles.

Been there, I want to tell them. Done that.

Maybe it's Fertility Hollis wanting to talk about dancing with me today. Ready to give me her second impression of me.

Maybe she'll tell me in secret what's so terrible she does to earn money.

All the way from the elevator doors coming open, I run to answer the phone.

Hello.

The apartment door to the hallway is still open behind me. The fish needs to be fed. The curtains are still open, and it's almost dark outside. Anyone could see in here.

A man on the other end says, "May you be of complete service in your lifetime."

Without a thought I respond, *Praise and glory to the Lord for this day through which we labor.*

He says, "May our efforts bring all those around us to Heaven."

I ask, Who is this?

And he says, "May you die with all your work complete."

And he hangs up.

There's a way to polish chrome with club soda. To clean the ivory or bone handles on cutlery, rub them with lemon juice and salt. To get the shine off a suit, dampen the cloth with a weak mixture of water and ammonia, then iron with a damp pressing cloth.

The secret for making perfect boeuf Bourguignon is to add some orange peel.

To remove cherry stains, rub them with a ripe tomato and wash as usual.

The key is not to panic.

To make pants keep a sharp crease, turn them inside out

and rub a bar of soap on the inside of the crease. Turn them right-side out and iron as usual.

The trick is to keep busy.

Despite the fact the killer called, I'm doing everything as usual.

The secret is to not let your imagination get carried away.

All night long, I'm cleaning. I can't sleep. To clean the oven, I'm baking a pan of ammonia. Another way to put a lasting crease in pants is to dampen your pressing cloth with water and vinegar. I dig today's dirt out from under each fingernail. If I don't open a window, I'm going to suffocate from the smell of baked ammonia.

Here, I have to just spit it out.

The caseworker is missing. Every ten minutes, I call the case-worker at her office and all I get is her message. Here's the first time in ten years I've called her, and this is all I hear. "Please leave a message at the beep."

I say, that crazy psycho she told me about, well, he called.

All night, I'm phoning her office every ten minutes.

Please leave a message at the beep.

She needs to get me some protection.

And her message machine keeps cutting me off. So I call back.

Please leave a message.

I need an armed, twenty-four-hour police escort.

Please leave a message.

Somebody could be in the hallway, and I need to use the bath-room.

Please leave a message.

The killer she told me about knows who I am. He called. He knows where I live. He has my telephone number.

Please leave a message.

Call me. Call me. Call me.

Please leave a message.

If I turn up suicided in the morning, it was murder.

Please leave a message.

If I end up dead from some murderer holding my head in the oven, it's because she never checks her messages.

Please leave a message.

Listen, I tell her machine. This is for real. This is not a paranoid delusion. She cured me of those, remember?

Please leave a message.

This isn't a schizoid fantasy. I'm not hallucinating. Take my word for it.

Please leave a message. Then her message tape runs out.

All night, I'm awake and listening with the refrigerator moved halfway in front of the hall door. I need to use the bathroom but not bad enough to risk my life. People go down the hallway, but nobody stops. Nobody touches my doorknob all night. The phone just rings and rings, and I have to answer it in case it's the caseworker, but it's never her. It's just the regular parade of human misery. Pregnant unweds. Chronic sufferers. Substance abusers. They have to dash off their confessions pretty fast before I hang up. I have to keep the line free.

Every phone call I get fills me with joy and terror since this could be the caseworker or the killer.

Approach or avoidance.

Positive and negative reinforcement for answering the phone.

In the middle of my panic, Fertility calls to say, "Hi, me again. I've been thinking about you all week. I wanted to ask if it's against the rules for us to meet. I'd really like to meet you."

Still listening for footsteps, expecting a shadow to fall across the crack of light under the hallway door, I'm lifting the window shade to see if anyone's on the fire escape. I ask her, what about her friend? Wasn't she supposed to meet him again today?

"Oh, him," Fertility says. "Yes, I saw him today."

And?

"He smells like women's perfume and hair spray," Fertility says. "I don't see what my brother ever saw in him."

The perfume and hair spray were from spraying the roses, but I can't tell her that.

"The other thing is he had chipped red nail polish on his finger-nails."

It was red spray paint from me touching up the roses.

"And he's a terrible dancer."

Right now, me getting killed would be redundant.

"And his teeth are weird, not rotten, but crooked and little."

You could stab a knife right through my heart and you'd be too late.

"And he has these gross little monkey hands."

Right now, getting killed would be a breath of spring.

"That's supposed to mean he has a little wiener dick."

If Fertility keeps talking, my caseworker will have one less client in the morning.

"And he's not obese," Fertility says, "he's not a whale, but he's too fat for me."

In case there's a sniper outside, I open the blinds and stand my gross obese body in the window. Please, anybody with a rifle and a scope. Shoot me right here. Right in my big fat heart. Right in my little wiener.

"He's not anything like you," Fertility says.

Oh, I think she'd be surprised how much we're alike.

"You're so mysterious."

I ask, if she could change any one thing about this guy at the mausoleum, what would it be?

"Just so he'd quit pestering me," she says, "I'd kill him."

Well, she's not alone there. Be my guest. Take a number, and stand in line.

"Forget about him," she says, and her voice is sinking deeper in her throat. "I called because I want to get you off. Tell me what you want me to do. Make me do something terrible."

Opportunity knocks.

Here's the next part of my big plan.

This is something I'll go to Hell for, but I tell her, That guy you don't like, I want you to go screw his brains out and then tell me what it was like.

She says, "No way. No day."

Then I'm hanging up.

She says, "Wait. What if I call you and lie? I could just make the whole thing up. You wouldn't know."

No, I say, I'd know. I could tell.

"No way am I going to sleep with that geek."

What if she just kissed him?

Fertility says, "No."

What if she just took him out on a date? They could just go out for the afternoon. Get him out of the mortuary and he might look better. Take him on a picnic. Do something fun.

Fertility says, "Then will you get together with me?"

Definitely.

35

The sun wakes me up where I'm crouched next to the stove with a butcher knife in my fist. The way I feel, the idea of getting killed isn't so bad. My back hurts. My eyes feel cut open with a razor. I get dressed, and I go to work.

I sit in the back of the bus so no one can sit behind me with a knife, a poison dart, a piano-wire garrote.

At the house where I work, the regular caseworker's car is in the driveway. On the lawn are some normal red-looking birds walking around in the grass. The sky is blue-colored the way you'd expect. Nothing looks out of the ordinary.

In the house, the caseworker is on all fours scrubbing the kitchen tile with bleach and ammonia so strong it makes the air around her go all wavy with toxins that bring tears to my eyes.

"I hope you don't mind," she says, still scrubbing. "This was in your daily planner for you to do today. I came over early."

Bleach plus ammonia equals deadly chlorine gas.

The tears rolling down my cheeks, I ask, did she get my messages?

The caseworker does most of her breathing through a cigarette. The fumes must be nothing to her.

"No, I called in sick," she says. "This cleaning things is just so fulfilling. There's some coffee and homemade muffins I just baked. Why don't you just relax?"

I ask, doesn't she want to hear all about my problems? Take some notes? The killer called me last night. I was awake all night. He's picked me out to kill me. God forbid she should stop scrubbing the floor and get up and call the police for my sake.

"Don't worry," she says. She dips her scrub brush in her bucket of cleaning water. "The suicide rate took a big jump last night. That's why I couldn't face the office this morning."

The way she's scrubbing the floor, it will never come clean again. Once you scrub the clear gloss coat off a vinyl floor with an oxidizer like bleach, you're fucked. When she's done, the floor will be so porous, everything will stain. God forbid I should try and tell her this. She thinks she's doing a great job.

I ask, So how does the high suicide rate keep me alive?

"Don't you get it? We lost eleven more clients last night. Nine the night before. Twelve the night before that. We're looking at a landslide here," she says.

So?

"With numbers like that every night, if there is a killer, he doesn't need to kill anybody."

She starts singing. Maybe the deadly chlorine gas is having its effect. Her scrubbing does a little soft-shoe dance to go with her song. She says, "This won't sound appropriate, but congratulations."

I'm the last Creedish.

"You're almost the last survivor."

I ask how many others.

"In this town, one," she says. "Nationwide, only five."

Let's play like old times, I say. I tell her, Let's us get out the old *Diagnostic and Statistical Manual of Mental Disorders* and pick out a new way for me to go crazy. Let's do it. Just for old times' sake. Get the book.

The caseworker sighs and looks down at me reflected with my face wet with tears in her puddle of dirty scrub water on the floor. "Listen," she says, "I've got some real work to do here. Besides, the DSM is lost. I haven't seen it in a couple days."

She scrubs back and forth, saying, "Not that I miss it."

Okay, this has been a tough ten years. Almost all her clients are gone. She's stressed out. Burned out. No, incinerated. Cremated. She sees herself as a failure.

She's suffering from what's called Learned Helplessness.

"Besides," she says, scrubbing hard, here and there at the last spots where the vinyl is still intact, "I can't hold your hand forever. If you're going to kill yourself, I can't stop you, and it's not my fault. According to my records, you're perfectly happy and adjusted. We have the tests. There's empirical evidence to prove it."

The fumes in here make it so I have to sniff back my tears.

She says, "Kill yourself or don't kill yourself, but stop torturing me. I'm trying to move on with my life."

She says, "Every day in America people kill themselves. The problem isn't worse just because you know most of them."

She says, "Don't you think it's time you cut your own meat?"

The rumor was you had to squeeze a frog to death with your bare hand. You had to eat a live earthworm. To prove you could obey just as Abraham did when he tried to kill his son to make God happy, you had to cut off your little finger with an ax.

That was the rumor.

After that, you had to cut off someone else's little finger.

You never saw anybody after they were baptized so you couldn't tell if they still had a little finger. You couldn't ask them if they had had to squeeze the frog.

Right after you were baptized, you got on a truck and

left the colony. You'd never see the colony again. The truck was headed out into the wicked outside world where they already had your first work assignment lined up for you. The big outside world with all its wonderful new sins, and the better you did on the tests, the better the job you'd get.

You could figure out what some of the tests were going to be.

The church elders told you right up front if you were too skinny or too fat for how tall you were. They set aside the whole year before your baptism for you to get yourself perfect. You were excused from work at home so you could go to special lessons all day. Bible lessons. Cleaning lessons. Etiquette, fabric care, and you know all the rest. If you were fat you ate to lose weight, and if you were too skinny you just ate.

That whole year before baptism, every tree, every friend, everything you saw had the halo around it of your knowing you'd never see it again.

By what you studied, you knew about most of the tests you'd get.

Beyond that, the rumor was there was more we didn't know would happen.

We knew by rumor that you'd be bare naked for part of the baptism. One church elder would put his hand on you and tell you to cough. Another elder would slide a finger up your anus.

Another church elder would follow along with you and write on a card how well you did.

You didn't know how you were supposed to study for a prostate exam.

We all knew the baptisms took place in the meetinghouse basement. The daughters went to baptism in the spring with only the church women in attendance. Sons went in the fall with only the men there to tell you to get up on the scale naked and be weighed or ask you to recite a chapter and verse from the Bible.

Job, Chapter Fourteen, Verse Five:

"Seeing his days are determined, the number of his months are with thee, thou hast appointed his bounds that he cannot pass."

And you had to recite it naked.

Psalm 101, Psalms of David, Verse Two:

"I will behave myself wisely in a perfect way. . . . I will walk within my house with a perfect heart."

You had to know how to make the best dust cloths (soak rags in diluted turpentine, then hang them to dry). You had to figure how deep to set a six-foot-tall gatepost so it could support a five-foot-wide gate. Another church elder would blindfold you and give you cloth samples to feel, and you had to say which was cotton or wool or a poly-cotton blend.

You had to identify houseplants. Stains. Insects. Fix small appliances. Do elegant handwriting for invitations.

We guessed about the tests from what we had to study in school. Other parts came from sons who weren't too bright. Sometimes your father would tell you inside information so you might score a little higher and get a better job assignment instead of a lifetime of misery. Your friends would tell each other, and then everybody would know.

Nobody wanted to embarrass their family. And nobody wanted a lifetime of removing asbestos.

The church elders were going to stand you in one place and you'd have to read a chart at the far end of the meeting hall.

The church elders would give you a needle and thread and time how long you took to sew on a missing button.

We knew about what kind of jobs we were headed for in the wicked outside world from what the elders said to scare or inspire us. To make us work harder, they told us about wonderful jobs in gardens bigger than anything we could picture this side of Heaven. Some jobs were in palaces so enormous you'd forget you were indoors. These gardens were called amusement parks. The palaces, hotels.

To make us study even harder, they told us about jobs where

you'd spend years pumping cesspools, burning offal, spraying poisons. Removing asbestos. There were jobs so terrible, they told us we'd be glad to run up and meet death halfway.

There were jobs so boring, you'd find ways to cripple yourself so you couldn't work.

So you memorized every minute of your last year in the church district colony.

Ecclesiastes, Chapter Ten, Verse Eighteen:

"By much slothfulness the building decayeth; and through idleness of the hands the house droppeth through."

Lamentations, Chapter Five, Verse Five:

"Our necks are under persecution: we labour, and have no rest."

To keep bacon from curling, chill it a few minutes in the freezer before frying.

Rub the top of your meat loaf with an ice cube, and the loaf won't crack while it bakes.

To keep lace crisp, iron it between sheets of waxed paper.

We were kept busy learning. We had a million facts to remember. We memorized half the Old Testament.

We thought all this teaching was to make us smart.

What it did was make us stupid.

With all the little facts we learned, we never had the time to think. None of us ever considered what life would be like cleaning up after a stranger every day. Washing dishes all day. Feeding a stranger's children. Mowing a lawn. All day. Painting houses. Year after year. Ironing bedsheets.

Forever and ever.

Work without end.

We were all of us so excited about passing tests, we never looked beyond the night of the baptism.

We were all so worried about our worst fears, squeezing frogs, eating worms, poisons, asbestos, we never considered how boring life would be even if we succeeded and got a good job.

Washing dishes, forever.

Polishing silver, forever.

Mowing the lawn.

Repeat.

The night before the baptism, my brother Adam took me out on the back porch of our family's house and gave me a haircut. Every other family in the church district colony with a seventeen-year-old son was giving him the exact same haircut.

In the wicked outside world, they call this product standardization.

My brother told me not to smile, but to stand straight up and down and answer any questions in a clear voice.

In the outside world, they call this marketing.

My mother was putting my clothes together in a bag for me to take with me. We were all of us pretending to sleep that night.

In the wicked outside world, my brother told me, there were sins the church didn't know enough to forbid. I couldn't wait.

The next night was our baptism, and we did everything we'd expected. Then nothing else. Just when you were ready to hack off your little finger and the finger of the son next to you, nothing happened. After you'd been poked and felt and weighed and questioned about the Bible and housework, then they told you to get dressed.

You took your bag with your extra clothes inside, and you walked from the meetinghouse into a truck that was idling outside.

The truck drove out into the wicked outside world, into the night, and nobody you knew would ever see you again.

You never found out how high you scored.

Even if you knew you'd done well, that good feeling didn't last very long.

There was already a work assignment waiting for you.

God forbid you should ever get bored and want more.

It was church doctrine that the rest of your life would be the same work. The same being alone. Nothing would change. Every day. This was success. Here was the prize.

Mowing the lawn.

And mowing the lawn.

And mowing the lawn.

Repeat.

33

On the bus on the way to our third date, Fertility and I are sitting in front of some guy when we overhear the joke.

The temperature is eighty, ninety degrees, too hot for June anywhere, and the bus windows are open, with the smell of traffic making me a little sick. The vinyl seats are hot the way touching anything will feel in Hell, hot. The bus is Fertility's idea for going downtown. On a date, she told me. Downtown. It's the afternoon so only people without jobs or with night jobs or crazy people with Tourette's Syndrome are going anywhere.

Here's the date she has to take me on since she won't sleep with me and won't even kiss me, no way, no day.

Who's sitting behind us I can't imagine. He was nobody to notice, just a guy in a shirt. Blond hair. If you pressed me, I'd have to say ugly. I don't remember. The bus comes by the mausoleum every fifteen minutes, and we just got on. We met at Crypt 678, the same as every time.

I do remember the joke. It's an old joke. Houses of the city are going by outside the bus, behind cars parked along the curb and between fences to mark the property lines, and the joker leans his head between Fertility and me and whispers, "What's harder than getting a camel through the eye of a needle?"

These jokes are all over. No matter how not funny they are, you can't not hear them.

Neither Fertility or me says anything back.

And the joker whispers, "Buying life insurance to cover a Creedish church member."

The truth is, nobody laughs at these jokes except me, and I only laugh so I'll fit in. I laugh so I won't not fit in. The main thing I worry about in public is maybe people can tell I'm a survivor. The church costume I got rid of years ago. God forbid I should look like one of those stupid crazy people in the Midwest who all killed themselves because they thought their God was calling them home.

My mother, my father, my brother Adam, my sisters, my other brothers, they're all dead and in the ground getting laughed at, but I'm alive. I still have to live in this world and get along with people.

So I laugh.

Because I have to do something, make some noise, shout, scream, cry, swear, howl, I laugh. It's all just different ways to vent.

These jokes are everywhere this morning, and you have to do something not to start crying all the time. Nobody laughs harder than me.

The joker whispers, "Why did the Creedish cross the road?"

Maybe he's not even talking to Fertility and me.

"Because he couldn't get any cars to hit him."

Behind everybody is the roar of the bus, pushed down the street by its engine in the back, putting out stink-colored smoke.

Today, all the jokes are because of the newspaper. From where I sit, I can see the headline below the fold on the front pages of five people hiding behind today's morning edition. It says:

"Cult Survivors Dwindle"

The article says how the curtain is almost closed on the tragedy of the Creedish church mass suicide ten years ago. The article says how the last surviving members of the Creedish church, the cult based in central Nebraska that committed mass suicide rather than face an FBI investigation and national attention, well, the newspaper says only six church members are known to still exist. They don't name names, but I must be one of the last half-dozen.

The rest of the story jumps to page A9, but you get the gist. When you read between the lines, it says, Good riddance.

They don't write anything about suspect deaths where it looked like murder. There's nothing about how a killer is maybe stalking those last six church survivors.

Behind me, the joker whispers, "What do you call a Creedish with blond hair?"

In my head I tell him, Dead. I've heard all these jokes.

"What do you call a Creedish with red hair?"

Dead.

"With brown hair?"

Dead.

The guy whispers, "What's the difference between a Creedish and a corpse?"

Just a matter of hours.

The guy whispers, "What did the Creedish yell when the hearse drove by?"

Taxi!

The guy whispers, "How can you pick out a Creedish on a crowded bus?"

Someone pulls the cord for the next stop and rings the bell.

And Fertility twists around to say, "Shut up." She goes loud enough to bring people out from behind their newspapers, she says, "You're joking about suicide, about people that people loved that are dead. So just shut up."

It's really loud she says this. How bright her eyes are, gray but looking silver, it makes me wonder if Fertility isn't Creedish or if she's still peeved about her brother being dead. She's being such an overreaction.

The bus pulls to the curb right then, and the joker gets up in the aisle and starts out. The same as in church, we're sitting in the bench seats with the aisle down the middle of the bus. The guy waiting in line to get off, his pants are the baggy brown wool only a survivor would wear in this heat. The church costume suspenders crisscross his back. The brown wool jacket is folded over his arm. He shuffles up the aisle of the bus, he stops a minute while other people get off, and he turns and just touches the brim of his straw hat. He's familiar from somewhere, but it's been so long. His smell is sweat and wool and straw of a farm.

Where I know him from I can't remember. His voice, I remember. His voice, just his voice, over my shoulder, into my telephone.

May you die with all your work done.

His face is the face I see in the mirror.

Not even thinking, I say his name out loud.

Adam. Adam Branson.

The joker says, "Do I know you from somewhere?"

But I say, No.

The line moves a few steps, taking him farther away, and he says, "Didn't we grow up together?"

And I say, No.

Standing at the door of the bus, he shouts, "Aren't you my brother?"

And I shout, No.

And he's gone.

Luke, Chapter Twenty-two, Verse Thirty-four:

". . . thou shalt thrice deny that thou knowest me."

The bus starts back into traffic.

The only way to describe the guy is ugly. Geeky. A tad overweight. A loser. Pathetic at best. A victim. My big brother by three minutes. A Creedish.

According to her body language, the psychology textbooks would say Fertility is pissed off at me for laughing. Her legs are crossed at the knee and ankle. She looks out the window as if where we're at is any different.

According to my daily planner, right now I should be waxing the dining-room floor. There's the gutters to clean. There's a stain to clean up in the driveway where I work. I should be peeling the white asparagus for dinner tonight.

I shouldn't be out on a date with a lovely and angry Fertility Hollis even if I killed her brother and she has the secret hots for my voice on the phone at night but can't stand me in person.

The truth is, it doesn't matter what I should do. What any survivor should do. According to everything we grew up believing, we're corrupt and evil and unclean.

The air moving along downtown in the bus with us is hot and dense, mixed in with bright sunlight and burning gasoline. Flowers move by, planted in the ground, roses that should have a smell, red, yellow, orange all the way open but without effect. The six lanes of traffic move along relentless as a conveyor belt.

Everything we can do is wrong as long as we're still alive.

The feeling is you have no control. The feeling is that we're being delivered.

It's not like we're traveling. We're being processed. It's more like we're just waiting. It's just a matter of time.

There's nothing I can do right, and my brother's out there to kill me.

The buildings of downtown start to pile up along the sidewalk. The traffic gets slow. Fertility lifts her arm to pull the cord, ding, and the bus stops to let us out in front of a department store. Artificial men and women are posed in the windows wearing clothes. Smiling. Laughing. Pretending to have a good time. I know just how they feel.

The clothes I'm wearing are just pants and a plaid shirt, but they belong to the man who I work for. All morning, I was upstairs trying on different combinations of clothes and going downstairs to where the caseworker was vacuuming lampshades to ask her what she thought.

There's a big clock above the doors into the store, and Fertility looks up. She says to me, "Hurry. We have to be there by two o'clock."

She takes my hand in her amazing cold hand, cold and dry even in the heat, and we push in through the doors, into the air conditioning and first floor with piles of what's there to buy on tables and inside glass cases, locked.

"We have to be on the fifth floor," Fertility says, her hand tight around mine and pulling. We charge up the escalators. Second floor, Men's. Third floor, Children's. Fourth floor, Junior Miss. Fifth floor, Women's.

That kind of recorded music comes out the vents in the ceiling. It's a Cha-Cha. Two slow steps and three fast. There's a crossover step and a women's under-arm turn. Fertility taught me.

This is less of a date than I thought. Clothes on racks, hanging on hangers. Salespeople walk around dressed really well and asking if they can help. None of this is anything I haven't seen before.

I ask, does she want to dance, here?

"Wait a minute," Fertility says. "Just wait."

What happens first is the smell of smoke.

"Back here," Fertility says, and leads me into the forest of long dresses for sale.

Then what happens is bells start ringing, and people head for the escalators, stepping down them the way they would ordinary stairs since the escalators are stopped. People are walking down the up escalator, and this looks as wrong as breaking a law. A saleslady empties out her register into a zippered bag, and looks across the floor at some people by the elevators, standing, looking up at the elevator numbers, holding big glossy shopping bags with handles and stuff folded inside.

The bells are still ringing. The smoke is thick enough for us to watch it roll across the lights in the ceiling.

"Don't use the elevators," the saleslady shouts. "When it's a fire, the elevators don't work. You'll have to use the stairs."

She rushes over to them through the maze of clothes on racks, the zippered bag tucked in her arm, quarterback-style, and she herds them through a door marked EXIT.

Then it's just Fertility and me, and the lights flicker and go out.

In the dark, the smoke and the feel of satin all around us, the rub of cut velvet, the cold of silk, the smooth of polished cotton, the bells ringing, all the dresses, the scratch of wool, the cold of Fertility's hand on mine, she says, "Don't worry."

The little green signs shine at us across the dark, saying EXIT.

The bells ringing.

"Just stay calm," Fertility says.

The bells ringing.

"Any minute now," Fertility says.

Bright orange flashes in the dark on the other side of the floor, breaking everything into strange shapes of orange against black. The dresses and pants between here and there are hanging black shapes of people with arms and legs that burst into flame.

The shapes of a thousand people burning and collapsing head toward us. The bells are ringing so loud you feel it, and only Fertility's cold hand is keeping me here.

"It's any second now," she says.

The heat's close enough to feel. The smoke's thick enough to taste. Not twenty feet away, the scarecrow shapes of women made by clothes on hangers start smoldering and slump to the floor. Breathing gets hard, and my eyes won't stay open.

And the bells ring.

My clothes feel ironed hot and dry against me.

The fire is that close.

Fertility says, "Isn't this great? Don't you just love it?"

I put my hand up and it makes a shadow of cool between my face and the rack of rayon burning next to us.

This is the way to tell about fabric content. Pull a few threads off a garment, and hold them over a flame. If they don't burn, it's wool. If they burn slowly, it's cotton. If they torch the way the slacks next to us are blazing, the fabric is synthetic. Polyester. Rayon. Nylon.

Fertility says, "It's right now."

Then it's cold before I can think why. It's wet. Water pours down. The orange light flickers, lower, lower, gone. The smokes washes out of the air.

One by one, spotlights blink on to show what's left in huge shadows of black and white. The ringing bells stop. The recorded Cha-Cha music comes back on.

"I saw this all happen in a dream," Fertility says. "We were never in any real danger."

This is the same as her and Trevor on the ocean liner that only sank halfway.

"Next week," Fertility says, "there's a commercial bakery that's going to explode. You want to go watch? I see at least three or four people getting killed."

My hair, her hair, my clothes, her clothes, there isn't a smudge or burn on us.

Daniel, Chapter Three, Verse Twenty-seven:

". . . the fire had no power, nor was an hair of their head singed, neither were their coats changed, nor the smell of fire had passed on them."

Been there, I'm thinking. Done that.

"Hurry," she says. "Some firemen will be coming up here in a few minutes." She takes my hands in hers and says, "Let's not let this Cha-Cha go to waste."

One, two, cha cha cha. We dance, three, four, cha cha cha.

The wreckage, the burned arms and legs of the clothes tangled on the floor around us, the ceiling hanging down, the water still falling, everything soaking wet, we dance one, two, cha cha cha.

And that's just how they find us.

32

There's a gas station going to explode next week. There's a pet store where all the canaries, their whole inventory of hundreds of canaries, will escape. Fertility has previewed all this in dream after dream. There's a hotel where a water pipe is leaking right this moment. For weeks, the water has been dripping inside the walls, dissolving plaster, rotting wood, rusting metal, and at 3:04 next Tuesday afternoon, the mammoth crystal chandelier in the middle of the lobby ceiling will drop.

In her dream, there's a rattle of lead crystal thingamabobs, then a spray of plaster dust. Some bracket will pop the head off a rusted bolt. In Fertility's dream, the bolt head lands, plop, on the carpet next to an old man with luggage. He picks it up and turns it over in his palm, looking at the rust and the shining steel inside the stress fracture.

A woman pulling her luggage on wheels stops next to the man and asks if he's waiting in line.

The old man says, "No."

The woman says, "Thank you."

A clerk at the desk hits a bell and says, "Front please!"

A bellhop steps forward.

At that moment the chandelier falls.

That's how exact Fertility's dreams get, and in each dream she looks for another detail. The woman is wearing a red suit, jacket and skirt with a Christian Dior gold chain belt. The old man has blue eyes. His hand holding the bolt head has a gold wedding band. The bellhop has a pierced ear, but he's got the earring out.

Behind the desk clerk, Fertility says, there's a complicated French Baroque clock inside a frou-frou case of gilded lead with seashells and dolphins supporting the clock dial. The time is 3:04 p.m.

Fertility told me all this with her eyes closed. Remembering it or making it up, I couldn't tell.

I Thessalonians, Chapter Five, Verse Twenty:

"Despise not prophesyings."

The chandelier will blink out at the second it falls so everybody underneath will look up. What happens after that, she can't say. She always wakes up. The dreams always end there, at the moment the chandelier falls or the plane crashes. Or the train derails. The lightning strikes. The earth quakes.

She's started keeping a calendar of upcoming disasters. She shows it to me. I show her the daily planner book the people I work for keep. On tap for next week, she has a bakery explosion, the loose canaries, the gas station fire, the hotel chandelier.

Fertility says to take my pick. We'll pack a lunch and make a real day out of it.

For next week, I have mowing the lawn, twice. Polishing the brass fireplace tool set. Checking the dates on everything in the freezer. Rotating the canned goods in the pantry. Buying the people I work for wedding anniversary gifts to give each other.

I say, Sure. Whatever she wants.

This was right after the firemen discovered us doing the Cha-Cha inside the burned-out fifth-floor women's department without a mark on us. After they took our statements and made us sign insurance forms letting them off the hook, they escorted us down to the street. We're back outside when I ask Fertility, Why?

Why doesn't she call anybody and warn them before a disaster?

"Because nobody wants bad news," she says and shrugs. "Trevor told people every time he had a dream, and it just got him in trouble."

Nobody wanted to believe in a talent this incredible, she said. They'd accuse Trevor of being a terrorist or an arsonist.

A pyromaniac, according to the *Statistical Manual of Mental Disorders*.

In another century, they'd have accused him of being a warlock.

So Trevor killed himself.

With a little help from yours truly.

"So that's why I don't tell people anymore," Fertility says. "Maybe if it was an orphanage that was going to burn down, maybe I'd tell, but these people killed my brother, so why should I do them any favors?"

The way I can save human lives here is to tell Fertility the truth, I killed her brother, but I don't. We sit at the bus stop not talking until her bus is within sight. She writes me her phone number on a sales receipt she picks up off the ground. This is good for three-hundred-plus dollars if I take it back to the store and work my scam. Fertility says to pick a disaster and give her a call. The bus takes her away to wherever, to work, to dinner, to dream.

According to my daily planner, I'm dusting baseboards. I'm clipping hedges right now. I'm mowing the lawn. I'm detailing the cars. I should be ironing, but I know the caseworker is getting my work done.

According to the *Statistical Manual of Mental Disorders,* I should go into a store and shoplift. I should go work off some pent-up sexual energy.

According to Fertility, I should pack a lunch to eat while we watch strangers get killed. I can picture us on a velvet love seat in the hotel lobby, sipping tea Tuesday afternoon in our front-row seat.

According to the Bible, I should be, I don't know what.

According to Creedish church doctrine, I should be dead.

None of the above really catches my fancy so I just walk around downtown. Outside the commercial bakery there's the smell of bread where in five days Fertility says, boom. In the back of the pet store, the hundreds of canaries flutter from side to side of their stinking crowded cage. Next week, they'll all be free. Then what? I want to tell them, stay in the cage. There are better things than freedom. There are worse things than living a long bored life in some stranger's house and then dying and going to canary heaven.

At the gas station Fertility says will explode, the attendants pump gas, happy enough, not unhappy, young, not knowing that next week they'll be dead or unemployed depending on who works what shift.

It gets dark pretty fast.

Outside the hotel, in through the big plate glass lobby windows, the chandelier looms over victim after victim. A woman with a pug dog on a leash. A family: mother, father, three little kids. The clock behind the desk says it's still a long ways from 3:04 next Tuesday afternoon. It would be safe to stand there for days and days but not for one second too long.

You could go in past the doormen in their gold braid and tell the manager his chandelier was going to fall.

Everyone he loves will die.

Even he will die, someday.

God will come back to judge us.

All his sins will dog him into Hell.

You can tell people the truth, but they'll never believe you until the event. Until it's too late. In the meantime, the truth will just piss them off and get you in a lot of trouble.

So you just walk home.

There's dinner to start. There's a shirt you need to iron for tomorrow. Shoes to shine. You have dishes to wash. New recipes to master.

There's something called Wedding Soup that takes six pounds of bone marrow to make. Organ meats are big this year. The people I work for want to eat right on the cutting edge. Kidneys. Livers. Inflated pig bladders. The intermediate cow stomach stuffed with watercress and fennel, cud-style. They want animals stuffed with the most unlikely other animals, chickens stuffed with rabbit. Carp stuffed with ham. Goose stuffed with salmon.

There's so much I need to get home and perfect.

To bard a steak, you cover it with strips of fat from some other animal to protect it while it cooks. This is what I'm up to when the phone rings.

Of course, it's Fertility.

"You were right about that weird guy," she says.

I ask, About what?

"That guy, Trevor's boyfriend," she says. "He really needs somebody. I took him out on a date like you wanted, and one of those cult people was on the bus with us. They had to be twin brothers. They looked that much alike."

I say, maybe she's wrong. Most of those cult people are dead. They were crazy and stupid and almost all of them are dead. It's in the newspaper. Everything they believed in turned out to be wrong.

"The guy on the bus asked if they were related, and Trevor's boyfriend said no."

Then they weren't related, I say. You'd have to recognize your own brother.

Fertility says, "That's the sad part. He did recognize the guy. He even said a name, Brad or Tim or something."

Adam.

I say, So how is that sad?

"Because it was such an obvious, pathetic denial," she says. "It's so obvious he's trying to pass as a normal happy person. It was so sad I even gave him my phone number. I felt sorry for him. I mean I want to help him embrace his past. Besides," Fertility says, "I have a feeling he's headed for some terrible shit."

Like what shit, I ask. What does she mean, shit?

"Misery," she says. "It's still pretty vague. Disasters. Pain. Mass murder. Don't ask me how I know. It's a long story."

Her dreams. The gas station, the canaries, the hotel chandelier, and now me.

"Listen," she says. "We still need to talk about us getting together, but not right now."

Why?

"My evil job is getting a little thick right now, so if somebody called Dr. Ambrose calls to ask if you know Gwen, say you don't know me. Tell him we never met, okay?"

Gwen?

I ask, Who's Dr. Ambrose?

"That's just his name," Fertility says. Gwen says. "He's not a real doctor, I don't think. He's more like my booking agent. This isn't what I want to be doing, but I work on contract for him."

I ask, what is it she does on contract?

"It's nothing not legal. I have it all under control. Pretty much."

What?

And she tells me, and the alarms and sirens start going off.

How I'm feeling is smaller and smaller.

The alarms and flashing lights and sirens are all around me.

How I'm feeling is less and less.

Here in the cockpit of Flight 2039, the first of the four engines has just flamed out. Where we're at right here is the beginning of the end.

31

P art of her doing suicide intervention is my caseworker has to mix me another gin and tonic. This is while I'm talking long-distance on the telephone. A producer for *The Dawn Williams Show* is holding on line two. All the lines are blinking blinking. Somebody from Barbara Walters is holding on line three. Top priority is my getting somebody to handle the buzz. The breakfast dishes are piled up in the sink not washing themselves.

Top priority is my hooking up with a good agent.

Upstairs, the beds are still unmade.

The garden needs to be repainted.

Over the telephone, this one top agent is stressing about what if I'm not the sole survivor. This has to be the case is what I'm saying. The caseworker wouldn't be dropping by for a breakfast gin and tonic if there hadn't been another suicide last night. Right here on the kitchen table I have spread out in front of me all the other case history folders.

The government's whole Survivor Retention Program is what you'd call a washout. It's the caseworker mixing me gin and tonics who needs some suicide intervention.

Just to make sure I don't go south on her, the caseworker is eyeing me. Just to keep her out of my way, I have her slicing a lime. Get me some cigarettes. Mix me a fresh drink, I say, or I'll kill myself. I swear. I'll go in the bathroom and hack all my veins open with a razor.

The caseworker brings my new gin and tonic back to where we're sitting at the kitchen table and asks if I want to help identify some bodies. This is supposed to help me achieve closure. After all, she says, they are my people, my flesh and blood. My kith and kin.

She's fanning the same ten-year-old government photos out on the table. Staring up at me are hundreds of dead people laid out shoulder to shoulder in rows on the ground. Their skin is all bruised black from the cyanide. They're bloated so much the dark home-made clothes on them are tight. Ashes to ashes. Dust to dust. The whole recycling process should be that quick and easy, but it's not. The bodies lying there stiff and rank. This is the caseworker trying to jump-start my emotions. I'm repressing my grief, she says.

Would I like to wade in and what you'd call ID these dead people?

If there is a killer out there, she says, I can help her find the person who should be pictured here dead but isn't.

Thanks, I say. No, thanks. Without even looking, I know Adam Branson won't be dead in any of her pictures.

As the caseworker goes to sit down, I ask would she mind closing the curtains. There's a van from a network affiliate outside shooting video for a satellite feed through the kitchen window. The dirty breakfast dishes piled up in the foreground, that's not how I want to look on the news tonight. The dirty dishes in the sink, me and the caseworker sitting at the kitchen table with the telephone and all her manila folders spread out on the yellow-and-white-check tablecloth, gin and tonics in hand at ten a.m.

The voice-over of the newscaster will be saying how the sole survivor of America's latest death cult, the Creedish, is on suicide watch following the tragic string of suicides that one by one have claimed the lives of the remaining cult survivors.

Then, cut to commercial.

The caseworker goes through her last client folders. Brannon, deceased. Walker, deceased. Phillips, deceased. Everybody, deceased. Everybody except me.

The girl last night, the only other remaining survivor of the Creedish church district, she ate dirt. There's even a name for it. They call it geophagy. This was popular among the Africans brought to America as slaves. Popular probably isn't the right word.

She knelt down in the backyard of the house where she'd served for eleven years, and she spooned the dirt out of a rose bed and right into her mouth. This is all in the caseworker's report. Then something called an esophageal rupture happened, then peritonitis, then around sunrise she was dead.

The girl before that one died with her head in the oven. The boy before her cut his throat. This is exactly what the church taught. One day the wickedness of the kings of the world would destroy us, oh sorrow, and armies of the world would march upon us, wailing, and the purest children of God would have to deliver themselves unto the Lord by their own hand.

The Deliverance.

Yea, and everybody not delivered unto the Lord among the first leavings should follow behind as soon as possible.

So for the past ten years, one after another, men and women, maids and gardeners and factory workers all over the country, have been giving themselves up. Despite the Survivor Retention Program.

Except for me.

I ask the caseworker, would she mind making the beds? If I have to make one more hospital corner, I swear, I'll stick my head in the food processor. If she agrees, I promise to be alive when she gets back.

Upstairs she goes. I say, Thanks.

After the caseworker told me about everybody in the Creedish district colony being dead and all, the first thing I did was start smoking. The smartest thing I've ever done is start smoking. When the caseworker dropped by to say rise and shine, and the only other surviving Creedish went south last night, then I sat myself in the kitchen and upped my suicide process with a good stiff drink.

It's church doctrine that says I have to kill myself. They don't say it has to be a hurry-hurry instant quick death.

The newspaper's still out on the doorstep. The breakfast dishes, unwashed. The people I work for, they've gone off to escape the spotlight. This is after years of my rewinding their rental porn and presoaking their stains. He's a banker. She's a banker. They have cars. They own this lovely house. They own me to make the beds and mow the lawn. The truth be told, they probably left so they wouldn't come home one night and find me suicided on the kitchen floor.

Their four telephone lines are still holding. *The Dawn Williams Show.* Barbara Walters. The agent is saying to get a hand mirror and practice looking sincere and innocent.

One of the manila folders has my name on the tab. The top sheet inside the folder is all the basics about the documented persons who survived the Creedish colony disaster.

The agent is saying: product endorsements.

The agent is saying: my own religious program.

It's documented in the folder how for more than two hundred years, Americans had considered the Creedish the most pious, the most hardworking, decent, sensible people left on Earth.

The agent is saying: A million-dollar advance for my life story in hardcover.

The background sheet says how ten years ago a local sheriff served the elders of the Creedish church district with a search warrant. There were charges of child abuse. It was some crazy anonymous allegation that families in the church district were having children and having children and having children. And none of these children were documented, no birth certificates, no social security numbers, nothing. All of these births occurred within the church district. All of these children had attended church district schools. None of these children would ever be allowed to marry or raise children. When they turned seventeen, they were all baptized as adult church members and then sent off into the world.

This has all become what you would call public knowledge.

The agent is saying: my own exercise video.

The agent is saying: an exclusive for the cover of *People* magazine.

Somebody leaked these crazy rumors to some child welfare peon, and the next thing is the sheriff and two carloads of deputies are being dispatched to the Creedish church district in Bolster County, Nebraska, to count heads and make sure everything is official. It was the sheriff who called in the FBI.

The agent on the phone is saying: talk show circuit.

The FBI learned how children sent out into the world were considered labor missionaries by the Creedish. It was the government investigation that called it white slavery. The television people called it the Child Slave Cult.

These kids would be placed when they turned seventeen by Creedish overseers in the outside world who found them jobs as manual labor or domestic help on a cash-pay basis. Temp jobs that could last for years.

It was the newspapers who called it the Church of Slave Labor.

The church district would pocket the cash, and the outside world got an army of clean, honest little Christian maids and gardeners and dishwashers and housepainters who'd been raised to believe the only way they could earn a soul is if they worked to death for nothing more than room and board.

The agent is saying to me: syndicated newspaper column.

When the FBI moved in to make arrests, they found the entire population of the district colony shut up in the meetinghouse. Maybe the same person who leaked this crazy story about child slaves as a cash crop, it could be this same person had let the colony know the government was about to invade. Every farm going into Bolster County was deserted. It would come out later that every cow, every pig, chicken, pigeon, cat, and dog was dead. Even goldfish in fishbowls were poisoned. Every Creedish perfect little farm with its white farmhouse and red barn was silent as the National Guard drove past. Every field of potatoes was silent and empty under blue sky and a few clouds.

The agent is saying: my very own Christmas Special.

According to the background report, here with the manila folders, the kitchen table, the caseworker making beds upstairs, the heat of the lighter as I light another cigarette, this practice of sending labor missionaries had gone on for more than a hundred years. The Creedish had just gotten richer and bought more land and had more children. More children had disappeared out of the valley every year. Girls were shipped out in the spring and boys in the fall.

The agent is saying: my own fragrance.

The agent is saying: my own line of autographed Bibles.

The missionaries were invisible in the outside world. The church wasn't troubled with paying taxes. According to church doctrine, the most noble you could be was to just do your work and hope to live long enough to show the district an enormous profit. The rest of your life was supposed to be a burden, making the beds of other people. Caring for other people's babies. Cooking food for other people.

Forever and ever.

Work without end.

The plan was little by little to bring about a Creedish paradise by acquiring the whole world an acre at a time.

Until the FBI vans rolled to a stop an official three hundred feet outside the doors of the church district meetinghouse. The air was still, according to the official investigation into the massacre. No sound came from the church.

The agent is saying: inspirational Tapes.

The agent is saying: Caesars Palace.

It was then that everybody in the world started calling the Creedish the Old Testament Death Cult.

The cigarette smoke chokes past the point where my throat would close it out and sits thick in my chest. The caseworker folders document the stragglers. Survivor Retention Client Number Sixty-three, Biddy Patterson, age approximately twenty-nine, killed herself by ingesting cleaning solvent three days after the colony district incident.

Survivor Retention Client Tender Smithson, age forty-five, killed himself by stepping out of a window of the building where he worked as a janitor.

The agent is saying: my own 1-976 salvation hotline.

The smoke hot and dense inside me feels the way I would if I had a soul.

The agent is saying: my own infomercial.

The people black and swollen with their giving up. Long rows of people the FBI carried dead out of the meetinghouse, they lie there black with the cyanide in their last communion. These are the people who whatever they imagined was coming down the road, they'd rather die than meet it.

They died together in one mass, holding each other by the hand so tight the FBI had to pry at their dead fingers to take them apart.

The agent is saying: Celebrity Superstar.

It's church doctrine that right now while the caseworker is gone, I should take a knife from the dishes in the sink and hack out my windpipe. I should spill my guts out onto the kitchen floor.

The agent says he'll handle the buzz with *The Dawn Williams Show* and Barbara Walters.

Among the deceased is a manila folder with my own name on it. In it, I write:

Survivor Retention Client Number Eighty-four has lost everyone he ever loved and everything that gave his life meaning. He is tired and sleeps most of the time. He has started drinking and smoking. He has no appetite. He seldom bathes and hasn't shaved in weeks.

Ten years ago, he was the hardworking salt of the earth. All he wanted was to go to Heaven. Sitting here today, everything that he worked for in the world is lost. All his external rules and controls are gone.

There is no Hell. There is no Heaven.

Still, just dawning on him is the idea that now anything is possible.

Now he wants everything.

I shut the folder and slip it back in the pile.

Just between him and me, the agent asks, is there any chance I'm going to off myself soon?

Staring up through my gin and tonic, the sunken faces of everybody from my past are dead in the government pictures under my drink. After moments like this, you're whole life is gravy.

I freshen my drink.

I light another cigarette.

Really, my life no longer has a point. I'm free. This and I stand to inherit twenty thousand acres of central Nebraska.

How this feels is just like ten years ago, when I rode with the police downtown. And once again, I am weak. And minute by minute I'm moving away from salvation and into the future.

Kill myself?

Thanks, I say. No, thanks.

Let's not rush anything here.

30

What I'm busy telling the police all morning is I left the caseworker still alive and scrubbing the brick around the fireplace in the den. The problem is the flue doesn't open right and smoke comes out the front. The people who I work for burn wet wood. What I tell the police is I'm innocent.

I didn't kill anybody.

According to my daily planner, I was supposed to scrub the brick yesterday.

This is how my day's gone so far.

First the police are hammering me about why did I kill

my caseworker. Then the agent's calling to promise me the world. Fertility, Fertility, Fertility is out of the picture. Let's just say I'm not comfortable with how she earns a living. Plus, I'd just as soon not know about all the misery in my future.

So I lock myself in the bathroom to try to collate what's all happened. The downstairs green bathroom.

How my statement to the police goes is first the caseworker was dead facedown on the bricks in front of the fireplace in the den with her black capri pants still on and all bunched up around her ass from the way she's fallen there. Her white shirt's untucked with the sleeves rolled up to each elbow. The room's choking with deadly chlorine gas and the sponge is still squeezed in her dead fish white hand.

Before that, I was climbing in through the basement window we left unlocked so I could come and go without the television people dogging me with their cameras and paper cups of coffee and their professional concern as if they're getting paid enough to really care. As if this doesn't happen with another feature story for them to cover every two days. It does.

So I'm locked in the bathroom and now the police are outside the door to ask if I'm throwing up and say the man who I work for is on the speakerphone yelling at them for directions on how to eat a salad.

The police are asking, did the caseworker and I have a fight?

Look at my daily planner book for yesterday, I tell them. We never had time.

From starting work until eight in the morning, I was supposed to be caulking windows. The planner's open on the kitchen counter next to the speakerphone. I was supposed to be painting trim.

From eight until ten I was scrubbing the oil stains out in the driveway. From ten until lunch was for cutting back the hedges. Lunch until three was for sweeping porches. Three until five was for changing the water in all the flower arrangements. Five to seven was for scrubbing the fireplace brick.

Every last minute of my life has been preordained, and I'm sick and tired of it.

How this feels is I'm just another task in God's daily planner: the Italian Renaissance penciled in for right after the Dark Ages.

To everything there is a season.

For every trend, fad, phase. Turn, turn, turn.

Ecclesiastes, Chapter Three, Verses something through something.

The Information Age is scheduled immediately after the Industrial Revolution. Then the Postmodern Era, then the Four Horsemen of the Apocalypse. Famine. Check. Pestilence. Check. War. Check. Death. Check. And between the big events, the earthquakes and tidal waves, God's got me squeezed in for a cameo appearance. Then maybe in thirty years, or maybe next year, God's daily planner has me finished.

Through the bathroom door, the police are asking me, did I hit her? The caseworker. Did I ever steal her case history files and her DSM? All her files are missing.

She drank, is what I tell them. She took psychotropic drugs. She mixed bleach with ammonia inside closed unventilated areas. I don't know how she spent her free time, but she talked about dating a wide variety of lowlifes.

And she had those files yesterday.

The last thing I said to her was you can't get brick clean without sandblasting it, but she was so sure muriatic acid would do the job. One of her boyfriends swore by it.

When I climbed in through the basement window this morning she was dead on the floor with chlorine gas and muriatic acid all over half the brick wall, and it was still as dirty as ever, only now she was part of the mess.

Between her black capri pants and her little white socks and red canvas shoes, her calf muscles are smooth and white with every-thing of her that used to be red turned blue, her lips, her cuticles, the rim of each eye.

The truth is I didn't kill the caseworker, but I'm glad someone did.

She was my only connection to the last ten years. She was the last thing holding me onto my past.

The truth is you can be orphaned again and again and again.

The truth is you will be.

And the secret is, this will hurt less and less each time until you can't feel a thing.

Trust me on this.

With her lying there dead after our ten years of heart-to-heart talks every week, my first thought was, here's just something else for me to pick up.

The police are asking through the bathroom door, why did I make a batch of strawberry daiquiris before I called them?

Because we were out of raspberries.

Because, can't they see, it just does not matter. Time was not of the essence.

Think of this as valuable on-the-job training. Think of your life as a sick joke.

What do you call a caseworker who hates her job and loses every client?

Dead.

What do you call the police worker zipping her into a big rubber bag?

Dead.

What do you call the television anchor on camera in the front yard?

Dead.

It does not matter. The joke is we all have the same punch line.

The agent is holding on line one with what only looks like a whole new future to offer.

The man who I work for is shouting over the speakerphone that he's at a business lunch in some restaurant only he's calling from his cell phone in the toilet because he doesn't know how to eat the hearts of palm salad. As if this is really important.

Hey, I shout back. Me too.

Hiding in the toilet, I mean.

There's a terrible dark joy when the only person who knows all your secrets is finally dead. Your parents. Your doctor. Your therapist. Your caseworker. The sun's outside the bathroom window trying to show us we're all being stupid. All you have to do is look around.

What they teach you in the church district colony is to desire nothing. Keep a mild and downcast countenance. Preserve a modest posture and demeanor. Speak in a simple and quiet tone.

And just look how well their philosophy has turned out.

Them dead. Me alive. The caseworker dead. Everybody dead.

I rest my case.

Here in the bathroom with me are razor blades. Here is iodine to drink. Here are sleeping pills to swallow. You have a choice. Live or die.

Every breath is a choice.

Every minute is a choice.

To be or not to be.

Every time you don't throw yourself down the stairs, that's a choice. Every time you don't crash your car, you reenlist.

If I let the agent make me famous that wasn't going to change anything important.

What do you call a Creedish who gets his own talk show?

Dead.

What do you call the Creedish who goes around in a limousine and eats steak?

Dead.

Whatever direction I go in, I really don't have anything to lose.

According to my daily planner I should burn zinc in the fireplace to clear the chimney of soot.

Outside the bathroom window, the sun is watching police workers with the caseworker zipped inside a rubber bag belted to a gurney they're wheeling between them down the driveway to an ambulance with the lights not on.

For a long time after I found her, I stood over the body drinking my strawberry daiquiri and just looking at her there, blue and facedown. You didn't have to be Fertility Hollis to see this coming from way back. Her black hair was poking out the red bandanna tied around her head. A little drool had dripped outside the corner of her dead mouth onto a brick. Her whole body looked covered in dead skin.

All along, you could've guessed this would happen. Someday it would happen to us all.

Behaving myself just was not going to work anymore. It was time to make trouble.

So I made another blender full of daiquiris and called the police and told them not to hurry, nobody here was going anywhere.

Then I called the agent. The truth is there's always been someone to tell me what to do. The church. The people who I work for. The caseworker. And I can't stand the idea of being alone. I can't bear the thought of being free.

The agent said to hold on and give my statement to the police. The second I could leave, he'd send a car. A limousine.

My black-and-white stickers are all over town still telling people: Give Yourself, Your Life, Just One More Chance. Call Me for Help. Then my phone number.

Well, all those desperate people were on their own.

The limousine would take me to the airport, the agent said. The airplane would take me to New York. Already a team of people I'd never met, people in New York who knew nothing about me, were writing my autobiography. The agent said the first six chapters

would be faxed to me in the limousine so I could commit my childhood to memory before I give any interviews.

I told the agent I already knew my childhood.

Over the phone he said, "This version's better."

Version?

"We'll have an even hotter version for the movie." The agent asks,
"So who do you want to be you?"

I want to be me.

"In the movie, I mean."

I ask him to hold please. Already being famous was turning into
less freedom and more of a schedule of decisions and task after task
after task. The feeling isn't so great but it's familiar.

Then the police were at the front door and then they were inside
the den with the dead caseworker, taking her picture with a camera
from different angles and asking me to put down my drink so they
could ask questions about the night before.

It's right then I locked myself in the bathroom and had what the
psychology textbooks would call a quickie existential crisis.

The man who I work for calls from his restaurant bathroom
about his hearts of palm salad, and my day is pretty much complete.

Live or die?

I come out the bathroom door past the police and go right to the
phone. To the man who I work for, I tell him to use his salad fork.
Skewer each heart. Tines down. Lift the heart to his mouth and
suck out the juice. Then, place it in the breast pocket of his dou-
ble-breasted, Brooks-Brothered, pin-striped suit jacket.

He says, "Got it." And my job in this house is finished.

My one hand is holding the telephone, and with my other I'm
motioning for the police to put more rum in the next batch of
daiquiris.

The agent tells me not to bother with any luggage. New York has
a stylist already building a wardrobe of marketable all-cotton sack-
cloth-style religious sportswear they want me to promote.

Luggage reminds me of hotels reminds me of chandeliers reminds me of disasters reminds me of Fertility Hollis. She's the only thing I'm leaving behind. Only Fertility knows anything about me, even if she doesn't know much. Maybe she knows my future, but she doesn't know my past. Now nobody knows my past.

Except maybe Adam.

Between the two of them, they know more about my life than me.

According to my itinerary, the agent says, the car will be here in five minutes.

It's time to keep living.

It's time to reenlist.

In the limousine, there should be dark sunglasses. I want to be obviously incognito. I want black leather seats and tinted windows. I tell the agent, I want crowds at the airport chanting my name. I want more blender drinks. I want a personal fitness trainer. I want to lose fifteen pounds. I want my hair to be thicker. I want my nose to look smaller. Capped teeth. A cleft chin. High cheekbones. I want a manicure, and I want a tan.

I try to remember everything else Fertility doesn't like about how I look.

29

It's somewhere above Nebraska I remember I left my fish behind.

And it must be hungry.

It's part of Creedish tradition that even labor missionaries had something, a cat, a dog, a fish, to care for. Most times it was a fish. Just something to need you home at night. Something to keep you from living alone.

The fish is something to make me settle in one place. According to church colony doctrine, it's why men marry women and why women have children. It's something to live your life around.

It's crazy, but you invest all your emotion in just this one tiny goldfish, even after six hundred and forty goldfish, and you can't just let the little thing starve to death.

I tell the flight attendant, I've got to go back, while she's fighting against my one hand that's holding her by the elbow.

An airplane is just so many rows of people sitting and all going in the same direction a long ways off the ground. Going to New York's a lot the way I imagine going to Heaven would be.

It's too late, the flight attendant says. Sir. This is a nonstop. Sir. Maybe after we land, she says, maybe I could call someone. Sir.

But there isn't anybody.

Nobody will understand.

Not the apartment manager.

Not the police.

The flight attendant yanks her elbow away. She gives me a look and moves up the aisle.

Everyone else I could call is dead.

So I call the only person who can help. I call the last person I want to talk to, and she picks up on the first ring.

An operator asks if she'd accept the charges, and somewhere hundreds of miles behind me Fertility said yes.

I said hi, and she said hi. She doesn't sound at all surprised.

She asked, "Why weren't you at Trevor's crypt today? We had a date."

I forgot, I say. My whole life is about forgetting. It's my most valuable job skill.

It's my fish, I say. It's going to die if nobody feeds it. Maybe this doesn't sound important to her, but that fish means the whole world to me. Right now, that fish is the only thing I care about, and Fertility needs to go there and feed it, or better yet, take it home to live with her.

"Yeah," she says. "Sure. Your fish."

Yes. And it needs to be fed every day. There's the kind of food it likes best next to the fish bowl on my fridge, and I give her the address.

She says, "Enjoy going off to become a big international spiritual leader."

We're talking from farther and farther away as the plane takes me east. The sample chapters of my autobiography are on the seat next to me, and they're a complete shock.

I ask, how did she know?

She says, "I know a lot more than you give me credit for."

Like what for instance? I ask, what else does she know?

Fertility says, "What are you afraid I might know?"

The flight attendant goes on the other side of a curtain and says, "He's worried about a goldfish." Some women behind the curtain laugh and one says, "Is he retarded?"

As much to the flight crew as to Fertility I say, It just so happens that I'm the last survivor of an almost extinct religious cult.

Fertility says, "How nice for you."

I say, And I can't ever see her again.

"Yeah, yeah, yeah."

I say, People want me in New York by tomorrow. They're planning something big.

And Fertility says, "Of course they are."

I say, I'm sorry I won't ever get to dance with her anymore.

And Fertility says, "Yes, you will."

Since she knows so much, I ask her, what's the name of my fish?

"Number six forty-one."

And miracle of miracles, she's right.

"Don't even try keeping a secret," she says. "With all the dreams I've been having every night, not much surprises me."

28

After just the first fifty flights of stairs, my breath won't stay inside me long enough to do any good. My feet fly out behind me. My heart is jumping against the ribs it's behind inside my chest. The insides of my mouth and tongue are thick and stuck together with dried-up spit.

Where I'm at is one of those stair climbing machines the agent has installed. You climb and climb forever and never get off the ground. You're trapped in your hotel room. It's the mystical sweat lodge experience of our time, the only sort of Indian vision quest we can schedule into our daily planner.

Our StairMaster to Heaven.

Around the sixtieth floor, sweat is stretching my shirt down to my knees. The lining of my lungs feels the way a ladder looks in nylon stockings, stretched, snagged, a tear. In my lungs. A rupture. The way a tire looks before a blowout, that's how my lungs feel. The way it smells when your electric heater or hair dryer burns off a layer of dust, that's how hot my ears feel.

Why I'm doing this is because the agent says there's thirty pounds too much of me for him to make famous.

If your body is a temple, you can pile up too much deferred maintenance. If your body is a temple, mine was a real fixer-upper.

Somehow, I should've seen this coming.

The same way every generation reinvents Christ, the agent's giving me the same makeover. The agent says nobody is going to worship anybody with my role of flab around his middle. These days, people aren't going to fill stadiums to get preached at by somebody who isn't beautiful.

This is why I'm going nowhere at the rate of seven hundred calories an hour.

Around the eightieth floor, my bladder feels nested between the top of my legs. When you pull plastic wrap off something in the microwave and the steam sunburns your fingers in an instant, my breath is that hot.

You're going up and up and up and not getting anywhere. It's the illusion of progress. What you want to think is your salvation.

What people forget is a journey to nowhere starts with a single step, too.

It's not as if the great coyote spirit comes to you, but around the eighty-first floor, these random thoughts from out of the ozone just catch in your head. Silly things the agent told you, now they add up. The way you feel when you're scrubbing with pure ammonia fumes and right then while you're scrubbing chicken skin off the barbecue grill, every stupid thing in the world, decaffeinated coffee, alcohol-free beer, StairMasters, makes perfect sense, not because you're any smarter, but because the smart part of your brain's on vacation. It's that kind of faux wisdom. That kind of Chinese food enlightenment where you know that ten minutes after your head clears, you'll forget it all.

Those clear plastic bags you get a single serving of honey-roasted peanuts in on a plane instead of a real meal, that's how small my lungs feel. After eighty-five floors, the air feels that thin. Your arms pumping, your feet jam down on every next step. At this point, your every thought is so profound.

The way bubbles form in a pan of water before it comes to a boil, these new insights just appear.

Around the ninetieth floor, every thought is an epiphany.

Paradigms are dissolving right and left.

Everything ordinary turns into a powerful metaphor.

The deeper meaning of everything is right there in your face.

And it's all so significant.

It's all so deep.

So real.

Everything the agent's been telling me makes perfect sense. For instance, if Jesus Christ had died in prison, with no one watching and with no one there to mourn or torture him, would we be saved?

With all due respect.

According to the agent, the biggest factor that makes you a saint is the amount of press coverage you get.

Around the one hundredth floor, it all comes clear. The whole universe, and this isn't just the endorphins talking. Any higher than the hundredth floor and you enter a mystical state.

The same as if a tree falls in the forest and no one is there to hear it, you realize, if no one had been there to witness the agony of Christ, would we be saved?

The key to salvation is how much attention you get. How high a profile you get. Your audience share. Your exposure. Your name recognition. Your press following.

The buzz.

Around the one hundredth floor, the sweat is parting your hair all over. The boring mechanics of how your body works are all too clear, your lungs are sucking air to put in your blood, your heart pumps blood to your muscles, your hamstrings pull themselves short, cramping to pull your legs up behind you, your quadriceps cramp to put your knees out in front of you. The blood delivers air and food to burn inside the mito-whatever in the middle of your every muscle cell.

The skeleton is just a way to keep your tissue off the floor. Your sweat is just a way to keep you cool.

The revelations come at you from every direction.

Around the one hundred and fifth floor, you can't believe you're the slave to this body, this big baby. You have to keep it fed and put it to bed and take it to the bathroom. You can't believe we haven't invented something better. Something not so needy. Not so time-consuming.

You realize that people take drugs because it's the only real personal adventure left to them in their time-constrained, law-and-order, property-lined world.

It's only in drugs or death we'll see anything new, and death is just too controlling.

You realize that there's no point in doing anything if nobody's watching.

You wonder, if there had been a low turnout at the crucifixion, would they have rescheduled?

You realize the agent was right. You've never seen a crucifix with a Jesus who wasn't almost naked. You've never seen a fat Jesus. Or a Jesus with body hair. Every crucifix you've ever seen, the Jesus could be shirtless and modeling designer jeans or men's cologne.

Life is every way the agent said. You realize that if no one's watching, you might as well stay home. Play with yourself. Watch broadcast television.

It's around the one hundred and tenth floor you realize that if you're not on videotape, or better yet, live on satellite hookup in front of the whole world watching, you don't exist.

You're that tree falling in the forest that nobody gives a rat's ass about.

It doesn't matter if you do anything. If nobody notices, your life will add up to a big zero. Nada. Cipher.

Fake or not, it's these kinds of big truths that swarm inside you.

You realize that our mistrust of the future makes it hard to give up the past. We can't give up our concept of who we were. All those adults playing archaeologist at yard sales, looking for childhood artifacts, board games, CandyLand, Twister, they're terrified. Trash becomes holy relics. Mystery Date. Hula Hoops. Our way of getting nostalgic for what we just threw in the trash, it's all because we're afraid to evolve. Grow, change, lose weight, reinvent ourselves. Adapt.

That's what the agent says to me on the StairMaster. He's yelling at me, "Adapt!"

Everything's accelerated except me and my sweaty body with its bowel movements and body hair. My moles and yellow toenails. And I realize I'm stuck with my body, and already it's falling apart. My backbone feels hammered out of hot iron. My arms swing thin and wet on each side of me.

Since change is constant, you wonder if people crave death because it's the only way they can get anything really finished.

The agent's yelling that no matter how great you look, your body is just something you wear to accept your Academy Award.

Your hand is just so you can hold your Nobel Prize.

Your lips are only there for you to air-kiss a talk show host.

And you might as well look great.

It's around the one hundred and twentieth floor you have to

laugh. You're going to lose it anyway. Your body. You're already losing it. It's time you bet everything.

This is why when the agent comes to you with anabolic steroids, you say yes. You say yes to the back-to-back tanning sessions. Electrolysis? Yes. Teeth capping? Yes. Dermabrasion? Yes. Chemical peels? According to the agent, the secret to getting famous is you just keep saying yes.

27

It's in the car coming from the airport the agent shows me his cure for cancer. It's called ChemoSolv. It's supposed to dissolve a tumor, he says and opens his briefcase to take out a brown prescription bottle with dark capsules inside.

This is jumping back a little ways to before I met the stair climbing machine, to my first face-to-face with the agent the night he picks me up at the airport in New York. Before he tells me I'm too fat to be famous yet. Before I'm a product being launched. It's dark outside when my plane first lands in New York. Nothing's too spectacular. It's night, with the same moon as we have back home, and the agent's just a regular man standing where I get off the plane, wearing glasses with his brown hair parted on one side.

We shake hands. A car drives up to the curb outside, and we get in the back. He pinches the crease in each trouser leg to lift it as he steps into the car. How he looks is custom-tailored.

How he looks is eternal and durable. Just meeting him, there's that guilt I feel whenever I buy something impossible to recycle.

"This other cancer cure we have is called Oncologic," he says and hands another brown bottle across to me sitting next to him in the backseat. This is a nice car, the way it's black leather and padded all over inside. The ride is smoother than on the airplane.

It's more dark capsules inside the second bottle, and pasted around the bottle is a pharmacy label the way you always see. The agent takes out another bottle.

"This is one of our cures for AIDS," he says. "This is our most popular one." He takes out bottle after bottle. "Here we have our leading cure for antibiotic-resistant tuberculosis. Here's liver cirrhosis. Here's Alzheimer's. Multiple Neuritis. Multiple Myeloma. Multiple Sclerosis. The rhinovirus," he says, shaking each one so the pills inside rattle, and handing them over to me.

ViralSept, it says on one bottle.

MaligNon, another bottle says.

CerebralSave.

Kohlercaine.

Nonsense words.

These are all same-sized brown plastic bottles with white child-guard caps and prescription labels from the same pharmacy.

The agent comes packaged in a medium-weight gray wool suit and is equipped with only his briefcase. He features two brown eyes behind glasses. A mouth. Clean fingernails. Nothing is remarkable about him except what he's telling me.

"Just name a disease," he says, "and we have a cure ready for it."

He lifts two more handfuls of brown bottles from his briefcase and shakes them. "I brought all these to prove a point."

Every second, the car we're in slides deeper and deeper through the dark into New York City. Around us, other cars keep pace. The moon keeps pace. I say how I'm surprised all these diseases still exist in the world.

"It's a shame," the agent says, "how medical technology is still lagging behind the marketing side of things. I mean, we've had all the sales support in place for years, the coffee mug giveaways to physicians, the feel-good magazine ads, the total product launch, but it's the same old violin in the background. R&D is still years behind. The lab monkeys are still dropping like flies."

His two perfect rows of teeth look set in his mouth by a jeweler.

The pills for AIDS look just like the pills for cancer look just like the pills for diabetes. I ask, So these things really aren't invented?

"Let's not use that word, 'invented,' " the agent says. "It makes everything sound so contrived."

But they aren't real?

"Of course they're real," he says and plucks the first two bottles out of my hands. "They're copyrighted. We have an inventory of almost fifteen thousand copyrighted names for products that are still in development," he says. "And that includes you."

He says, "That's just my point."

He's developing a cure for cancer?

"We're a total concept marketing slash public relations organization," he says. "Our job is to create the concept. You patent a drug. You copyright the name. As soon as someone else develops the product they come to us, sometimes by choice, sometimes not."

I ask him, Why sometimes not?

"The way this works is we copyright every conceivable combination of words, Greek words, Latin, English, what-have-you. We get the legal rights to every conceivable word a pharmaceutical company might use to name a new product. For diabetes alone, we have an inventory of one hundred forty names," he says. He hands me stapled-together pages from out of his briefcase in his lap.

GlucoCure, I read.

InsulinEase.

PancreAid. Hemazine. Glucodan. Growdenase. I turn to the next page, and bottles slip out of my lap and roll along the car floor with the pills inside rattling.

"If the drug company that ever cures diabetes wants to use any combination of words even vaguely related to the condition, they'll have to lease that right from us."

So the pills I have here, I say, these are sugar pills. I twist one bottle open and shake a tablet, dark red and shining, into my palm. I lick it, and it's candy-coated chocolate. Others are gelatin capsules with powdered sugar inside.

"Mock-ups," he says. "Prototypes."

He says, "My point is that every bit of your career with us is already in place, and we've been prophesying your arrival for more than fifteen years."

He says, "I'm telling you this so you can relax."

But the Creedish church district disaster was only ten years ago.

And I put a pill, an orange Geriamazone, in my mouth.

"We've been tracking you," he says. "As soon as the Creedish survival numbers dipped below one hundred, we started the campaign rolling. The whole media countdown over the last six months, that was our doing. It needed some fine-tuning. It wasn't anything specific at first, all the copy is pretty much search-and-replace, fill-in-the-blank, universal-change stuff, but it's all in the can. All we needed was a warm body and the survivor's name. That's where you enter the picture."

From another bottle, I shake out two dozen Inazans and hold them under my tongue until their black candy shells dissolve. Chocolate melts out.

The agent takes out more sheets of printed paper and hands them to me.

Ford Merit, I read.

Mercury Rapture.

Dodge Vignette.

He says, "We have names copyrighted for cars that haven't been designed, software that's never been written, miracle dream cures for epidemics still on the horizon, every product we can anticipate."

My back teeth crunch a sweet overdose of blue Donnadons.

The agent eyes me sitting there and sighs. "Enough with the empty calories, already," he says. "Our first big job is to modify you so you'll fit the campaign." He asks, "Is that your real hair color?"

I pour a million milligrams of Jodazones in my mouth.

"Not to mince words," the agent says, "but you're about thirty pounds heavier than we need you to be."

The bogus pills I can understand. What I don't understand is how he could begin planning a campaign around something before it happened. No way could he have a campaign planned before the Deliverance.

The agent takes off his glasses and folds them. He sets them inside his briefcase and takes back the printed lists of future miracle products, drugs and cars, and he puts the lists in his briefcase. He tug-of-wars the pill bottles out of my hands, all of them silent and empty.

"The truth is," he says, "nothing new ever happens."

He says, "We've seen it all."

He says, "Listen."

In 1653, he says, the Russian Orthodox church changed a few old rituals. Just some changes in the liturgy. Just words. Language. In Russian, for God's sake. Some Bishop Nikon introduced the changes as well as the western manners that were becoming popular in Russian court life at the time, and the bishop started excommunicating anyone who rebelled against these changes.

Reaching around in the dark by my feet, he picks up the other pill bottles.

According to the agent, the monks who didn't want to change the way they worshiped fled to remote monasteries. The Russian authorities hunted and persecuted them. By 1665, small groups of monks began burning themselves to death. These group suicides in northern Europe and western Siberia continued through the 1670s. In 1687, some two thousand seven hundred monks captured a monastery, locked themselves inside, and burned it. In 1688, another fifteen hundred "Old Believers" burned themselves alive in their locked monastery. By the end of the seventeenth century, an estimated twenty thousand monks had killed themselves instead of submitting to the government.

He snaps his briefcase shut and leans forward.

"These Russian monks kept killing themselves until 1897," he says. "Sound familiar?"

You have Samson in the Old Testament, the agent says. You have the Jewish soldiers who killed themselves in the Masada. You have seppuku among the Japanese. Sati among the Hindu. Endura among the Cathari during the twelfth century in southern France. He ticked off group after group on his fingertips. There were the Stoics. There were the Epicureans. There were the tribes of Guiana Indians who killed themselves so they could be reborn as white men.

"Closer to here and now, the People's Temple mass suicide of 1978 left nine hundred twelve dead."

The Branch Davidian disaster of 1993 left seventy-six dead.

The Order of the Solar Temple mass suicide and murder in 1994 killed fifty-three people.

The Heaven's Gate suicide in 1997 killed thirty-nine.

"The Creedish church thing was just a blip in the culture," he says. "It was just one more predictable mass suicide in a world filled with splinter groups that limp along until they're confronted.

Maybe their leader is about to die, as was the case with the Heaven's Gate group, or they're challenged by the government, like what happened around the Russian monks or the People's Temple or the Creedish church district."

He says, "Actually, it's awfully boring stuff. Anticipating the future based on the past. We might as well be an insurance company; nevertheless, it's our job to make cult suicide look fresh and exciting every time around."

After knowing Fertility, I wonder if I'm the last person in the world who ever gets caught by surprise. Fertility with her dreams of disaster and this guy with his clean shave and his closed loop of history, they're two peas trapped in the same boring pod.

"Reality means you live until you die," the agent says. "The real truth is nobody wants reality."

The agent closes his eyes and presses his open palm to his forehead. "The truth is the Creedish church was nothing special," he says. "It was founded by a splinter group of Millerites in 1860 during the Great Awakening, during a period when in California alone, splinter religions founded more than fifty utopian communities."

He opens one eye and points a finger at me. "You have something, a pet, a bird or a fish."

I ask how he knows this, about my fish.

"It's not necessarily true, but it's probable," he says. "The Creedish granted their labor missionaries what was known as Mascot Privilege, the right to own a pet, in 1939. It was the year a Creedish biddy stole an infant from the family where she worked. Having a pet was supposed to sublimate your need to nurture a dependent."

A biddy stole somebody's baby.

"In Birmingham, Alabama," he says. "Of course, she killed herself the minute she was found."

I ask what else does he know.

"You have a problem with masturbation."

That's easy, I say. He read that in my Survivor Retention record.

"No," he says. "Lucky for us, all the client records for your case-worker are missing. Anything we say about you will be uncontested. And before I forget, we took six years off your life. If anyone asks, you're twenty-seven."

So how does he know so much about my, you know, about me?

"Your masturbation?"

My crimes of Onan.

"It seems that all you labor missionaries had a problem with masturbation."

If he only knew. Somewhere in my lost case history folder are the records of my being an exhibitionist, a bipolar syndrome, a mysophobic, a shoplifter, etc. Somewhere in the night behind us, the caseworker is taking my secrets to her grave. Somewhere half the world behind me is my brother.

Since he's such an expert, I ask the agent if there are ever murders of people who were supposed to kill themselves but just didn't. In these other religions, did anyone ever go around killing the survivors?

"With the People's Temple there was an unexplained handful of survivors murdered," he says. "And the Order of the Solar Temple. It was the Canadian government's trouble with the Solar Temple that prompted our government's Survivor Retention Program. With the Solar Temple, little groups of French and Canadian followers kept killing themselves and killing each other for years after the original disaster. They called the killings 'Departures.' "

He says, "Members of the Temple Solaire burned themselves alive with gasoline and propane explosions they thought would blast them to eternal life on the star Sirius," and he points into the night sky. "Compared to that, the Creedish mess was infinitely tame."

I ask, has he anticipated anything about a surviving church member hunting down and killing any leftover Creedish?

"A surviving church member, other than you?" the agent asks.

Yes.

"Killing people, you say?"

Yes.

Looking out the car at the New York lights going by, the agent says, "A killer Creedish? Oh heavens, I hope not."

Looking out at the same lights behind tinted glass, at the star Sirius, looking past my own reflection with chocolate smeared around my mouth, I say, yeah. Me too.

"Our whole campaign is based on the fact that you're the last survivor," he says. "If there's another Creedish alive in the world, you're wasting my time. The entire campaign is down the tubes. If you're not the only living Creedish in the world, you're worthless to us."

He opens his briefcase a crack and takes out a brown bottle. "Here," he says, "take a couple Serenadons. These are the best antianxiety treatment ever invented."

They just don't exist yet.

"Just pretend," he says, "for the placebo effect." And he shakes two into my hand.

26

People are going to say it's the steroids that made me go crazy.

The Durateston 250.

The Mifepristone abortion pills from France.

The Plenastril from Switzerland.

The Masterone from Portugal.

These are the real steroids, not just the copyrighted names of future drugs. These are the injectables, the tablets, the transdermal patches.

People will be so sure the steroids made me into this, this crazy plane hijacker flying around the world until I kill myself. As if people know anything about being a celebrated famous celebrity spiritual leader. As if any one of those people isn't already looking around for a new guru to make sense out of their risk-free boredom of a lifestyle while they watch the news on television and pass judgment on me. People are all looking for that, a hand to hold. Reassurance. The promise that everything will be all right. That's all they wanted from me. Stressed, desperate, celebrated me. Under-pressure me. None of these people know the first thing about being a big, glamorous, big, charismatic, big role model.

It's stair climbing around floor number one hundred and thirty you start raving, ranting, speaking in tongues.

Not that any one person except maybe Fertility knows the kind of day-in and day-out effort it took to be me at this point.

Imagine how you'd feel if your whole life turned into a job you couldn't stand.

No, everybody thinks their whole life should be at least as much fun as masturbation.

I'd like to see these people even try to live out of hotel rooms and find low-fat room service and do a halfway convincing job of faking a deep inner peace and at-oneness with God.

When you get famous, dinner isn't food anymore; it's twenty ounces of protein, ten ounces of carbohydrates, salt-free, fat-free, sugar-free fuel. This is a meal every two hours, six times a day. Eating isn't about eating anymore. It's about protein assimilation.

It's about cellular rejuvenation cream. Washing is about exfolia-tion. What used to be breathing is respiration.

I'd be the first to congratulate anybody if they could do a better job of faking flawless beauty and delivering vague inspiring mes-sages:

Calm down. Everyone, breathe deep. Life is good. Be just and kind. Be the love.

As if.

At most events, those deep inner messages and beliefs went

from the writing team to me in the last thirty seconds before I went onstage. That's what the silent opening prayer was all about. It gives me a minute to look down on the podium and read over my script.

Five minutes go by. Ten minutes. The 400 milligrams of Deca-Durabolin and testosterone cypionate you just spiked backstage is still a round little bolus in the skin on your ass. The fifteen thousand paying faithful are kneeling right there in front of you with their heads bowed. The way an ambulance screams down a quiet street, that's how those chemicals feel going into your bloodstream.

The liturgical robes I started wearing onstage are because with enough Equipoise in your system, half the time you're packing wood.

Fifteen minutes go by with all those people on their knees.

Whenever you're ready, you just say it, the magic word.

Amen.

And it's showtime.

"You are children of peace in a universe of everlasting life and a limitless abundance of love and well-being, blah, blah, blah. Go in peace."

Where the writing team comes up with this copy, I don't know.

Let's not even mention the miracles I performed on national television. My little halftime miracle during the Super Bowl. All those disasters I predicted, the lives I saved.

You know the old saying: It's not *what* you know.

It's *who* you know.

People think it's so simple to be me and go up in front of people in a stadium and lead them in prayer and then be seat-belted on a jet headed for the next stadium within the hour, all the time preserving a vibrant, healthy facade. No, but these people will still call you crazy for hijacking a plane. People don't know the first thing about vibrant dynamic healthy vibrancy.

Let them even try to find enough of me to autopsy. It's nobody's business if my liver function is impaired. Or if maybe my spleen and gallbladder are enormous from the effects of human growth hormone. As if they themselves wouldn't inject anything sucked from the pituitary glands of dead cadavers if they thought they could look as good as I did on television.

The risk of being famous is you have to take levothyroxine sodium to stay thin. Yes, you have your central nervous system to worry about. There's the insomnia. Your metabolism ramps up. Your heart pounds. You sweat. You're nervous all the time, but you look terrific.

Just remember, your heart is only beating so you can be a regular dinner guest at the White House.

Your central nervous system is just so you can address the UN General Assembly.

Amphetamines are the most American drug. You get so much done. You look terrific, and your middle name is Accomplishment.

"Your whole body," the agent is yelling, "is just how you model your designer line of sportswear!"

Your thyroid shuts down natural production of thyroxine.

But you still look terrific. And you are, you're the American Dream. You are the constant-growth economy.

According to the agent, the people out there looking for a leader, they want vibrant. They want massive. They want dynamic. Nobody wants a little skinny god. They want a thirty-inch drop between your chest and waist sizes. Big pecs. Long legs. Cleft chin. Big calves.

They want more than human.

They want larger than life size.

Nobody wants just anatomically correct.

People want anatomical enhancement. Surgically augmented. New and improved. Silicone-implanted. Collagen-injected.

Just for the record, after my first three-month cycle of Deca-Durabolin I couldn't reach down far enough to tie my shoes; my arms were that big. Not a problem, the agent says, and he hires someone to tie all my shoes for me.

After I cycled some Russian-made Metahapoctehosich for seventeen weeks all my hair fell out, and the agent bought me a wig.

"You have to meet me halfway on this," the agent tells me. "Nobody wants to worship a God who ties his own shoes."

Nobody wants to worship you if you have the same problems, the same bad breath and messy hair and hangnails, as a regular person. You have to be everything regular people aren't. Where they fail, you have to go all the way. Be what people are too afraid to be. Become whom they admire.

People shopping for a messiah want quality. Nobody is going to follow a loser. When it comes to choosing a savior, they won't settle for just a human being.

"For you, a wig is better," the agent said. "It's got the level of consistent perfection we can trust. Getting out of helicopters, the wash of the prop, every minute in public, you can't control how real hair is going to look."

How the agent explained his plan to me was, we weren't targeting the smartest people in the world, just the most.

He said, "Think of yourself from now on as a diet cola."

He said, "Think of those young people out in the world struggling with outdated religions or with no religions, think of those people as your target market."

People are looking for how to put everything together. They need a unified field theory that combines glamour and holiness, fashion and spirituality. People need to reconcile being good and being good-looking.

After day after day of no solid food, limited sleep, climbing thousands of stairs, and the agent yelling his ideas to me over and over, this all made perfect sense.

The music team was busy writing hymns even before I was under contract. The writing team was putting my autobiography to bed. The media team was doing press releases, merchandise licensing agreements, the skating shows: The Creedish Death Tragedy on Ice, the satellite hookups, tanning appointments. The image team has creative control on appearance. The writing team has control of every word that comes out of my mouth.

To cover the acne I got from cycling Laurabolin, I started wearing makeup. To cure the acne, someone on the support team got me a prescription for Retin-A.

For the hair loss, the support team was spritzing me with Rogaine.

Everything we did to fix me had side effects we had to fix. Then the fixes had side effects to fix and so on and so on.

Imagine a Cinderella story where the hero looks in the mirror and who's looking back is a total stranger. Every word he says is written for him by a team of professionals. Everything he wears is chosen or designed by a team of designers.

Every minute of every day is planned by his publicist.

Maybe now you're starting to get a picture.

Plus your hero is spiking drugs you can only buy in Sweden or Mexico so he can't see down past his own jutting-out chest. He's tanned and shaved and wigged and scheduled because people in Tucson, people in Seattle, or Chicago or Baton Rouge, don't want an avatar with a hairy back.

It's around floor number two hundred that you reach the highest state.

You're gone anaerobic, you're burning muscle instead of fat, but your mind is crystal-clear.

The truth is that all this was just part of the suicide process. Because tanning and steroids are only a problem if you plan to live a long time.

Because the only difference between a suicide and a martyrdom really is the amount of press coverage.

If a tree falls in the forest and nobody is there to hear it, doesn't it just lie there and rot?

And if Christ had died from a barbiturate overdose, alone on the bathroom floor, would He be in Heaven?

This wasn't a question of whether or not I was going to kill myself. This, this effort, this money and time, the writing team, the drugs, the diet, the agent, the flights of stairs going up to nowhere, all this was so I could off myself with everyone's full attention.

25

This one time, the agent asked me where I saw myself in five years.

Dead, I told him. I see myself dead and rotting. Or ashes, I can see myself burned to ashes.

I had a loaded gun in my pocket, I remember. Just the two of us were standing in the back of a crowded, dark auditorium. I remember it was the night of my first big public appearance.

I see myself dead and in Hell, I said.

I remember I was planning to kill myself that night.

I told the agent, I figured I'd spend my first thousand

years of Hell in some entry-level position, but after that I wanted to move into management. Be a real team player. Hell is going to see enormous growth in market share over the next millennium. I wanted to ride the crest.

The agent said that sounded pretty realistic.

We were smoking cigarettes, I remember. Down onstage, some local preacher was doing his opening act. Part of his warm-up was to get the audience hyperventilated. Loud singing does the job. Or chanting. According to the agent, when people shout this way or sing "Amazing Grace" at the top of their lungs, they breathe too much. People's blood should be acid. When they hyperventilate the carbon dioxide level of their blood drops, and their blood become alkaline.

"Respiratory alkalosis," he says.

People get light-headed. People fall down with their ears ringing, their fingers and toes go numb, they get chest pains, they sweat. This is supposed to be rapture. People thrash on the floor with their hands cramped into stiff claws.

This is what passes for ecstasy.

"People in the religion business call it 'lobstering,' " the agent says. "They call it speaking in tongues."

Repetitive motions add to the effect, and the opening act down onstage runs through the usual drills. The audience claps in unison. Long rows of people hold hands and sway together in their delirium. People do that rainbow hands.

Whoever invented this routine, the agent tells me, they pretty much run things in Hell.

I remember the corporate sponsor was SummerTime Old-Fashioned Instant Lemonade.

My cue is when the opening act calls me down onto the stage, my part of the show is putting a spell on everybody.

"A naturalistic trance state," the agent says.

The agent takes a brown bottle out of his blazer pocket. He says, "Take a couple Endorphinols if you feel any emotion coming on."

I tell him to give me a handful.

To get ready for tonight, staffers went and visited local people to give them free tickets to the show. The agent is telling me this for the hundredth time. The staffers ask to use the bathroom during their visit and jot down notes about anything they find in the medicine cabinet. According to the agent, the Reverend Jim Jones did this and it worked miracles for his People's Temple.

Miracles probably isn't the right word.

Up on the pulpit is a list of people I've never met and their life-threatening conditions.

Mrs. Steven Brandon, I just have to call out. Come down and have your failing kidneys touched by God.

Mr. William Doxy, come down and put your crippled heart in God's hands.

Part of my training was how to press my fingers into somebody's eyes hard and fast so the pressure registered on their optic nerve as a flash of white light.

"Divine light," the agent says.

Part of my training was how to press my hands over somebody's ears so hard they heard a buzzing noise I could tell them was the eternal Om.

"Go," the agent says.

I've missed my cue.

Down onstage, the opening preacher is shouting Tender Branson into a microphone. The one, the only, the last survivor, the great Tender Branson.

The agent tells me, "Wait." He plucks the cigarette out of my mouth and pushes me down the aisle. "Now, go," he says.

All the hands reach out into the aisle to touch me. The spotlight's so bright onstage in front of me. In the dark around me are the smiles of a thousand delirious people who think they love me. All I have to do is walk into the spotlight.

This is dying without the control issues.

The gun is heavy and banging my hip in my pants pocket.

This is having a family without being familiar. Having relations without being related.

Onstage, the spotlights are warm.

This is being loved without the risk of loving anyone in return.

I remember this was the perfect moment to die.

It wasn't Heaven, but it was as close as I was ever going to get.

I raised my arms and people cheered. I lowered my arms and people were silent. The script was there on the podium for me to read. The typewritten list told me who out in the dark was suffering from what.

Everybody's blood was alkaline. Everybody's heart was there for the taking. This is how it felt to shoplift. This is how it felt to hear confessions over my crisis hotline. This is how I imagined sex.

With Fertility on my mind, I started to read the script:

We are all the divine products of creation.

We are each of us the fragments that make up something whole and beautiful.

Each time I paused, people would hold their breath.

The gift of life, I read from the script, is precious.

I put my hand on the gun loaded with bullets in my pocket.

The precious gift of life must be preserved no matter now painful and pointless it seemed. Peace, I told them, is a gift so perfect that only God should grant it. I told people, only God's most selfish children would steal God's greatest gift, His only gift greater than life. The gift of death.

This lesson is to the murderer, I said. This is to the suicide. This is to the abortionist. This is to the suffering and sick.

Only God has the right to surprise His children with death.

I had no idea what I was saying until it was too late. And maybe it was a coincidence, or maybe the agent knew what I had in mind when I'd asked him to get me some bullets and a gun, but what happened is the script really screwed up my whole plan. There was no way I could read this and then kill myself. It would just look so stupid.

So I never did kill myself.

The rest of the evening went as planned. People went home feeling saved, and I told myself I'd kill myself some other time. The moment was all wrong. I procrastinated, and timing was everything.

Besides.

Eternity was going to seem like forever.

With the crowds of smiling people smiling at me in the dark, me who spent my life cleaning bathrooms and mowing the lawn, I told myself, why rush anything?

I'd backslid before, I'd backslide again. Practice makes perfect.

If you could call it that.

I figured, a few more sins would help round out my résumé.

This is the upside of already being eternally damned.

I figured, Hell could wait.

24

Before this plane goes down, before the flight recorder tape runs out, one of the things I want to apologize for is the *Book of Very Common Prayer*.

People need to know the *Book of Very Common Prayer* was not my idea. Yes, it sold two hundred million copies, worldwide. It did. Yes, I let them put my name on it, but the book was the agent's brainchild. Before that the book was the idea of some nobody on the writing team. Some copywriter trying to break into the big time, I forget.

What's important is the book was not my idea.

What happened is one day, the agent comes up to me with that dancing light in his brown eyes that means a deal. According to my publicist, I'm booked solid. This is after we did that line of Bibles I was autographing in bookstores. We had a million plus feet of guaranteed shelf space in bookstores, and I was on tour.

"Don't expect a book tour to be something fun," the agent tells me.

The thing about book signings, the agent says, is they're exactly the same as the last day of high school when everyone wants you to write in their high school annual, only a book tour can go on for the rest of your life.

According to my itinerary, I'm in a Denver warehouse signing stock when the agent pitches me on his idea for a weeny book of meditations people can use in their everyday lives. He sees this as a paperback of little prose poems. Fifty pages, tops. Little tributes to the environment, children, safe stuff. Mothers. Pandas. Topics that step on nobody's toes. Common problems. We put my name on the spine, say I wrote it, run the product up a flagpole.

What else people need to know is I never saw the finished book until after the second press run, after it had sold more than fifty thousand copies. Already people weren't not just a little pissed off, but all the fuss only upped sales.

What happened is one day I'm in the green room waiting to co-host some daytime television project. This is way fast forward, after the autographed Bible book tour. The idea here is if I co-host and enough people tune in, I'll spin off with a vehicle of my own. So I'm in the green room trading toenail secrets with somebody, the actress Wendi Daniels or somebody, and she asks me to sign her copy of the book. The *Book of Very Common Prayer*. This is the first time I ever see a copy, I swear. On a stack of my own autographed Bibles, I swear.

According to Wendi Daniels, I can smooth out the swelling under my eyes by rubbing in a dab of hemorrhoid cream.

Then she hands it to me, the *Book of Very Common Prayer,* and my name is just so right there on the spine. Me, me, me. There I am.

There inside are the prayers people think I wrote:

The Prayer to Delay Orgasm

The Prayer to Lose Weight

The feeling, the way it feels when laboratory product-testing animals are ground up to make hot dogs, that's how hurt I felt.

The Prayer to Stop Smoking

> Our most Holy Father,
> Take from me the choice You have given.
> Assume control of my will and habits.
> Wrest from me power over my own behavior.
> May it be Your decision how I act.
> May it be by Your hands, my every failing.
> Then if I still smoke, may I accept that my smoking is
> Your will.
> Amen.

The Prayer to Remove Mildew Stains

The Prayer to Prevent Hair Loss

> God of ultimate stewardship,
> Shepherd of thine flock,
> As You would succor the least of Your charges,
> As You would rescue the most lost of Your lambs,
> Restore to me the full measure of my glory.
> Preserve in me the remainder of my youth.
> All of Creation is Yours to provide.
> All of Creation is Yours to withhold.
> God of limitless bounty,
> Consider my suffering.
> Amen.

The Prayer to Induce Erection

The Prayer to Maintain an Erection

The Prayer to Silence Barking Dogs

The Prayer to Silence Car Alarms

The way all this felt, I looked terrible on television. My spin-off television show, well, I had to kiss that goodbye. One minute after we were off the air, I was being all over the telephone long-distance to the agent in New York. Everything on my end of the conversation was furious.

All he cared about was the money.

"What's a prayer?" he says. "It's an incantation," he says, and he's yelling back at me over the phone. "It's a way for people to focus their energy around a specific need. People need to get clear on a single intention and accomplish it."

The Prayer to Prevent Parking Tickets

The Prayer to Stop Plumbing Leaks

"People pray to solve problems, and these are the honest-to-God problems that people worry about," the agent's still yelling at me.

The Prayer for Increased Vaginal Sensitivity

"A prayer is how the squeaky wheel gets greased," he says. That's how made out of cheese his heart is. "You pray to make your needs known."

The Prayer Against Drivetrain Noise

The Prayer for a Parking Space

> Oh, divine and merciful God,
> History is without equal for how much I will adore
> You, when You give me today, a place to park.
> For You are the provider.
> And You are the source.
> From You all good is delivered.
> Within You all is found.

In Your care will I find respite. With Your
guidance, will I find peace.
To stop, to rest, to idle, to park.
These are Yours to give me. This is what I ask.
Amen.

Seeing how I'm just about to die here, people need to know that
my personal intention all along has been to serve the glory of God.
Pretty much. Not that you can find this in our mission statement,
but that's my general overall plan. I want to at least make an effort.
This new book just looked so not at all pious. So not even a little
devout.

The Prayer Against Excessive Underarm Wetness

The Prayer for a Second Interview

The Prayer to Locate a Lost Contact Lens

Still, even Fertility says I'm way off base about the book. Fertility
wanted a second volume.

It's Fertility who says, some stadiums when I'm up front praising
God, I'm the same as people wearing clothes printed with Mickey
Mouse or Coca-Cola. I mean, it's so easy. It's not even a real choice.
You can't go wrong. Fertility says, praising God is just such a safe
thing to do. You don't even have to give it any thought.

"Be fruitful and multiply," Fertility says to me. "Praise God.
There's no real risk. This is just our default setting."

What saved the *Book of Very Common Prayer* was, people were
using every prayer. Some people were pissed off, mostly religious
people who resented the competition, but by this point our cash
flow was down. Our total revenues were leveling off. It was market
saturation. People had the prayers committed to memory. People
were stuck in traffic reciting the *Prayer to Make Traffic Move*. Men
were reciting the *Prayer to Delay Orgasm*, and it worked at least as
well as multiplication tables. My best option seemed to be to just
keep my mouth shut and smile.

Besides, the attendance figures were down at my personal appearances, this looked to be the beginning of the end. My *People* magazine cover was already three months behind me.

And there's no such thing as Celebrity Outplacement.

You don't see faded movie stars or whoever going back to community college for retraining. The only field left to me was doing the game show circuit, and I'm not that smart.

I'd peaked, and timing-wise, this looked like another good window to do my suicide, and I almost did. The pills were in my hand. That's how close I came. I was planning to overdose on meta-testosterone.

Then the agent calls on the telephone, loud, real loud, the way it sounds when a million screaming Christians are screaming your name in Kansas City, that's the kind of excitement that's in his voice.

Over the phone in my hotel room the agent tells me about the best booking of my career. It's next week. It's a thirty-second slot between a tennis shoe commercial and a national taco restaurant spot, prime time during sweeps week.

It amazes me to think those pills were almost in my mouth.

This is just so not boring anymore.

Network television, a million billion people watching, this would be the prime moment, my last chance to pull a gun and shoot myself with a decent audience share.

This would be such a totally not-ignored martyrdom.

"One catch," the agent tells me over the phone. He's shouting, "The catch is I told them you'd do a miracle."

A miracle.

"Nothing too big. You don't have to part the Red Sea or anything," he says. "Turning water into wine would be enough, but remember, no miracle and they won't run the spot."

23

Enter Fertility Hollis back into my life in Spokane, Washington, where I'm eating pie and coffee, incognito in a Shari's restaurant, when she comes in the front door and heads straight for my table. You can't call Fertility Hollis anybody's fairy godmother, but you might be surprised where she turns up.

But most times you wouldn't.

Fertility with her old-colored gray eyes as bored as the ocean.

Fertility with her every exhale an exhausted sigh.

She's the blasé eye of the hurricane that's the world around her.

Fertility with her arms and face hanging slack as some jaded survivor, some immortal, an Egyptian vampire after watching the million years of television repeats we call history, she slumps into the seat across from me being glad since I needed her for a miracle anyway.

This is back when I could still give my entourage the slip. I wasn't a nobody yet, but I was on the cusp. Thanks to my media slump. My publicity doldrums.

The way Fertility slouches with her elbows on the table and her face propped in her hands, her bored-colored red hair hanging limp in her face, you'd guess she's just arrived from some planet with not as much gravity as Earth. As if just being here, as skinny as she is she weighs eight hundred pounds.

How she's dressed is just separates, slacks and a top, shoes, dragging a canvas tote bag. The air-conditioning is working, and you can smell her fabric softener, sweet and fake.

How she looks is watered-down.

How she looks is disappearing.

How she looks is erased.

"Don't stress," she says. "This is just me not wearing any makeup. I'm here on an assignment."

Her job.

"Right," she says. "My evil job."

I ask, How's my fish?

She says, "Fine."

No way could meeting her here be a coincidence. She has to be following me.

"What you forget is I know everything," Fertility says. She asks, "What time is it?"

I tell her, One fifty-three in the afternoon.

"In eleven minutes the waitress will bring you another piece of pie. Lemon meringue, this time. Later, only about sixty people will

120

show up for your appearance tonight. Then, tomorrow morning, something called the Walker River Bridge will collapse in Shreveport. Wherever that is."

I say she's guessing.

"And," she says and smirks, "you need a miracle. You need a miracle, bad."

Maybe I do, I say. These days, who doesn't need a miracle? How does she know so much?

"The same way I know," she says and nods toward the other side of the dining room, "that waitress over there has cancer. I know the pie you're eating will upset your stomach. Some movie theater in China will burn in a couple minutes, give or take what time it is in Asia. Right now in Finland, a skier is triggering an avalanche that will bury a dozen people."

Fertility waves and the waitress with cancer is coming over.

Fertility leans across the table and says, "I know all this because I know everything."

The waitress is young and with hair and teeth and everything, meaning nothing about her looks wrong or sick, and Fertility orders a chicken stir-fry with vegetables and sesame seeds. She asks, does it come with rice?

Spokane is still outside the windows. The buildings. The Spokane River. The sun we all have to share. A parking lot. Cigarette butts.

I ask, so why didn't she warn the waitress?

"How would you react if a stranger told you that kind of news? It would just wreck her day," Fertility says. "And all her personal drama would just hold up my order."

It's cherry pie I'm eating that's going to upset my stomach. The power of suggestion.

"All you have to do is pay attention to the patterns," Fertility says. "After you see all the patterns, you can extrapolate the future."

According to Fertility Hollis, there is no chaos.

There are only patterns, patterns on top of patterns, patterns that affect other patterns. Patterns hidden by patterns. Patterns within patterns.

If you watch close, history does nothing but repeat itself.

What we call chaos is just patterns we haven't recognized. What we call random is just patterns we can't decipher. What we can't understand we call nonsense. What we can't read we call gibberish.

There is no free will.

There are no variables.

"There is only the inevitable," Fertility says. "There's only one future. You don't have a choice."

The bad news is we don't have any control.

The good news is you can't make any mistakes.

The waitress across the dining room looks young and pretty and doomed.

"I pay attention to the patterns," Fertility says.

She says she can't not pay attention.

"They're in my dreams more and more every night," she says. "Everything. It's the same as reading a history book about the future, every night."

So she knows everything.

"So I know you need a miracle to go on television with."

What I need is a good prediction.

"That's why I'm here," she says and takes a fat daily planner book out of her tote bag. "Give me a time window. Give me a date for your prediction."

I tell her, Any time during the week after next.

"How about a multiple-car accident," she says, reading from her book.

I ask, How many cars?

"Sixteen cars," she says. "Ten dead. Eight injured."

Does she have anything flashier?

"How about a casino fire in Las Vegas," she says. "Topless show-girls in big feather headdresses on fire, stuff like that."

Any dead?

"No. Minor injuries. A lot of smoke damage, though."

Something bigger.

"A tanning salon explosion."

Something dazzling.

"Rabies in a national park."

Boring.

"Subway collision."

She's putting me to sleep.

"A fur activist strapped with bombs in Paris."

Skip it.

"Oil tanker capsizes."

Who cares about that stuff?

"Movie star miscarries."

Great, I say. My public will think I'm a real monster when that comes true.

Fertility pages around in her daily planner.

"Geez, it's summer," she says. "We don't have a lot of choices in disasters."

I tell her to keep looking.

"Next week, Ho Ho the giant panda the National Zoo is trying to breed will pick up a venereal disease from a visiting panda."

No way am I going to say that on television.

"How about a tuberculosis outbreak?"

Yawn.

"Freeway sniper?"

Yawn.

"Shark attack?"

She must really be scraping the bottom of the barrel.

"A broken racehorse leg?"

"A slashed painting in the Louvre?"

"A ruptured prime minister?"

"A fallen meteorite?"

"Infected frozen turkeys?"

"A forest fire?"

No, I tell her.

Too sad.

Too artsy.

Too political.

Too esoteric.

Too gross.

No appeal.

"A lava flow?" Fertility asks.

Too slow. No real drama. Mostly just property damage.

The problem is disaster movies have everybody expecting too much from nature.

The waitress brings the chicken stir-fry and my lemon meringue pie and fills our coffee cups. Then she smiles and goes off to die.

Fertility pages back and forth in her book.

In my guts, the cherry pie is putting up a fight. Spokane is outside. The air conditioning is inside. Nothing even looks like a pattern.

Fertility Hollis says, "How about killer bees?"

I ask, Where?

"Arriving in Dallas, Texas."

When?

"Next Sunday morning, at ten past eight."

A few? A swarm? How many?

"Zillions."

I tell her, Perfect.

Fertility lets out a sigh and digs into her chicken stir-fry. "Shit," she says, "That's the one I knew you'd pick all along."

22

So a zillion killer bees buzz into Dallas, Texas, at ten past eight on Sunday morning, right on schedule. This is despite the fact I only had a crummy fifteen percent market share of the television audience for my spot.

The next week, the network slots me for a full minute, and some heavy hitters, the drug companies, the car makers, the oil and tobacco conglomerates, are lining up as definite maybe sponsors if I can come up with an even bigger miracle.

For all the wrong reasons, the insurance companies are very interested.

Between now and next week, I'm on the road making weeknight appearances in Florida. It's the Jacksonville–Tampa–Orlando–Miami circuit. It's the Tender Branson Miracle Crusade. One night each.

My Miracle Minute, that's what the agent and the network want to call it, well it takes about zero effort to produce. Someone points a camera at you with your hair combed and a tie around your neck, and you look somber and talk straight into the lens:

The Ipswich Point Lighthouse will topple tomorrow.

Next week, the Mannington Glacier in Alaska will collapse and capsize a cruise ship that's sightseeing too close.

The week after that, mice carrying a deadly virus will turn up in Chicago, Tacoma, and Green Bay.

This is exactly the same as being a television newscaster, only before the fact.

The way I see the process happening is I'll get Fertility to give me a couple dozen predictions at a time, and I'll just tape a season's worth of Miracle Minutes. With a year in the can, I'll be free to make personal appearances, endorse products, sign books. Maybe do some consulting. Do cameo walk-ons in movies and television.

Don't ask me when because I don't remember, but somewhere along the way I keep forgetting to commit suicide.

If the publicist ever put killing myself on my schedule I'd be dead. Seven p.m., Thursday, drink drain cleaner. No problem. But what with the killer bees and the demands on my time, I keep stressing about what if I can't find Fertility again. This, and my entourage is with me every step of the way. The team's always dogging me, the publicist, the schedulers, the personal fitness trainer, the orthodontist, the dermatologist, the dietician.

The killer bees got less accomplished than you'd expect. They didn't kill anybody, but they got a lot of attention. Now I needed an encore.

A collapsing stadium.

A mining cave-in.

A train derailment.

The only moment I'm ever alone is when I go sit on the toilet, and even then I'm surrounded.

Fertility is nowhere.

In almost every public men's room, there's a hole chipped in the wall between one toilet stall and the next. This is chipped through solid wood an inch thick by somebody with just their fingernails. This is done over days or months at a time. You see these holes scratched through marble, through steel. As if someone in prison is trying to escape. The hole is only big enough to look though, or talk. Or put a finger through or a tongue or a penis, and escape just that little bit at a time.

What people call these openings is "glory holes."

It's the same as where you'd find a vein of gold.

Where you'd find glory.

I'm on a toilet in the Miami airport, and right at my elbow there's the hole in the stall wall, and all around the hole are messages left by men who sat here before me.

John M was here 3/14/64.

Carl B was here Jan. 8, 1976.

Epitaphs.

Some of them are scratched here fresh. Some are covered up but scratched so deep they're still readable under decades of paint.

Here are the shadows left behind by a thousand moments, a thousand moods, of needs traced here on the wall by men who are gone. Here is the record of their being here. Their visit. Their passing. Here's what the caseworker would call a primary source document.

A history of the unacceptable.

Be here tonight for a free blow job. Saturday, June 18, 1973.

All this is scratched in the wall.

Here are words without pictures. Sex without names. Pictures without words. Scratched here is a naked woman with her long legs spread wide, her round staring breasts, her long flowing hair and no face.

Squirting huge teardrops toward her hairy vagina is a severed penis as big as a man.

Heaven, the words say, is an all-you-can-eat pussy buffet.

Heaven is getting fucked up the ass.

Go to Hell faggot.

Been there.

Go suck shit.

Done that.

These are only a few of the voices around me when a real voice, a woman's voice, whispers, "You need another disaster, don't you?"

The voice is coming through the hole, but when I look, all you can see are two lipsticked lips. Red lips, white teeth, a flash of wet tongue says, "I knew you'd be here. I know everything."

Fertility.

At the hole now is a plain gray-colored eye made big with blue shadow and eyeliner and blinking lashes heavy with mascara. The pupil pulses large and then small. Then the mouth appears to say, "Don't sweat it. Your plane will be delayed for another couple hours."

On the wall next to the mouth it says, I suck and swallow.

Next to that it says, I only want to love her if she'd just give me the chance.

There's a poem that starts, Warm inside you is the love . . . The rest of the poem is washed down the wall and erased by ejaculate.

The mouth says, "I'm here on an assignment."

It must be her evil job.

"It's my evil job," she says. "It's the heat."

It's not something we talk about.

She says, "I don't want to talk about it."

Congratulations, I whisper. About the killer bees, I mean.

Scratched on the wall is, What do you call a Creedish girl who goes down?

Dead.

What do you call a Creedish fag who takes dick up the ass?

The mouth says, "You need another disaster, don't you?"

More like fifteen or twenty, I whisper.

"No," the mouth says. "You're turning out just like every guy I've ever trusted," she says. "You're greedy."

I just want to save people.

"You're a greedy pig."

I want to save people from disasters.

"You're just a dog doing a trick."

This is only so I can kill myself.

"I don't want you dead."

Why?

"Why what?"

Why does she want me alive? Is it because she likes me?

"No," the mouth says. "I don't hate you, but I need you."

But she doesn't not like me?

The mouth says, "Do you have any idea how boring it is to be me? To know everything? To see everything coming from a million miles away? It's getting unbearable. And it's not just me."

The mouth says, "We're all bored."

The wall says, I fucked Sandy Moore.

All around that, ten others have scratched, Me too.

Someone else has scratched, Has anybody here not fucked Sandy Moore?

Next to that is scratched, I haven't.

Next to that is scratched, Faggot.

"We all watch the same television programs," the mouth says. "We all hear the same things on the radio, we all repeat the same talk to each other. There are no surprises left. There's just more of the same. Reruns."

Inside the hole, the red lips say, "We all grew up with the same television shows. It's like we all have the same artificial memory implants. We remember almost none of our real childhoods, but we remember everything that happened to sitcom families. We have the same basic goals. We all have the same fears."

The lips say, "The future is not bright.

"Pretty soon, we'll all have the same thoughts at the same time. We'll be in perfect unison. Synchronized. United. Equal. Exact. The way ants are. Insectile. Sheep."

Everything is so derivative.

A reference to a reference to a reference.

"The big question people ask isn't 'What's the nature of existence?'" the mouth says. "The big question people ask is *'What's that from?'*"

I listened at the hole the way I listened to people confess over the telephone, the way I listened at crypts for signs of life. I asked, so why does she need me?

"Because you grew up in a different world," the mouth says.

"Because if anybody is going to surprise me, it's going to be you. You're not part of the mass culture, not yet. You're my only hope of seeing anything new. You're the magic prince that can break this spell of boredom. This trance of day-after-day sameness. Been there. Done that. You're a control group of one."

But no, I whisper, I'm not all that different.

"Yes, you are," the mouth says. "And your staying different is my only hope."

So give me some predictions.

"No."

Why not?

"Because I'll never see you again. The world of people will eat you up, and I'll lose you. From now on, I'll give you one prediction each week."

How?

"This way," the mouth says. "Just like right now. And don't worry. I'll find you."

According to my itinerary, I'm in a dark television studio on a brown sofa, a 60/40 poly-wool blend by the feel of it, a broadloom weave, treated to resist stains and fading at the center of a dozen stage lights. My hair styled by. My clothes designed by. My jewelry provided by.

My autobiography says I've never been more joyful and fulfilled in my joy of living life every day to its fullest. The press releases say I'm taping a new television program, a half hour every late night when I'll take calls from people needing advice. I'll offer new perspectives. According to the press releases, every so often the show will include a new prediction. A disaster, an earthquake, tidal wave, rain of locusts could be headed your way, so you'd better tune in, just in case.

It's sort of the evening news before the fact. The press release calls the new show *Peace of Mind.*

If you could call it that.

It's Fertility who said I'd be famous someday. She said I'd be telling the whole world about her so I'd better get my facts straight.

Fertility said, after I was famous to describe her eyes as catlike. Her hair, she said, was storm-tossed. Those were her exact words. Yeah, and her lips were bee-stung.

She said her arms are as smooth as a skinless chicken breast.

According to Fertility, the way she walked was fun-loving.

"After you're famous," she told me, "don't make me look like a monster or a victim or anything." Fertility said, "You're going to sell out your entire religion and everything you believe in, just don't lie about me. Okay? Please."

So part of my being famous is I do this weekly sit-down program with a famous television journalist to introduce me. She segues to commercial break. She feeds me the people calling in with questions. The TelePrompTer feeds me the answers. People call in on the toll-free line. Help me. Heal me. Feed me. Hear me. It's what I used to do in my doggy apartment at night only broadcast nationwide.

Messiah. Savior. Deliver us. Save us.

The confessions to me in my apartment, the confessions to me on national television, they're all just the same as my story right now into the cockpit flight recorder. My confessional.

With the kinds of drugs I was taking at that point in my career, if you want to sleep at night, you don't want to read the package insert. The side effects include nothing you'd do on national television.

Vomiting, flatulence, diarrhea.

The side effects include: headache, fever, dizziness, rashes, sweating.

I could tick them all off:

Dyspepsia.

Constipation.

Malaise.

Somnolence.

Taste perversions.

According to my personal trainer, it's the Primabolin that's making my head buzz. My hands shake. Sweat stands on the back of my neck. It could be a drug interaction.

According to my personal trainer, this is a good thing. Just sitting here, I'm losing weight.

According to my personal trainer, the best way to get illegal steroids is you find a cat sick with leukemia and take it around to veterinarians who will prescribe preloaded syringes of animal steroids equivalent to the best steroids for human use. He said if the cat lives long enough, you can stockpile a year's worth.

When I asked him what happens to the cat, he asked, why should he care?

The journalist sits across from me. How her legs look with the rest of her body is not too long. She shows just enough ear for earrings. All her problems are hidden inside. All her flaws are underneath. The only smell she gives off, even her breath, is hair spray. How she's folded into her chair, her legs crossed at the knee, her hands folded in her lap, is less good posture than it is some flesh-and-blood origami.

According to the storyboards, I'm on a sofa in the island of hot light surrounded by television cameras and cables and silent technicians doing their jobs around me in the dark. The agent is there in the shadows with his arms crossed and looking at his watch. The agent turns to where some writers are marking last-minute revisions to the copy before it appears on the TelePrompTer.

On a little table next to the sofa is a glass of ice water, and if I pick it up my hand shakes so much the ice cubes ring until the agent shakes his head at me, his mouth making a silent no.

We're taping.

According to the journalist, she feels my pain. She's read my autobiography. She knows all about my humiliation. She's read all about the humiliating ordeal it must've been to be naked and sold as a slave, naked. Me being just seventeen or eighteen years old and all those people, everyone in the cult, being there to see me, naked. A naked slave, she says, in slavery. Naked.

The agent is in my line of sight just over the journalist's shoulder, with the writers crowded around him in the dark, clothed.

Next to the agent, the TelePrompTer screen tells me: I FELT VIO-LATED BY BEING AUCTIONED NAKED AS A SLAVE.

According to the TelePrompTer: I FELT DEEPLY HUMILIATED.

According to the TelePrompTer: I FELT USED AND DEFILED . . . MOLESTED.

The staff writers bunch up around the TelePrompTer and mouth the words as I read them aloud.

While I read all this out loud with the cameras watching me, the journalist looks off into the darkness at the director and touches her wrist. The director holds up two fingers, then eight fingers. A tech-nician steps into the light and pats a curl back over the journalist's ear.

The TelePrompTer tells me: I WAS SEXUALLY ABUSED. SEXUAL ABUSE WAS COMMONPLACE AMONG THE CREEDISH CULT MEMBERS. INCEST WAS AN EVERYDAY PART OF FAMILY LIFE. SO WAS SEX WITH ALL SORTS OF ANIMALS. SATAN WORSHIP WAS POPULAR. THE CREEDISH SACRIFICED CHILDREN TO SATAN ALL THE TIME, BUT NOT BEFORE ABUSING THEM LIKE CRAZY. THEN THE CREEDISH CHURCH ELDERS KILLED THEM. DRANK THEIR BLOOD. THESE WERE KIDS I SAT NEXT TO IN SCHOOL EVERY DAY. THE CHURCH ELDERS ATE THEM. WHEN THERE WAS A FULL MOON, CHURCH ELDERS DANCED NAKED, WEARING JUST THE SKINS OF DEAD CREEDISH CHILDREN.

Yeah, I say, it was all really, really stressful.

The TelePrompTer says: YOU CAN FIND ALL THE VIVID ACCOUNTS

OF THE CREEDISH SEX CRIMES IN MY BOOK. IT'S CALLED *SAVED FROM SALVATION* AND IT'S IN BOOKSTORES EVERYWHERE.

In the shadows, the agent and the writers give each other silent high fives. The agent gives me a big thumbs-up.

My hands are numb. I can't feel my face. My tongue belongs to somebody else. My lips are dead with circumoral paresthesia.

Side effects.

Peripheral paresthesia kills any feeling in my feet. My whole body feels as far away and detached as the picture of me wearing a black suit and sitting on a brown sofa on the studio monitor, the way it's supposed to feel as your soul goes up to Heaven and watches the rest of you, the flesh and blood of you, die.

The director is waving his fingers at me, two fingers on his one hand and four on his other. What he's trying to tell me I don't know.

Most of what's on the TelePrompTer is from my autobiography I didn't write. The terrible childhood I didn't have. According to the TelePrompTer, the Creedish are all burning in Hell.

The TelePrompTer tells me: I'LL NEVER GET OVER THE PAINFUL HUMILIATING PAIN NO MATTER HOW RICH I GET WHEN I INHERIT THE CREEDISH CHURCH DISTRICT LAND.

According to the TelePrompTer: MY NEWEST BOOK, THE *BOOK OF VERY COMMON PRAYER,* IS AN IMPORTANT TOOL FOR COPING WITH STRESSES WE ALL EXPERIENCE. IT'S CALLED THE *BOOK OF VERY COMMON PRAYER* AND IT'S IN BOOKSTORES EVERYWHERE.

According to the journalist watching the director watch the agent watch me watch the TelePrompTer, according to her I'm very happy and fulfilled now that I'm free of the Creedish Death Cult. When we come back, she tells the cameras, we'll take calls from viewers at home.

The journalist breaks to commercial.

During the commercial, she asks me if my growing up was really all that terrible. The agent steps up and says, yes. It was. It was terrifying. A technician trailing wires from his belt and from around his head steps up and asks, do I need some water? The agent says, no. The director asks if I need to use the bathroom, and the agent says I'm fine. He says I don't like dealing with a crowd of strangers asking me questions. I've evolved beyond physical needs. Then the camera techs roll their eyes, and the director and journalist look at each other and shrug as if I'm the one who sends them away.

Then the director says we're taping, and the journalist says that caller number one is on the air.

"If I'm in a crowded restaurant," the caller is a woman's voice coming over the studio speakers, "this is a very expensive restaurant, and someone eating next to me passes gas, not just once but over and over, and it's horrible, what should I do?"

The journalist cups one hand over her face. The director turns his back. The agent looks at the writers writing my response for the TelePrompTer.

To stall for time, the journalist asks what the caller was eating.

"Something with pork," the caller says. "It doesn't matter. The smell was so bad I couldn't taste anything else."

The TelePrompTer says: THE LORD GOD HAS GIVEN US MANY SENSES.

The TelePrompTer is stalling for time, too.

AMONG THESE IS THE SENSE OF SMELL AND THE SENSE OF TASTE.

As the lines of copy appear on the TelePrompTer, I just read them aloud.

BUT ONLY MAN JUDGES WHICH GIFTS ARE GOOD AND BAD. TO GOD THE SMELL OF OFFAL IS EQUAL TO THE SMELL OF FINE PORK OR WINE.

I have no idea where they're going with this.

DO NOT SUFFER AND DO NOT REJOICE. BE NOT COMPLIMENTED OR OFFENDED BY SUCH GIFTS. JUDGE NOT, LEST YE BE JUDGED.

The director mouths the words Burma Shave. The journalist says caller number two, you're on the air.

Caller number two asks what I think of thong swimwear.

The TelePrompTer says: ABOMINATION.

I say, After years of presoaking for rich people, I think the people who make thong swimwear and underwear should just make the thong part black to begin with.

The journalist says caller number three, you're on the air.

"There's a guy I like, but he's avoiding me."

It's Fertility, it's her voice, on loudspeakers, talking to me, talking about me all over North America. Is she going to force a spat here on television? My thoughts branch into a flow chart of the lies I've told and my possible responses to what she might start.

Is she going to expose me and my disaster predictions?

Has she put two and two together and guessed that I coached her brother to commit suicide? Or has she known that all along? And if she knows I killed her brother, then what?

"This guy who won't call me, I told him about what I do," she says. "My job. And he disapproves, but he pretends he's okay with it."

The journalist asks, what exactly is Fertility's job?

The TelePrompTer is blank.

Then all of America is about to know a big secret about either Fertility or me. Her evil job. My murderous suicide hotline. Her disaster dreams. My borrowed predictions.

"I have an agent named Dr. Ambrose," Fertility says, "except he's not a real doctor."

Fertility told me one time that everyone in the world, even garbage haulers and dishwashers, will be signed by an agent someday. Her Dr. Ambrose would find couples with money looking for someone to have their baby. A surrogate mother. Dr. Ambrose calls it the procedure. It's conducted in utero with the birth father in bed with Fertility and his wife waiting outside the door.

"The wife will be in the hallway, knitting or listing baby names," Fertility says, "and the husband will be carefully emptying the teeny-weeny contents of his testicles into me."

The first time she told me about her job, back when I was a

nobody doing crisis intervention at home, she told me Fertility Hollis is a stage name. She said her real name was Gwen, but she hated that.

"My being with the birth father is more naturopathic, says Dr. Ambrose. That's his pitch to desperate couples. It isn't adultery. It's holistic."

It wasn't fraud or prostitution, she told me.

"It's in the Bible," Fertility says.

It costs five thousand dollars.

"You know, Genesis Chapter Thirty, Rachel and Bilhah, Leah and Zilpah."

Bilhah didn't use birth control, I want to tell her. Zilpah didn't make five grand, tax-free. They were real slaves. They didn't travel all over the nation getting plugged by would-be fathers hungry for an heir.

Fertility will live with a couple for up to one full week, but every time they conduct the procedure it's another five grand. With some men, this can mean fifteen grand in one night. Plus the couple has to pay her airfare.

"Dr. Ambrose is just a voice on the telephone that arranges the arrangement," Fertility says. "It's not as if he's a real person. The couple pays him and he sends me half the money in cash. There's never a return address. He's such a coward."

I know that feeling.

The TelePrompTer says: SLUT.

"All I have to do is not conceive, and I'm a big success."

It's her vocation, she told me, being barren.

The TelePrompTer says: HARLOT.

Over the speakers she says it, "I'm sterile."

The TelePrompTer says: WHORE.

It's her one marketable job skill. It's her calling.

Here's the job she was born to do.

She pays no taxes. She loves to travel. She lives on the road in rich places, and the hours are flexible. She told me, some nights, she falls asleep during the procedure. With some birth fathers, she dreams of arson, of falling bridges and landslides.

"I don't think I'm doing anything wrong," she says. "I think I'm making lemons into lemonade."

The TelePrompTer says: BURN IN THE HOT ETERNAL FIRES OF HELL YOU HEATHEN DEVIL SLATTERN.

Fertility says, "So what do you think?"

The journalist is staring at me so hard she hasn't noticed some hair that's slipped down over her forehead. The director is staring at me. The agent is staring. The journalist gulps. The writers are feeding copy into the TelePrompTer.

PRAY TO DIE ADULTEROUS DEVIL WHORE.

All of America is tuned in.

YOU ARE BEYOND FORGIVENESS EVIL DEVIL GIRL.

The agent shakes his head, no.

The TelePrompTer screen goes blank for a moment. The writers write. The copy reappears.

YOU ARE BEYOND FORGIVENESS EVIL DEVIL WOMAN.

Says Fertility's voice, "So what do you think?"

HARLOT

The agent points at me, points at the TelePrompTer screen, points at me, over and over, fast.

TROLLOP

"You're not going to pass some big judgment on me, are you?"

JEZEBEL

There's just dead air going out to the satellite. Somebody has to say something.

With my numb mouth I read the words on the TelePrompTer. With no feeling in my lips, I just say what they tell me to say.

The journalist asks, "Caller number three? Are you still there?"

The director is flashing his fingers at us, five, four, three, two, one. Then he pulls his index finger across his throat.

20

What else I want people to know before my plane crash is I didn't dream up the idea for the PornFill.

The agent is always pushing paper in front of me and saying, sign this.

He tells me, sign here.

And here.

Here.

And here.

The agent tells me to just initial next to each paragraph. He tells me, don't bother reading this bit, I won't understand.

That's how the PornFill happened.

It was not my idea to take all twenty thousand acres of the Creedish church district and turn it into the repository for this nation's outdated pornography. Magazines. Playing cards. Videocassettes. Compact disks. Worn-out dildos. Punctured blow-up dolls. Artificial vaginas. The bulldozers are out there twenty-four hours a day pushing mountains of that around. This is twenty thousand acres. Two-zero-zero-zero-zero acres. Every square foot of Creedish property. Wildlife is displaced. The groundwater is contaminated.

It's being compared to Love Canal, and it's not my fault.

Before the flight recorder tape runs out, people need to know who to blame. It's the agent. The *Book of Very Common Prayer*. The *Peace of Mind* television show. The American PornFill Corporation. The Genesis Campaign. The Tender Branson Dashboard Statuette. Even my botched Super Bowl halftime special, the agent brainstormed them all.

And they all made tons of money.

But what's important is none of them was my idea.

With the PornFill, the agent pitches it to me one day in Dallas or Memphis. My whole life at that point was stadiums and hotel rooms separated by time on airplanes instead of real distance. The whole world was just carpet patterns rushing by under my feet. Low-pile poly-nylon florals or corporate logos on a field of dark blue or gray that won't show cigarette burns or dirt.

The whole world was just public toilets with Fertility in the stall next to mine, whispering:

"There's a cruise ship hitting an iceberg tomorrow night."

Whispering, "At two o'clock p.m., eastern standard time, next Wednesday, the Bolivian gray panther will become extinct."

The agent is saying, a major problem for most Americans is disposing of pornographic material in a safe, private manner. Throughout America, he says, are vast collections of *Playboy* magazines or *Screw* magazines that don't excite anybody anymore. There are warehouses and shelves full of videotaped nobodies with long sideburns or blue eye shadow humping away to bad pirated music. What America needs, he says, is a place to ship this stale smut where it can decompose out of the sight of children and prudes.

His pitch to me comes after the agent's already run a feasibility study on landfilling paper, plastic, elastic, latex, rubber, leather, steel fasteners, zippers, chrome rings, Velcro, vinyl, petroleum- and water-based lubricants, and nylon.

His idea is to set up collection sites where people can drop off porno, no questions asked. From there, local franchises will ship the porno in the same type of specialized biohazard containers used for sharps and dressings contaminated with infectious disease. The porno will be hauled to the former Creedish church district colony in central Nebraska where it'll be sorted. The three categories will include:

Soft Core.

Hard Core.

And Child.

The first category will be allowed to rot on the surface of the ground. The second category will be bulldozed into the ground. The third will be handled only by uninterested people wearing full-body disposable rip-stop coveralls including 50-mil rubber gloves and boots and breathing through masks, who'll seal the kiddie porn in underground vaults where it can sit out its bazillion-year half-life.

According to the agent, we need to get people panicking about the porno threat.

We're going to push for government action that makes it mandatory to dispose of porno in safe, clean ways. Our ways. The same as used motor oil or asbestos, if people want to get rid of it, they'll have to pay.

We'll show people discarded porno filling the streets, corrupting children, inspiring sex crimes.

We'll charge by the ton to accept the stuff. The local collection franchises will pass the cost on to their customers, plus an extra margin for profit. We make money. The local franchises make money. Joe Blow is free to shop for fresh porno. The porno industry gets rich.

Okay, the agent told me. Richer.

According to the agent, it was all going to be a win, win, win, win situation.

Then it wasn't.

The agent was already drafting the federal law that now requires you to pay a deposit on all pornographic material. The deposit funnels back through the government to pay for the interment of pornographic materials found abandoned. Money from this special porno tax was earmarked for a porno superfund to clean up illegal dump sites. Some special user tax dollars were going to rehabilitate sex addicts, but not very much.

Before I ever heard word one about the PornFill, the environmental impact statement was already dummied up.

The perc tests were faked.

The publicist had faxes going out to church groups day and night, testing the waters. The lobbyists were making a discreet push.

There was the twenty thousand acres of the Creedish church district with its ghosts nobody wanted to buy. And there were the millions of personal stockpiles of pornography that no one wanted. It made sense to everybody except me.

It wasn't a decision I made. I explored some alternatives. I said *The Prayer to Create Extra Storage Space.* I swallowed 4000 milligrams of chocolate Gamacease prototypes. I thought that might solve the problem for America. I said *The Prayer to Recycle Accumulated Newspapers,* but this wasn't the same. I said *The Prayer to Procrastinate,* but the agent just would not let the issue drop.

According to the newspaper one morning, the Sensitive Materials Interment Bill had passed the House and the Senate and the president was signing it into law.

The agent just kept telling me, sign this.

Initial here. And here. And here.

I said the *Prayer for Signing Important Documents You Don't Read.*

According to Fertility, it was the PornFill that drove my brother Adam out of hiding.

My only part in the project was I signed some papers.

Since then, everybody in America thinks it's my fault they have to pay an extra two-dollar deposit when they buy a skin magazine.

After that, Adam Branson came out of hiding and put a gun to Fertility's bored head to force her to track me down.

As if Fertility couldn't see that coming.

Fertility knew everything.

Fertility said to describe my brother's threat to kill her as well-intentioned.

Later on, when it was my turn to hold the same gun to the pilot's head on this airplane, then I understood how fast these things happen.

Still. I'm the one people hate.

Me, I'm the brother with the Tender Branson National Sensitive Materials Sanitary Landfill named after me.

The last time Fertility saw the new buffed, bulked, tanned, and shaved me in person, she said I was improved beyond recognition. She said, "You need a disaster?"

She said, "Look in a mirror."

Adam was still out hunting me for sport. Adam is the brother Fertility told me to describe as "a saint."

19

Before this plane goes down or before the flight recorder tape runs out, some other mistakes I want to clean up include the following:

The *Peace of Mind* television show

The Tender Branson Dashboard Statuette

The board game Bible Trivia. As if anything God says is trivial.

The secret the agent told me was to have a lot of things in the pipeline. That way, when one failed you always have hope.

So there was:

The Bible Diet

The book *Money-Making Secrets of the Bible*

The book *Sex Secrets of the Bible*

The Bible Book of Remodeling Kitchens and Bathrooms

There was the Tender Branson Room Freshener.

There was the Genesis Campaign.

There was the *Book of Very Common Prayer,* Volume II, but the prayers were getting a little witchy:

For example, *The Prayer to Make Someone Love You.*

Or, *The Prayer to Strike Your Enemy Blind.*

All of these are brought to you by the good people of Tender Branson Enterprises. None of them was my idea.

The Genesis Campaign was the most not my idea. I fought the Genesis Campaign tooth and nail. The problem was, there were people asking if I was a virgin. Intelligent people were asking if it wasn't a little demented, my still being a virgin at my age.

People were asking, what was my problem with sex?

What was wrong with me?

The Genesis Campaign was the agent's quick fix. More and more everything in my life was a fix for an earlier fix for an earlier fix until I forget what the original problem was. The problem in this case was you just can't be a middle-aged virgin in America without something being wrong with you. People can't conceive of a virtue in someone else that they can't conceive in themselves. Instead of believing you're stronger, it's so much easier to imagine you're weaker. You're addicted to self-abuse. You're a liar. People are always ready to believe the opposite of what you tell them.

You're not just self-controlled.

You were castrated as a child.

The Genesis Campaign was a very iffy media event.

The quick fix was the agent decided to get me married.

The agent tells me this, riding in the limo one day.

Riding with us, the personal trainer tells me that tiny insulin needles are best because they don't snag against the inside of the vein. The publicist is there too, and she and the agent look out the tinted windows while the trainer sharpens a needle against the scratch pad of a matchbook and shoots me up with 50 milligrams of Laurabolin.

This doesn't not hurt, using insulin needles.

The thing about sex, the agent tells me, is no matter how much you crave it, you can forget. Back when he was a teenager, the agent developed an allergy to milk. He used to love milk, but he couldn't drink it. Years later, they developed lactose-free milk he can drink, but now he hates the taste of milk.

When he quit drinking alcohol because of a kidney problem, he thought he'd go crazy. Now he never thinks about having a drink.

To keep me from wrinkling the skin on my face, the team dermatologist has injected most of the muscles around my mouth and eyes with Botox, the botulinum toxin, to paralyze these muscles for the next six months.

With the peripheral paresthesia side effects of all my drug interactions, I can hardly feel my hands and feet. With the Botox injections, I can barely move my face. I can talk and smile, but only in a very limited way.

This is in the limo going to the plane going to the next stadium, God knows where. According to the agent, Seattle is just the general geographic area around the Kingdome. Detroit is the people who live around the Silverdome. We're never going to Houston, we're going to the Astrodome. The Superdome. The Mile High Stadium. RFK Stadium. Jack Murphy Stadium. Jacobs Field. Shea Stadium. Wrigley Field. All of these places have towns, but that doesn't matter.

The events coordinator is riding with us also, and gives me a list of names, applicants, women who want to marry me, and the agent gives me a list of questions to memorize. At the top of the page, the first question is:

"What woman in the Old Testament did God turn into a condiment?"

The events coordinator is planning a big romantic wedding on the fifty-yard line during Super Bowl halftime. The wedding colors will depend on which teams make it to the Super Bowl. The religion will depend on the bidding war, a very hush-hush bidding war going on for me to convert to Catholic or Jewish or Protestant now that the Creedish church is belly-up.

The second question on the list is:

"What woman in the Old Testament was eaten by dogs?"

The other option the agent is considering is that we avoid the middle man and found our own major religion. Establish our own brand recognition. Sell direct to the customer.

The third question on the list is:

"Did perpetual happiness in the Garden of Eden maybe get so boring that eating the apple was justified?"

In the limo, the six or seven of us sit facing each other on two bench seats with our knees mixed together between us.

According to the publicist, the wedding is set. A committee has already chosen a good nondenominational bride so my asking the questions will be a fake. The committee is in the limo with us. People are mixing drinks at the wet bar and passing them to each other. The bride is going to be the woman just hired as assistant events coordinator. She's in the limo with us, sitting in the seat across from me, and she leans forward.

Hi, she says. And she's sure we'll be very happy together.

The agent says, we need a big miracle to do at the wedding.

The publicist says, the biggest.

The agent says I need to come up with the biggest miracle of my career.

With Fertility pissed at me, with my brother still at large, with the Laurabolin needled into my bloodstream, the dating game scheme for choosing a sacred vessel, the Genesis Project, the complete stranger here to marry and deflower me, and the pressure for me to commit suicide, I don't know what.

The undersecretary to the media coordinator says we're out of vodka. He's in the limo with us. We're out of white wine, too. We have loads of tonic water.

Everybody looks at me.

No matter how much I do, they still want more, better, faster, different, newer, bigger. Fertility was right.

And now the agent's telling me I need the biggest miracle of my career. He says, "You need to get to completion on this."

Amen, I tell him. No kidding.

18

People are always asking me if I can operate a toaster. Do I know what a lawn mower does?

Do I know what hair conditioner is for?

People don't want for me to act too worldly. They're looking for me to have a kind of Garden of Eden, pre-apple innocence. A kind of baby Jesus naiveté. People ask, do I know how a television works?

No, I don't, but most people don't.

The truth is I wasn't a rocket scientist to begin with, and every day I'm losing ground. I'm not stupid, but I'm getting there. You can't live in the outside world all your adult life and not get the hang of things. I know how to work a can opener.

The hardest part of my being a famous celebrated celebrity religious leader is having to live down to people's expectations.

People ask, do I know what a hair dryer is for?

According to the agent, the secret to staying on top is to be non-threatening. Be nothing. Be a blank space people can fill in. Be a mirror. I'm the religious version of a lottery winner. America is full of rich and famous people, but I'm supposed to be that rare combination: celebrated and stupid, famous and humble, innocent and rich. You just live your humble life, people think, your Joan of Arc everyday life, your Virgin Mary life washing dishes, and one day your number will come up.

People ask, do I know what a chiropractor is?

People think sainthood is just something that happens to you. The whole process should be that easy. As if you can be Lana Turner at Schwab's drugstore when you're discovered. Maybe in the eleventh century you could be that passive. Nowadays there's laser resurfacing to remove those fine lines around your mouth before you tape your Christmas television special. Now we have chemical peels. Dermabrasion. Joan of Arc had it easy.

Nowadays, people are asking, do I know about checking accounts?

People ask all the time why I'm not married. Do I have impure thoughts? Do I believe in God? Do I touch myself?

Do I know what a paper shredder does?

I don't know. I don't know. I have my doubts. I won't tell. And I have the agent to tell me all about paper shredders.

Around this part of the story, a copy of the *Diagnostic and Statistical Manual of Mental Disorders* shows up in the mail. Some clerk on the incoming mail team directs it to an assistant media interface director who hands it off to a low-level publicist who routes it to the daytime scheduler who slips it onto my breakfast tray in the hotel suite. Alongside my morning's 430 grams of complex carbohydrates and 600 grams of egg albumin protein, here's the dead caseworker's missing DSM.

The mail comes in ten sacks at a time. I have my own zip code.

Help me. Heal me. Save me. Feed me, the letters say.

Messiah. Savior. Leader, they call me.

Heretic. Blasphemer. Antichrist. Devil, they call me.

So I'm sitting up in bed with my breakfast tray across my lap, and I'm reading the manual. There's no return address on the package it came in, but inside the cover is the signature of the caseworker. It's weird how the name outlives the person, the signifier outlasts the signified, the symbol the symbolized. The same as the name carved into stone on each crypt at the Columbia Memorial Mausoleum, only the caseworker's name is left.

We feel so superior to the dead.

For example, if Michelangelo was so damn smart, why'd he die?

How I feel reading the DSM is, I may be a fat stupid dummy, but I'm still alive.

The caseworker's still dead, and here's proof that everything she studied and believed in all her life is already wrong. In the back of this edition of the DSM are the revisions from the last edition. Already, the rules have changed.

Here are the new definions of what's acceptable, what's normal, what's sane.

Inhibited Male Orgasm is now Male Orgasmic Disorder.

What was Psychogenic Amnesia is now Dissociative Amnesia.

Dream Anxiety Disorder is now Nightmare Disorder.

Edition to edition, the symptoms change. Sane people are insane by a new standard. People who used to be called insane are the picture of mental health.

Without even knocking, the agent comes in with the morning newspapers and catches me in bed, reading. I tell him, Look what came in the mail, and he yanks the book out of my hands and asks me if I know what incriminating evidence is. The agent reads the caseworker's name inside the cover and asks, "Do you know what first-degree murder is?" The agent is holding the book with his one hand and smacking it with his other. "Do you know how it's going to feel to sit in the electric chair?"

Smack.

"Do you realize what a murder conviction will do to ticket sales at your upcoming events?"

Smack.

"Have you ever heard the phrase People's Exhibit A?"

I don't know what he's talking about.

The sound of vacuum cleaners in the hallway makes me feel lazy. It's almost noon, and I'm still in bed.

"I'm talking about this," the agent says and holds the book gripped in his two hands and pushed in my face. "This book," he says, "it's what the police would call a souvenir of the kill."

The agent says the police detectives are every day asking to talk to me about the caseworker's being found dead. The FBI is every day asking the agent what happened to the DSM that disappeared with her case history records the week before she choked to death on chlorine gas. The government isn't happy I fled the scene. The agent asks me, "Do you know how close you are to having a warrant out for your arrest?"

Do I know what a prime murder suspect is?

Do I know how me having this book will look?

I'm still sitting in bed eating toast, no butter, and oatmeal, no brown sugar. I'm stretching my arms and saying, Forget it. Relax. The book came in the mail.

The agent asks me if that seems more than a little convenient.

His point is it's possible I sent the book to myself. The DSM makes a good reminder of my old life. As rough as being me can feel, what with the drugs and schedule and zero personal integrity, it feels better than me cleaning toilets over and over. And it's not as if I've never stolen anything before. Another good way to shoplift is you find an item and cut off the price tag. This works best in really big stores with too many departments and clerks for any one person to know everything. Find a hat or gloves or an umbrella, cut off the price tag, and turn it in at the Lost and Found department. You don't even have to leave the store with it.

If the store finds out the item is stock, it just goes back on the sales floor.

Most times, the item just goes into a lost and found bin or a rack, and if no one claims it in thirty days, it's yours.

And since nobody lost it, nobody will come looking.

No big department store puts a genius in charge of the Lost and Found department.

The agent asks, "Do you know what money laundering is?"

This could be the same scam. As if I killed the caseworker and then mailed the book to myself. Laundered it, so to speak. As if I sent it to myself so I could act innocent about sitting here propped on my 200-thread-count Egyptian cotton pillows, gloating over my kill, eating breakfast until noon.

The idea of laundering anything makes me homesick for the sound of clothes with zippers going around and around in a clothes dryer.

Here in my hotel suite, you don't have to look very far to find a motive. The caseworker's file on me had all the records of how she cured me, me the exhibitionist, me the pedophile, me the shoplifter.

The agent asks, do I know what an FBI interrogation is like?

He asks, do I really think the police are that stupid?

"Assuming you're not the murderer," the agent asks, "do you know who sent the book? Who might try and set you up to take this fall?"

Maybe. Probably, yes, I do.

The agent's thinking it's someone from an enemy religion, a Catholic, Baptist, Taoist, Jewish, Anglican jealous rival.

It's my brother, I tell him. I have an older brother who might still be alive, and it's easy to picture Adam Branson out murdering survivors in ways the police would think was suicide. The caseworker was doing my job for me. It's easy to imagine her falling into a trap meant to kill me, a bottle of ammonia mixed with bleach and just waiting under the sink for me to unscrew the cap and drop dead from the smell.

The book drops out of the agent's one hand and lands open on the rug. The agent's other hand goes up to claw through his hair. "Mother of God," he says. He says, "You'd better not be telling me you have a brother still alive."

Maybe, I say. Probably, maybe, yes, I do. I saw him on a bus one time. This was maybe two weeks before the caseworker died.

The agent pins his eyes on me in bed covered with toast crumbs and says, "No, you didn't. You never saw anybody."

His name is Adam Branson.

The agent shakes his head, "No, it isn't."

Adam called me at home and threatened to kill me.

The agent says, "Nobody threatened to kill you."

Yes he did. Adam Branson is roaming the country, killing survivors, to take us all to Heaven, or to show the world Creedish unity, or to seek revenge on whoever blew the whistle on the labor missionary movement, I don't know.

The agent asks, "Do you understand the phrase *public backlash?*"

The agent asks, "Do you know what your career will be worth if people find out you're not the sole survivor of the legendary evil Creedish Death Cult?"

The agent asks, "What if this brother of yours is arrested and tells the truth about the cult? He'll blast everything the team of writers has been telling the world about your life growing up."

The agent asks, "What then?"

I don't know.

"Then you're nothing," he says.

"Then you're just another famous liar," he says.

"The whole world will hate you," he says.

He's yelling, "Do you know what the prison sentencing guidelines are for conducting a public hoax? For misrepresentation? For false advertising? For libel?"

Then he comes in close enough to whisper, "Do I need to tell you that prison makes Sodom and Gomorrah look like Minneapolis and St. Paul by comparison?"

He'll tell me what I know, the agent says. He picks up the DSM off the floor and wraps it in today's newspaper. He says I don't have a brother. He says I never saw the DSM. I never saw any brother. I regret the death of the caseworker. I miss my all-dead family. I deeply loved the caseworker. I'm forever grateful for her help and guidance, and I pray every minute my dead family isn't burning in Hell. He says I resent the police always attacking me because they're too lazy to go out and find the caseworker's real killer. He says I just want closure on all this tragic sad death stuff. He says I just want to get on with my life.

He says I trust and cherish the guidance I get every day from my wonderful agent. He tells me I'm deeply grateful.

Quick before the maid comes in to clean the room, the agent says, he's taking the DSM straight to the paper shredder.

He says, "Now get your ass out of bed, you lazy sack of shit, and remember what I just told you because someday soon you'll be telling it all to the police."

From the toilet stalls on either side of my stall come moans and breathing. Sex or bowel movements, I can't tell the difference. The stall I'm in has a hole in the partitions on each side of me, but I can't look.

If Fertility is here yet, I don't know.

If Fertility is here and sitting next to me, quiet until we're alone, I'll beg for my big miracle.

Next to the hole on my right is written, Here I sit all downhearted, tried to shit and only farted.

Next to that is written, Story of my life.

Next to the hole on my left is written, Show hard for hand job.

Next to that is written, Kiss my ass.

Next to that is written, With pleasure.

This is in the New Orleans airport, which is the airport closest to the Superdome, where tomorrow there's the Super Bowl, where at halftime I'm getting married.

And time is running out.

Outside in the hallway, my entourage and my new bride have been waiting more than two hours for me, while I've been sitting here so long my insides are ready to drop out of my ass. My pants are crushed around my ankles. The paper toilet seat liner is wicking water up from the toilet bowl to wet my bare skin. The smell of people's business is thick in every breath I take.

Toilet after toilet flushes, but every time the last man leaves another arrives.

On the wall is scratched, You know how both life and porno movies end. The only difference is life *starts* with the orgasm.

Next to that is scratched, It's getting to the end that's the exciting part.

Next to that is scratched, How tantric.

Next to that is scratched, It smells like shit in here.

The last toilet flushes. The last man washes his hands. The last footsteps go out the door.

Into the hole on my left, I whisper, Fertility? Are you there?

Into the hole on my right, I whisper, Fertility? Is that you?

There's nothing but my fear another man will walk in to read his newspaper and let loose with another spectacular six-course bowel movement.

Then from the hole on my right comes, "I hate that you called me a harlot on television."

I whisper back, I'm sorry. I was only reading the script they gave me.

"I know that."

I know she knows that.

The red mouth inside the hole says, "I called knowing you'd betray me. Free will had nothing to do with it. It was a Jesus/Judas thing. You're pretty much just my pawn."

Thanks, I say.

Footsteps come into the men's room and whoever it is, he settles in the stall on my left.

To the hole on my right, I whisper, We can't talk now. Someone's come in.

"It's okay," the red mouth says. "It's just big brother."

Big brother?

The mouth says, "Your brother, Adam Branson."

And through the hole on my left comes the barrel of a gun.

And a voice, a man's voice, says, "Hello, little brother."

The gun stuck through the hole aims around, blind, pointing at my feet, pointing at my chest, my head, the stall door, the toilet bowl.

Next to the barrel of the gun is scratched, Suck this.

"Don't freak," Fertility says. "He's not going to kill you. I know that much."

"I can't see you," Adam says, "but I have six bullets, and one of them is bound to find you."

"You're not going to kill anybody," the red mouth tells the black gun, the two of them talking back and forth across my bare white lap. "He was at my apartment all last night putting that gun against my head, and all he did was mess up my hair."

"Shut up," the gun says.

The mouth says, "He doesn't have any bullets in it."

The gun says, "Shut up!"

The mouth says, "I had another dream about you last night. I know what they did to you as a child. I know what happened to you was terrible. I understand why you're terrified of having sex."

I whisper, Nothing happened to me.

81

The gun says, "I tried to stop it, but just the idea of what the elders were doing to you kids made me sick."

I whisper, It wasn't that bad.

"In my dream," the mouth says, "you were crying. You were just a little boy the first time, and you had no idea what was about to happen."

I whisper, I've put all that behind me. I'm a famous celebrated religious celebrity.

The gun says, "No, you haven't."

Yes, I have.

"Then why are you still a virgin?" the mouth says.

I'm getting married tomorrow.

The mouth says, "But you won't have sex with her."

I say, She's a very lovely and charming girl.

The mouth says, "But you won't have sex with her. You won't consummate the marriage."

The gun says to the mouth, "That's how the church worked it with all the tenders and biddies so they'd never want sex in the outside world."

The mouth says to the gun, "Well, the whole practice was just sadistic."

Speaking of marriages, I say, I could use the biggest miracle you've got.

"You need more than that," the mouth says. "Tomorrow morning while you're getting married, your agent is going to drop dead. You're going to need a good miracle and a good lawyer."

The idea of my agent being dead isn't so bad.

"The police," the mouth says, "are going to suspect you."

But why?

"There's a bottle of that new cologne of yours, Truth, The Fragrance," the mouth says, "and he chokes to death breathing it."

"It's really bleach mixed with ammonia," the gun says.

I ask, Just like the caseworker?

"That's why the police will come after you," the mouth says.

But my brother killed the caseworker, I say.

"Guilty as charged," the gun says. "And I stole the DSM and your case history files."

The mouth says, "And he's the one who set things up for your agent to choke to death."

"Tell him the best part," the gun says to the mouth.

"More and more in my dreams," the mouth says, "the police have been suspecting you of murdering all the Creedish survivors whose suicides looked fake."

All the Creedish that Adam killed.

"Those are the ones," the gun says.

The mouth says, "The police think maybe you did all the killings to make yourself famous. Overnight, you went from being a fat ugly housecleaner to being a religious leader, and tomorrow you'll be accused of being the country's most successful serial killer."

The gun says, "Successful probably isn't the right word."

I say, I wasn't all that fat.

"What did you weigh?" the gun says, "And be honest."

On the wall it says, Today Is the Worst Day of the Rest of Your Life.

The mouth says, "You were fat. You are fat."

I ask, So why don't you just kill me now? Why don't you put some bullets in your gun and just shoot me?

"I have bullets loaded," the gun says, and the barrel swivels around to point at my face, my knees, my feet, Fertility's mouth.

The mouth says, "No, you don't have any bullets."

"Yes, I do," the gun says.

"Then prove it," the mouth says. "Shoot him. Right now. Shoot him. Shoot."

I say, Don't shoot me.

The gun says, "I don't feel like it."

The mouth says, "Liar."

"Well, maybe I wanted to shoot him a long time ago," the gun says, "but now the more famous he gets, the better. That's why I killed the caseworker and destroyed his mental health records. That's why I've set up the stupid phony bottle of chlorine gas for the agent to sniff."

I was only a pretend insane pervert with the caseworker, I say.

Scratched on the wall it says, Shit or get off the pot.

"It doesn't matter who kills the agent," the mouth says. "The police will be right on the fifty-yard line to arrest you for mass murder the second you step off camera."

"But don't worry," the gun says. "We'll be there to rescue you."

Rescue me?

"Just give them this miracle," the mouth says, "and there should be a few minutes of chaos so you can get out of the stadium."

I ask, Chaos?

The gun says, "Look for us in a car."

The mouth says, "A red car."

The gun says, "How do you know? We haven't stolen it yet."

"I know everything," the mouth says. "We'll steal a red car with an automatic transmission because I can't drive a stick."

"Okay," the gun says. "A red car."

"Okay," the mouth says.

I couldn't be more not excited. I say, Just give me the miracle.

And Fertility gives me the miracle. The biggest miracle of my career.

And she's right.

And there will be chaos.

There will be complete pandemonium.

16

At eleven o'clock the next morning, the agent is still alive.

The agent's alive at eleven-ten and at eleven-fifteen.

The agent's alive at eleven-thirty and eleven forty-five.

At eleven-fifty, the events coordinator chauffeurs me from the hotel to the stadium.

With everyone always around us, the coordinators and reps and managers, I can't ask the agent if he's brought a bottle of Truth, The Fragrance, and when he plans to sniff it next. I can't just tell him not to sniff any cologne today. That it's poison. That the brother I don't have and that I've never seen has got into the agent's luggage and set a trap. Every time I see the agent, every time he disappears into the bathroom or I have to turn my back for a minute, it could be the last time I see him.

It's not that I love the agent that much. I can easily enough picture myself at his funeral, what I'd wear, what I'd say in eulogy. Giggling. Then I see Fertility and me doing the Argentine Tango on his grave.

I just don't want to be on trial for mass murder.

It's what the caseworker would call an approach/avoidance situation.

Whatever I say about cologne, the entourage will repeat to the police if he turns up choked to death.

At four-thirty, we're backstage at the stadium with the folding tables and catered food and the rented wardrobe, the tuxes and the wedding dress hanging on racks, and the agent is still alive and asking me what I plan to proclaim as my big halftime miracle.

I'm not telling.

"But is it big?" the agent wants to know.

It's big.

It's big enough to make every man in this stadium want to kick my ass.

The agent looks at me, one eyebrow raised, frowning.

The miracle I have is so big it will take every policeman in this city to keep the crowds from killing me. I don't tell the agent that. I don't say how that's the idea. The police will have their hands so full keeping me alive, they won't be able to arrest me for murder. I don't tell the agent that part.

At five o'clock, the agent is still alive, and I'm getting strapped into a white tuxedo with a white bow tie. The justice of the peace comes up and tells me everything is under control. All I have to do is breathe in and out.

The bride comes over in her wedding dress, rubbing petroleum jelly up and down her ring finger, and says, "My name is Laura."

This isn't the girl who was in the limo from the day before.

"That was Trisha," the bride says. Trisha got sick so Laura is being her understudy. It's okay. I'll still be married to Trisha even though she's not here. Trisha is the one the agent still wants.

Laura says, "The cameras won't know." She's wearing a veil.

People are eating the food brought in by the caterer. Near the steel doors that open onto the sidelines, people from the florist are ready to hustle the altar out onto the football field. The candelabras. The bowers covered with white silk flowers. Roses and peonies and white sweet peas and stock, all of them brittle and sticky with hair spray to keep them stiff. The armload of silk bouquet for the bride to carry is silk gladioli and white poly-silk dahlias and tulips trailing yards of white silk honeysuckle.

All of it looks beautiful and real if you're far enough away.

The field lights are bright, the makeup artist says, and gives me a huge red mouth.

At six o'clock, the Super Bowl begins. It's football. It's the Cardinals against the Colts.

Five minutes into the first quarter, it's Colts six, Cardinals zero, and the agent is still alive.

Near the steel doors that open into the stadium are the altar boys and bridesmaids dressed as angels, flirting and smoking cigarettes.

With the Colts on their forty-yard line, it's their second down and six, and the post-event scheduler is briefing me how I'll spend my honeymoon on a seventeen-city tour to promote the books, the games, the dashboard statuette. Founding my own major world religion isn't out of the picture. A world tour is in the works now that the pesky question about my having sex is covered. The plan includes goodwill tours to Europe, Japan, China, Australia, Singapore, South Africa, Argentina, the British Virgin Islands, and New Guinea, with me getting back to the United States in time to see my first child born.

Just so there's nothing left to guesswork, the coordinator tells me the agent has taken certain liberties to make sure my wife will have our first child at the end of my nine-month tour.

Long-range planning calls for my wife to have six, maybe seven children, a model Creedish family.

The events coordinator says I won't have to lift a finger.

This will be immaculate conception, as far as I'm involved.

The field lights are way too bright, the makeup artist says, and smears my cheeks with red.

At the end of the first quarter, the agent comes by to make me sign some papers. Profit-sharing documents, the agent tells me. The party known as Tender Branson, to be hereafter known as The Victim, grants the party hereafter known as The Agent the power to receive and distribute all monies payable to the Tender Branson Media and Merchandising Syndicate, including but not limited to book sales, broadcast programming, artwork, live performances, and cosmetics, namely men's cologne.

"Sign here," the agent says.

And here.

Here.

And here.

Someone is pinning a white rose to my lapel. Someone is on his knees shining my shoes. The makeup artist is still blending.

The agent now owns the copyright to my image. And my name.

It's the end of the first quarter with the game tied seven to seven, and the agent's still alive.

The personal fitness trainer needles me with 10 cc's of adrenaline to put some sparkle in my eyes.

The senior events coordinator says all I have to do is walk the fifty-yard line out to where the wedding party is standing in the center of the stadium. The bride will walk in from the opposing side. We'll all of us be standing on a platform of wooden boxes with five thousand white doves hidden underneath. The audio for the ceremony was all prerecorded in a studio, so that's what the audience will hear. I don't have to say a word until my prediction.

When I step on a switch hidden by my foot, that will release the doves. Walk. Talk. Doves. It's a cinch.

The wardrobe supervisor announces that we need to use the corset to get the silhouette we're after and tells me to hurry and strip in front of everybody. The angels, the staff, the caterers, the florist people. The agent. Now. Everything except my shorts and socks. Now. The wardrobe supervisor stands with the rubber-and-wire torture of the corset ready for me to step into, and says here's my last chance to take a leak for the next three hours.

"You wouldn't have to wear that monster," the agent tells me, "if you could keep the weight off."

It's four minutes into the second quarter and nobody can find the wedding ring.

The agent blames the events coordinator blames the wardrobe supervisor blames the properties manager blames the jeweler who was supposed to donate a ring in return for advertising time on the blimp circling the stadium. Outside, the blimp is going around the sky flashing the jeweler's name. Inside the agent is threatening to sue for breach of contract and trying to radio the blimp.

The events coordinator is telling me, "Fake the ring."

They'll have the cameras do a head-and-shoulders on me and the bride. Just fake putting a ring on Trisha's finger.

The bride says she's not Trisha.

"And remember," the coordinator says, "just mouth the words, it's all prerecorded."

It's nine minutes into the second quarter and the agent is still alive and yelling into his phone.

"Shoot it down," he's yelling. "Pull the plug. Give me a gun and I'll do it," he's yelling. "Just get that damn blimp out of the air."

"No can do," the events coordinator says. The minute the wedding party comes out of the stadium, the crew in the blimp will dump fifteen thousand pounds of rice over the parking lot.

"If you'll come with me," the senior scheduler says. It's time for us to take our places.

The Colts and Cardinals go chugging off the field, the score twenty to seventeen.

The crowd is screaming for more football.

The angels and property staff rush out with the altar and silk flowers, the candelabras flaming and the platform full of doves.

The corset is squeezing all my internal organs up into my throat.

The clock is ticking down to the start of the second half, and the agent is still alive. I can only inhale in little half breaths.

The personal fitness trainer sidesteps up next to me and says, "Here, this will put some color in your cheeks."

He puts a little bottle under my nose and says for me to sniff hard.

The crowd is stomping their feet, the clock ticks, the score is so close, and I sniff.

"Now the other nostril," the trainer says.

And I sniff.

And everything's disappeared. Except for the hum of my blood chugging through veins in my ears and my heart pumping against the squeeze of my corset, I'm not aware of anything.

Feel no evil. See no evil. Hear no evil. Fear no evil.

In the distance, the coordinator is waving me out onto the artificial grass. He's pointing down at the line chalked into the field, then pointing out at a group of people standing on the wedding platform covered with white flowers in the center of the field.

The hum of my blood is fading until I hear music. I'm walking past the coordinator, out into the stadium with the thousands screaming in their seats. The music blares out of nowhere. The blimp circles outside, flashing:

Congratulations from the Many Fine Products of the Philip Morris Family of Products.

The bride, Laura, Trisha, whoever, arrives from the opposing side.

Without opening his mouth, the justice of the peace says:

DO YOU, TENDER BRANSON, TAKE TRISHA CONNERS TO BE YOURS TO HAVE AND TO HOLD AND BE FRUITFUL AND MULTIPLY WITH AS MANY TIMES AS POSSIBLE AS LONG AS YOU BOTH SHALL LIVE?

You can feel the reverb from a hundred speakers.

Without opening my mouth, I say:

I DO.

Without opening his mouth, the justice of the peace says:

WILL YOU, TRISHA CONNERS, TAKE TENDER BRAN-SON AS LONG AS YOU BOTH SHALL LIVE?

And Laura lip-synchs:

I DO.

With the television cameras zooming in, we fake the rings.

We fake the kiss.

The veil stays pretty much in place. Laura stays Trisha. From a distance everything looks perfect.

Outside the shot, the police are starting out onto the field. The agent must be dead. The cologne. Chlorine gas.

The police are at the ten-yard line.

I ask the justice of the peace for a microphone, to make my big prediction, my miracle.

The police are at the twenty-yard line.

I get the microphone, but it's dead.

The police are at the twenty-five-yard line.

I saying, Testing, testing, one, two, three.

Testing, one, two, three.

The police are at the thirty-yard line, their handcuffs open and ready to snap on me.

The microphone comes to life and my voice blares from the sound system.

The police are at the forty-yard line saying, You have the right to remain silent.

If you choose to give up that right, anything you say can and will be used against you . . .

And I give up my right.

I give my prediction.

The police are at the forty-five-yard line.

My voice blaring throughout the stadium, I say:

THE FINAL SCORE OF TODAY'S GAME WILL BE COLTS TWENTY-SEVEN, CARDINALS TWENTY-FOUR. THE COLTS WILL WIN TODAY'S SUPER BOWL BY THREE POINTS.

And all hell breaks loose.

What's worse than that, engine number two has just flamed out. Up here alone in Flight 2039, I only have two engines left.

15

To do the job right, you take one sheet of the goldenrod paper and fold it around a sheet of the white paper. Slip a coupon inside the folded papers. Hold a sheet of merchandise stamps alongside the folded papers. Then fold a sheet of the letterhead paper around all of it, and stuff this into an envelope.

Stick the corresponding address label on the envelope, and you've earned three cents.

Do this thirty-three times, and you've earned almost a dollar.

Where we're at tonight is Adam Branson's idea.

The letter I'm folding starts:

Is the water that comes into the WILSON house bringing with it dangerous parasites?

Where we're at is supposed to be safe.

The goldenrod around the white, the coupon inside, the sheet of stamps, the letterhead paper, it all goes inside the envelope, and I'm three cents closer to escaped.

Is the water that comes into the CAMERON house bringing with it dangerous parasites?

The three of us sit around the dining-room table, Adam and Fertility and me, stuffing these envelopes. At ten o'clock, the housemother locks the front door of the house and stops on her walk back to the kitchen to ask if our daughter is doing any better. Have the doctors upgraded her condition? Will she live?

Fertility with rice still in her hair says, "We're not out of the woods, not yet."

Of course, we don't have a daughter.

Us having a daughter was Adam Branson's idea.

Around us is the combination of three or four families, kids and parents talking about cancer and chemotherapy, burns and skin grafts. Staph infections. The housemother asks what we call our little girl.

Adam and Fertility and I look at each other, Fertility with her tongue stuck out to lick an envelope flap. Me looking at Adam is the same as looking at a picture of who I used to be.

All together, we say three different names.

Fertility says, "Amanda."

Adam says, "Patty."

I say, Laura. Only the three names all overlap.

Our daughter.

The housemother looks at me in the burned-up remains of my white tuxedo and asks, why is our little daughter in the hospital for treatment?

All together, we say three different problems.

Fertility says, "Scoliosis."

Adam says, "Polio."

I say, Tuberculosis.

The housemother watches us folding, the yellow in the white, the coupon, the stamps, the letterhead, her eyes coming back to the handcuffs snapped around one of my wrists.

Is the water that comes into the DIXON house bringing with it dangerous parasites?

It was Adam who brought us here. Just for one night, he says. It's safe here. Now that I'm a mass murderer, Adam knows how we can start north in the morning, north until we get to Canada, but for tonight we needed a place to hide. We needed food. We needed to earn a little cash, so he brought us here.

This is after the stadium and after the crowds were tearing to shreds the line of police crowd control. This is right after my sham marriage, when the agent was dead and the police were fighting to keep me alive so they could execute me for murder. The contents of the entire Superdome emptied down onto the field the minute I announced the Colts would win. One half of the handcuffs already clicked around my one wrist, the police were nothing against the running tide of drunks that rolled toward us from the sidelines.

The band was somewhere playing the national anthem.

Out of every direction, people are dropping onto the field from the bottom of the stands. People are running with their hands in fists out across the grass toward us. There are the Arizona Cardinals in their uniforms. There are the Indianapolis Colts still at their bench, slapping ass and giving each other high fives.

The moment the police get to the edge of the wedding platform, I kick the switch and five thousand white doves fly up in a solid wall around me.

The doves drive the police back long enough for the football mob to reach center field.

The police fight back the mob, and I grab the bride's bouquet.

Sitting here stuffing envelopes, I want to tell everybody how I made my great escape. How the crowd control cylinders of tear gas jet-trailed back and forth overhead. How the crowd roar echoed under the dome. How I grabbed the poly-silk white armload of silk flowers from the bride, tears streaming down her face. How I just touched the hair-sprayed bouquet to a burning candle and I had a torch to hold back any attacker.

Holding the torch of gladioli and whipping hot wires of fake honeysuckle out in front of me, I jumped off the wedding platform and fought my way down the football field. The fifty-yard line. The forty-yard line. The thirty. Me in my white tuxedo, I dodged and quarterbacked my way, sprinting and pivoting. The twenty-yard line. To keep from being tackled, I whipped the burning dahlias side-to-side in front of me. The ten-yard line.

Ten thousand tackles are out to sack me.

Some of them drunk, some of them professionals, none of them are jacked on the quality chemicals I'm riding.

Hands grab at my white tails.

Men dive for my legs.

It's the steroids that saved my life.

Then, touchdown.

I cross under the goalpost, still headed for the steel doors that will get me off the field.

My torch is burned down to just some tiny silk trilliums when I toss it back over my shoulder. I jam through the steel double doors and turn the deadbolt from the other side.

With the Super Bowl crowd pounding the locked doors, I'm safe here for a few minutes alone with the catered food and the make-up artist. The agent's dead body is under a white sheet on a gurney next to the buffet. The buffet is mostly just turkey sandwiches and bottled water, fresh fruit. Pasta salad. Wedding cake.

The makeup artist is eating a sandwich. She cocks her head sideways at the dead agent and says, "Good job." She says she always hated him too.

She's wearing the agent's heavy gold Rolex.

The makeup artist says, "You want a sandwich?"

I ask, Is it just turkey or do they have another kind?

The makeup artist hands me a bottle of mineral water and says my tuxedo is on fire in the back.

I ask, Where's the outside?

Take that door over there, the makeup artist says.

The steel doors behind me are buckling in their frame.

Go down the long hall, the makeup artist says.

Turn right at the end.

Go out the door marked Exit.

I say thanks.

She says there's a meat loaf sandwich left if I want it.

The sandwich in my one hand, I go out the door she said, go down the hall, go out the exit.

Outside in the parking lot is a red car, a red car with an automatic transmission, Fertility behind the wheel and Adam sitting next to her.

I get in the backseat and lock the door. To Fertility in the front seat, I tell her to roll up her window. Fertility fiddles with the controls for the radio.

Behind me, the crowd is pouring out the exits, running to surround us.

Their faces are getting close enough for me to feel spit on.

Then out of the sky comes the biggest miracle.

It starts raining.

A rain of white.

Manna from Heaven. I swear.

A rain comes down so slick and heavy the mob is falling, slipping and falling, fallen and sprawled. White bits of rain bounce in the car windows, into the carpet, into our hair.

Adam looks out in wonder at the miracle of this white rain that's helping us get away.

Adam says, "It's a miracle."

The back wheels spin, skid sideways, and then leave black as we escape.

"No," Fertility says and hits the gas, "it's rice."

The blimp circling the stadium says CONGRATULATIONS and HAPPY HONEYMOON.

"I wish they wouldn't do that," Fertility says. "That rice kills birds."

I tell her that rice that kills birds saved our lives.

We were on the street. Then we were on a freeway.

Adam twisted around in the front seat to ask me, "Are you going to eat all that sandwich?"

I say, It's meat loaf.

We needed a ride north, Adam said. He knew about a ride, but it wasn't leaving New Orleans until the next morning. He had almost ten years of doing this, traveling back and forth across the country with no money in secret.

Killing people, I say.

"Delivering people to God," he says.

Fertility says, "Shut up."

We need some cash, Adam tells us. We need some sleep. Food. And he knew where we could find some. He knew a place where people would have bigger problems than we did.

We only had to lie a little.

"From now on," Adam tells us, "you two have a child."

We do not.

"Your child is deathly ill," Adam says.

Our child is not.

"You're in New Orleans so your child can go to a hospital," Adam says. "That's all you need to say."

Adam says he'll handle the rest. Adam tells Fertility, "Turn here."

He says, "Now turn right here."

He says, "Go up two more blocks and turn left."

Where he's taking us, we can stay overnight for free. We can get food donated for us to eat. We can do some piecework, collating documents or stuffing envelopes, to earn a little cash. We can get showered. Watch ourselves on television, making our escape on the evening news. Adam tells me I'm too much of a mess to be recognized as an escaped mass murderer who ruined the Super Bowl. Where we're going, he says, people will have their own big problems to worry about.

Fertility says, "Like, how many people do you have to kill to make the jump from serial killer to mass murderer?"

Adam tells us, "Sit tight in the car, and I'll go inside to grease the skids. Just remember, your child is very sick."

Then he says, "We're here."

Fertility looks at the house and at Adam and says, "You're the one who's very sick."

Adams says, "I'm your poor child's godfather."

The sign in the front yard says, Ronald McDonald House.

14

I magine you live in a house only every day your house is
in a different town.

We had three ways out of New Orleans Adam knew
about. Adam took Fertility and me to a truck stop on the
edge of the city and said to take our pick. The airports were
being watched. The train and bus stations were staked out.
We couldn't all three of us hitchhike, and Fertility refused
to drive all the way to Canada.

"I flat out don't like driving," Fertility says. "Besides,
your brother's way to travel is just a lot more fun."

The day after the Ronald McDonald House, we're the

three of us standing in the acres of gravel parking lot outside a truck stop café when Adam pulls a linoleum knife out of his back pocket and slips the blade open.

"What will it be, people?" he says.

Nothing here is going due north. Adam's been inside talking up all the truck drivers. What we have to choose from is the following, Adam says, pointing at each.

There's a Westbury Estate going west out Highway 10 to Houston.

There's a Plantation Manor headed northeast on Highway 55 to Jackson.

There's a Springhill Castle going northwest to Bossier City on Highway 49, with stops at Alexandria and Pineville, then headed west on Highway 20 to Dallas.

Parked around us on the gravel are prefabricated houses, manufactured houses, trailer houses. These are broken into halves or thirds and hooked to the back of semi trucks. The open side of each modular piece is sealed with a sheet of translucent plastic and inside are the murky shapes of sofas, beds, rolls of rolled-up carpet. Major appliances. Dining-room sets. Easy chairs.

While Adam was chatting with the drivers, finding out where each is headed, Fertility was in the truck stop bathroom dyeing my blond hair black in the sink and washing the tanning bronzer off my face and hands. We stuffed enough envelopes to buy me thrift-store clothes and get a paper bag of fried chicken with paper napkins and coleslaw.

The three of us standing in the parking lot, Adam waves his knife in a circle and says, "Choose. The men who deliver these lovely homes won't be eating their dinner all night."

Most long-haul truck drivers drive at night, Adam tells us. There's less traffic. It's cooler. During the hot, busy day, the drivers pull off the highway and sleep in the sleeper boxes attached to the back of each truck cab.

Fertility asks, "What's the difference what we choose?"

"The difference," Adam says, "is your comfort level."

This is how Adam's been crossing and crisscrossing the country for the past ten years.

A Westbury Estate has a formal dining room and a built-in fireplace in the living room.

The Plantation Manor has walk-in closets and a breakfast nook.

The Springhill Castle has a whirlpool bathtub in the glamour bath. A glamour bath has two sinks and a wall of mirror. The living room and the master bedroom have skylights. The dining nook has a built-in china hutch with leaded-glass doors.

This is depending on which half you get. Again, these are just parts of homes. Broken homes.

Dysfunctional homes.

The half you get might be all bedrooms or just a kitchen and living room and no bedrooms. There might be three bathrooms and nothing else, or you might get no bathroom at all.

None of the lights work. All the plumbing is dry.

No matter how many luxuries you get, something will be missing. No matter how carefully you choose, you'll never be totally happy.

We choose the Springhill Castle, and Adam slices the knife along the bottom edge of the plastic sealing its open side. Adam slices only about two feet, only far enough for his head and shoulders to slip inside.

Stale air from inside the house comes out the slice hot and dry.

With Adam slid inside as far as his waist, his butt and his legs still outside with us, Adam says, "This one has the cornflower-blue interior." His voice coming from inside the wall of translucent plastic, he says, "Here we have the premium furniture package. A modular living room pit group. Built-in microwave in the kitchen. Plexiglas dining-room chandelier."

Adam boosts all of himself inside, then his blond head sticks out the slice in the plastic and grins at us. "California-king-sized beds.

Faux wood-grain countertops. Low-line Euro-style commode and vertical-blind window treatments," he says. "You've made an excellent choice for your starter home."

First Fertility and then me slide through the plastic.

The way the inside of the house, the furniture shapes and the colors, looked blurred and vague from outside, that's how the outside world, the real world, looks out of focus and unreal from inside the plastic. The neon lights of the truck stop are just coming on, dim and smeared outside the plastic. The noise of the highway sounds soft and muffled from inside.

Adam kneels down with a roll of clear strapping tape and seals the slice he made from the inside.

"We won't need this anymore," he says. "When we get where we're going, we'll walk out the front or the back door just like real people."

The wall-to-wall carpet is rolled up against one wall, awaiting the rest of the house before it's installed. The furniture and mattresses stand around covered with dry-cleaning-plastic-thin dust covers. The kitchen cabinets are each taped shut.

Fertility tries the light switch for the dining-room chandelier. Nothing happens.

"Don't use the toilet either," Adam says, "or we'll be living with your business until we move out."

Neon from the truck stop and headlights from the highway flicker through the dining-room French doors while we sit around the maple-veneer table eating our fried chicken.

This part of our broken home has one bedroom, the living room, kitchen, and dining room, and half a bath.

If we get all the way to Dallas, Adam tells us, we can move into a house headed up Interstate 35 to Oklahoma. Then we can catch houses up Interstate 35 to Kansas. Then north on Interstate 135 in Kansas to westbound Interstate 70 to Denver. In Colorado, we'll catch a house going northeast on Interstate 76 until it turns into Interstate 80 in Nebraska.

Nebraska?

Adam looks at me and says, "Yeah. Our old stomping grounds, yours and mine," he says with his mouth full of chewed-up fried chicken.

Why Nebraska?

"To get to Canada," Adam says and looks at Fertility who looks at her food. "We'll follow Interstate 80 to Interstate 29 across the state line in Iowa. Then we just cruise north up 29 through South Dakota and North Dakota, all the way to Canada."

"Right straight to Canada," Fertility says and gives me a smile that looks fake because Fertility never smiles.

When we say good night, Fertility takes the mattress in the bedroom. Adam falls asleep on one length of the blue velvet sectional pit group.

Pillowed in the blue velvet he looks dead in a casket.

For a long time, I lie awake on the other length of the sectional and wonder about the lives I left behind. Fertility's brother, Trevor. The caseworker. The agent. My all-dead family. Almost all dead.

Adam snores, and nearby a diesel truck engine rumbles to life.

I wonder about Canada, if running is going to resolve anything. Lying here in the cornflower-blue darkness, I wonder if running is just another fix to a fix to a fix to a fix to a fix to a problem I can't remember.

The whole house shudders. The chandelier swings. The leaves of the silk ferns in their wicker baskets vibrate. The window treatments sway. Quiet.

Outside the plastic, the world starts moving, sliding by, faster and faster until it's erased.

Until I fall asleep.

13

Our second day on the road, my teeth feel dull and yellow. My muscles feel less toned. I can't live my life as a brunette. I need some time, just a minute, just thirty seconds, under a spotlight.

No matter how much I try and hide this, bit by bit, I start to fall apart.

We're in Dallas, Texas, considering half a Wilmington Villa with faux tile countertops and a bidet in the master bath. It has no master bedroom, but it has a laundry room with washer/dryer hookups. Of course, it has no water or power or phone. It has almond-colored appliances in the kitchen. There isn't a fireplace, but the dining room has floor-length drapes.

This is after we look at more houses than I can remember. Houses with gas fireplaces. Houses with French Provincial furniture, vast glass-topped coffee tables, and track lighting.

This is with the sunset red and gold on the flat Texas horizon, in a truck stop parking lot outside Dallas proper. I wanted to go with a house that had separate bedrooms for each of us, but no kitchen. Adam wanted the house that had only two bedrooms, a kitchen, but no bathroom.

Our time was almost up. The sun was almost down and the drivers were about to start their all-night drives.

My skin felt cold and rolling with sweat. All of me, even the blond roots of my hair, ached. Right there in the gravel, I just started doing push-ups in the middle of the parking lot. I rolled onto my back and started doing stomach crunches with the intensity of convulsions.

The subcutaneous fat was already building up. My abdominal muscles were disappearing. My pecs were starting to sag. I needed bronzer. I needed to log some time in a sun bed.

Just five minutes, I beg Adam and Fertility. Before we hit the road again, just give me ten minutes in a Wolff tanning bed.

"No can do, little brother," Adam says. "The FBI will be watching every gym and every tanning salon and health food store in the Midwest."

After just two days, I was sick of the crap deep-fried food they serve at truck stops. I wanted celery. I wanted mung beans. I wanted fiber and oat bran and brown rice and diuretics.

"What I told you about," Fertility says, looking at Adam, "it's starting. We need to get him locked up someplace, stat. He's going into Attention Withdrawal Syndrome."

The two of them hustled me into a Maison d'Elégance just as the driver was putting his truck in gear. They pushed me into a back bedroom with just a bare mattress and a giant Mediterranean dress-er with a big mirror above it. Outside the bedroom door, I could hear them piling Mediterranean furniture, sofa groups and end tables, lamps made to look like old wine bottles, entertainment centers and bar stools against the outside of the bedroom door.

Texas is speeding past the bedroom window outside. In the twilight, a sign goes by the window saying, Oklahoma City 250 Miles. The whole room shakes. The walls are papered with tiny yellow flowers vibrating so fast they make me travel-sick. Anywhere I go in this bedroom, I can still see myself in the mirror.

My skin is going regular white without the ultraviolet light I need. Maybe it's just my imagination, but one of my caps feels loose. I try not to panic.

I tear off my shirt and study myself for damage. I stand sideways and suck in my stomach. I could really use a preloaded syringe of Durateston right about now. Or Anavar. Or Deca-Durabolin. My new hair color makes me look washed-out. My last eyelid surgery didn't take, and already my eye bags show. My hair plugs feel loose. I turn to study myself in the mirror for any hair growing on my back.

A sign goes by the window saying, Soft Shoulders.

The last of my bronzer is caked in the corners of my eyes and the wrinkles around my mouth and across my forehead.

I try and nap. I pick apart the mattress ticking with my finger-nails.

A sign goes by the window saying, Slower Traffic Keep Right.

There's a knock at the door.

"I have a cheeseburger if you want it," Fertility says through the door and all the piled-up furniture.

I don't want a greasy damn fatty damn cheeseburger, I yell back.

"You need to eat sugar and fat and salt until you get back to normal," Fertility says. "This is for your own good."

I need a full body wax, I yell. I need hair mousse.

I'm pounding on the door.

I need two hours in a good weight room. I need to go three hundred stories on a stair climbing machine.

Fertility says, "You just need an intervention. You're going to be fine."

She's killing me.

"We're saving your life."

I'm retaining water. I'm losing definition in my shoulders. My eye bags need concealer. My teeth are shifting. I need my wires tightened. I need my dietitian. Call my orthodontist. My calves are wasting away. I'll give you anything you want. I'll give you money.

Fertility says, "You don't have money."

I'm famous.

"You're wanted for mass murder."

Her and Adam have to get me some diuretics.

"Next time we stop," Fertility says, "I'll get you a skinny double americano."

That's not enough.

"It's more than you'd get in prison."

Let's rethink this, I say. In prison, I'd have weight equipment. I'd have time in the sun. They must have sit-up boards in prison. I could maybe get black-market Winstrol. I say, Just let me out. Just unblock this door.

"Not until you're making sense."

I WANT TO GO TO PRISON!

"In prison, they have the electric chair."

I'll take that risk.

"But they might kill you."

Good enough. I just need to be the center of a lot of attention. Just one more time.

"Oh, you go to prison, and you'll be the center of attention."

I need moisturizer. I need to be photographed. I'm not like regular people, to survive I need to be constantly interviewed. I need to be in my natural habitat, on television. I need to run free, signing books.

"I'm leaving you alone for a while," Fertility says through the door. "You need a time out."

I hate being mortal.

"Think of this as *My Fair Lady* or *Pygmalion,* only backward."

12

The next time I wake up, I'm delirious and Fertility is sitting on the edge of my bed, massaging cheap petrole-
um-based moisturizer into my chest and arms.

"Welcome back," she says. "We almost thought you
weren't going to make it."

Where am I?

Fertility looks around. "You're in a Maplewood Chateau
with the midrange interior package," she says. "Seamless
linoleum in the kitchen, no-wax vinyl floor covering in the
two bathrooms. It's got easy-clean patterned vinyl wall-

board instead of Sheetrock, and this one is decorated in the blue-and-green Seaside theme."

No, I whisper, where in the world?

Fertility says, "I knew that's what you meant."

A sign goes by the window saying, Detour Ahead.

The room around us is different than I remember. A wallpaper border of dancing elephants goes around next to the ceiling. The bed I'm in has a canopy and white machine-made lace curtains hanging around it and tied back with pink satin ribbons. White louvered shutters flank the windows. The reflection of Fertility and me is framed in a heart-shaped mirror on the wall.

I ask, What happened to the Maison?

"That was two houses ago," Fertility says. "We're in Kansas now. In half a four-bedroom Maplewood Chateau. It's the top of the line in manufactured houses."

So it's really nice?

"Adam says it's the best," she says, smoothing the covers over me. "It comes with color-coordinated bed linens, and there are dishes in the dining-room cabinets that match the mauve of the velvet sofa and love seat in the living room. There's even color-coordinated mauve towels in the bathroom. There's no kitchen though, at least not in this half. But I'm sure wherever it's at, the kitchen is mauve."

I ask, Where's Adam?

"Sleeping."

He wasn't worried about me?

"I told him how this was all going to work out," Fertility says. "Actually, he's very happy."

The bed curtains dance and swing with the movement of the house.

A sign goes by the window saying, Caution.

I hate that Fertility knows everything.

Fertility says, "I know that you hate that I know everything."

I ask if she knows I killed her brother.

As easy as that, the truth comes out. My whole deathbed confession.

"I know you talked to him the night he died," she says, "but Trevor killed himself."

And I wasn't his homosexual lover.

"I knew that, too."

And I was the voice on the crisis hotline she talked dirty to.

"I know."

She rubs a handful of moisturizer between her palms and then smooths it into my shoulders. "Trevor called your fake crisis hotline because he was looking for a surprise. I've been after you for the same thing."

With my eyes closed, I ask if she knows how this will all turn out.

"Long-term or short-term?" she asks.

Both.

"Long-term," she says, "we're all going to die. Then our bodies will rot. No surprise there. Short-term, we're going to live happily ever after."

Really?

"Really," she says. "So don't sweat it."

I look at myself getting older in the heart-shaped mirror.

A sign goes by the window saying, Drive to Stay Alive.

A sign goes by the window saying, Speed Checked by Radar.

A sign goes by the window saying, Lights On for Safety.

Fertility says, "Can you just relax and let things happen?"

I ask, does she mean, like disasters, like pain, like misery? Can I just let all that happen?

"And Joy," she says, "and Serenity, and Happiness, and Contentment." She says all the wings of the Columbia Memorial Mausoleum. "You don't have to control everything," she says. "You can't control everything."

But you can be ready for disaster.

A sign goes by saying, Buckle Up.

"If you worry about disaster all the time, that's what you're going to get," Fertility says.

A sign goes by saying, Watch Out for Falling Rocks.

A sign goes by saying, Dangerous Curves Ahead.

A sign goes by saying, Slippery When Wet.

Outside the window, Nebraska is getting closer by the minute.

The whole world is a disaster waiting to happen.

"I want you to know I won't always be here," Fertility says, "but I'll always find you."

A sign goes by the window saying, Oklahoma 25 Miles.

"No matter what happens," Fertility says, "no matter what you do or your brother does, it's the right thing."

She says, "You have to trust me."

I ask, Can I just have some Chap Stick? For my lips. They're chapped.

A sign goes by saying, Yield.

"Okay," she says. "I've forgiven your sins. If it helps you relax a little, I guess I can get you some Chap Stick."

11

Of course, we lose Fertility at a truck stop outside Denver, Colorado. Even I could see that coming. She sneaks off to get me some Chap Stick while the truck driver is out taking a leak. Adam and me are both asleep until we hear her screaming.

And of course she planned it this way.

In the dark, in the moonlight through the windows, I stumble through the furniture to where Adam has thrown open the two front doors.

We're pulling away from the truck stop, gaining speed as the driver upshifts with Fertility running after us. Her one hand outstretched with the little tube of Chap Stick. Her red hair is flagging out behind her. Her shoes slap the pavement.

Adam is stretching his one hand out to save her. His other hand is gripping the doorframe.

With the shaking of the house, a marble-topped little occasional table falls over and rolls past Adam out the doors. Fertility dodges as the table smashes in the street.

Adam is saying, "Take my hand. You can reach it."

A dining-room chair shakes out of the house and smashes, almost hitting Fertility, and she says, "No."

Her words almost lost in the roar of the truck engine, she says, "Take the Chap Stick."

Adam says, "No. If I can't reach you, we'll jump. We have to stay together."

"No," Fertility says. "Take the Chap Stick, he needs it."

Adam says, "He needs you more."

The windows we left open suck air inside, and the easy-living open floor plan channels this airstream out through the front doors. Embroidered throw pillows blow off the sofa and bounce out the front doors around Adam. They fly at Fertility, hitting her in the face and almost tripping her. Framed decorative art, botanical print reproductions mostly and tasteful racehorse prints, flap off the walls and sail out to explode into shards of glass and wood slivers and art.

The way I feel, I want to help, but I'm weak. I've lost too much attention in the last few days. I can hardly stand. My blood sugar levels are all over the map. I can only watch as Fertility falls behind and Adam risks leaning out farther and farther.

The silk flower arrangements topple and red silk roses, red silk geraniums, and blue iris sail out the door and flutter around Fertility. The symbols of forgetfulness, poppies, land in the road, and she sprints over them. The wind throws mock orange and sweet peas, white and pink, baby's breath and orchids, white and purple, at Fertility's feet.

"Don't jump," Fertility is saying.

She's saying, "I'll find you. I know where you're going."

For one instant, she almost makes it. Fertility almost reaches Adam's hand, but when he makes his grab to pull her inside, their hands miss.

Almost miss. Adam opens his hand, and inside is the tube of Chap Stick.

And Fertility has fallen back into the dark and the past behind us.

Fertility is gone. We must be going sixty miles an hour by now, and Adam turns and throws the tube at me so hard it ricochets off two walls. Adam snarls, "I hope you're happy now. I hope your lips recover."

The dining-room china cabinet comes open and dishes, salad plates, soup tureens, dinner plates, stemware, and cups bounce and roll out the front doors. All this smashes in the street. All this leaves a wide trail behind us sparkling in the moonlight.

Nobody is running behind us, and Adam wrestles a console color television with surround sound and near-digital picture quality toward the door. With a shout he shoves it off the front porch. Then he shoves a velvet love seat off the porch. Then the spinet piano. Everything explodes when it hits the road.

Then he looks at me.

Stupid, weak, desperate me, I'm groveling on the floor trying to find the Chap Stick.

His teeth bared, his hair hanging in his face, Adam says, "I should throw you out that door."

Then a sign goes by saying, Nebraska 98 miles.

And a smile, slow and creepy, cuts across Adam's face. He staggers to the open front doors, and with the night wind howling around him he shouts.

"Fertility Hollis!" he shouts.

"Thank you!" he shouts.

Into the darkness behind us, all the darkness and scraps and glass and wreckage behind us, Adam shouts, "I won't forget everything you told me must happen!"

10

The night before we get home, I tell my big brother everything I can remember about the Creedish church district.

In the church district, we raised everything we ate. The wheat and eggs and the sheep and cattle. I remember we tended perfect orchards and caught sparkling rainbow trout in the river.

We're on the back porch of a Casa Castile going sixty miles an hour through the Nebraska night down Interstate 80. A Casa Castile has cut-glass sconces on every wall and gold-plated fixtures in the bathroom, but no power or water. Everything is beautiful but none of it works.

"No electricity and no running water," Adam says. "It's just like when we were kids."

We're sitting on the back porch with our legs hanging over the edge and the pavement rushing under. The stinking diesel exhaust from the truck eddies around us.

In the Creedish church district, I tell Adam, people lived simple, fulfilling lives. We were a steadfast and proud people. Our air and water were clean. Our days were useful. Our nights were absolute. That's what I remember.

That's why I don't want to go back.

Nothing will be there except the Tender Branson Sensitive Materials Sanitary Landfill. How it will look, the stored-up years of pornography from all over the country sent here to rot, I don't want to see firsthand. The agent showed me the receipts. Tons of smut, dump trucks and hoppers full, garbage trucks and boxcars full of smut, were arriving there every month, where bulldozers spread it three feet deep across all twenty thousand acres.

I don't want to see that. I don't want Adam to see that, but Adam still has his gun, and I don't have Fertility here to tell me if it's loaded or not. Besides, I'm pretty used to getting told what to do. Where to go. How to act.

My new job is to follow Adam.

So we're going back to the church district. In Grand Island, we'll steal a car, Adam says. We'll get to the valley just around sunrise, Adam predicts. It's just a matter of hours. We'll be getting home on a Sunday morning.

Both of us looking out into the dark behind us and everything we've lost so far, Adam says, "What else do you remember?"

Everything in the church district was always clean. The roads were always in good repair. The summers were long and mild with rain every ten days. I remember the winters were peaceful and serene. I remember sorting seed we picked from marigolds and sun-flowers. I remember splitting wood.

Adam asks, "Do you remember my wife?"

Not really.

"She wasn't much to remember," Adam says. The gun's in his hands on his lap or I wouldn't be sitting here. "She was a Biddy Gleason. We should've been very happy together."

Until someone called the government and started the investigation.

"We should've bred a dozen children and made money hand over fist," Adam said.

Until the county sheriff was there asking about documentation for every child.

"We should've gotten old on that farm with every year just like the year before it."

Until the FBI launched its investigation.

"We should both have been church elders some day," Adam says.

Until the Deliverance.

"Until the Deliverance."

I remember life was calm and peaceful in the district valley. The cows and chickens all running free. The laundry hanging outside to dry. The smell of hay in the barn. Apple pies cooling on every windowsill. I remember it was a perfect way of life.

Adam looks at me and shakes his head.

He says, "That's how stupid you are."

How Adam looks in the dark is how I'd look if none of this chaos had ever happened to me. Adam is what Fertility would call a control group of me. If I'd never been baptized and sent into the outside world, if I'd never been famous and blown out of proportion, that would be me with Adam's simple blue eyes and clean blond hair. My shoulders would be squared and regular-sized. My manicured hands with clear polish on the nails would be his strong hands. My chapped lips would be like his. My back would be straight. My heart would be his heart.

Adam looks out into the dark and says, "I destroyed them."

The Creedish survivors.

"No," Adam says. "All of them. The entire district colony. I called the police. I left the valley one night and walked until I found a telephone."

There were birds in every Creedish tree, I remember. And we caught crawdads by tying a lump of bacon fat to a string and dropping it into the creek. When we pulled it out, the fat would be covered with crawdads.

"I must have pressed zero on the telephone," Adam says, "but I asked for the sheriff. I told someone who answered that only one out of every twenty Creedish children had a valid birth certificate. I told him the Creedish hid their children from the government."

The horses, I remember. We had teams of horses to plow with and pull buggies. And we called them by their color because it was a sin to give an animal a name.

"I told them the Creedish abused their children and didn't pay taxes on most of their income," Adam says. "I told them the Creedish were lazy and shiftless. I told them, to Creedish parents, their children were their income. Their children were chattel."

The icicles hanging on houses, I remember. The pumpkins. The harvest bonfires.

"I started the investigation," Adam says.

The singing in church, I remember. The quilting. The barn raisings.

"I left the colony that night and never went back," Adam says.

Being cherished and cared for, I remember.

"We never had any horses. The couple chickens and pigs we had were just for show," Adam says. "You were always in school. You just remember what they taught you Creedish life was like a hundred years ago. Hell, a century ago everybody had horses."

Being happy and belonging, I remember.

Adam says, "There were no black Creedish. The Creedish elders were a pack of racist, sexist white slavers."

I remember feeling safe.

Adam says, "Everything you remember is wrong."

Being valued and loved, I remember.

"You remember a lie," Adam says. "You were bred and trained and sold."

And he wasn't.

No, Adam Branson was a firstborn son. Three minutes, that made all the difference. He would own everything. The barns and chickens and lambs. The peace and security. He would inherit the future, and I would be a labor missionary, mowing the lawn and mowing the lawn, work without end.

The dark Nebraska night and the road slipping by fast and warm around us. With one good push, I say to myself, I could put Adam Branson out of my life for good.

"There was hardly anything we ate that we didn't buy from the outside world," Adam says. "I inherited a farm for raising and selling my children."

Adam says, "We didn't even recycle."

So that's why he called the sheriff?

"I don't expect you to understand," Adam says. "You're still the eight-year-old sitting in school, sitting in church, believing everything you're told. You remember pictures in books. They planned how you'd live your whole life. You're still asleep."

And Adam Branson is awake?

"I woke up the night I made that telephone call. That night I did something that couldn't be undone," Adam says.

And now everybody's dead.

"Everybody except you and me."

And the only thing left for me to do is kill myself.

"That's just what you've been trained to do," Adam says. "That would be the ultimate act of a slave."

So what's left I can do to make my life any different?

"The only way you'll ever find your own identity is to do the one thing the Creedish elders trained you most not to do," Adam says. "Commit the one biggest transgression. The ultimate sin. Turn your back on church doctrine," Adam says.

"Even the garden of Eden was just a big fancy cage," Adam says. "You'll be a slave the rest of your life unless you bite the apple."

I've eaten the entire apple. I've done everything. I've gone on television and denounced the church. I've blasphemed in front of millions of people. I've lied and shoplifted and killed, if you count Trevor Hollis. I've defiled my body with drugs. I've destroyed the Creedish church district valley. I've labored every Sunday for the past ten years.

Adam says, "You're still a virgin."

With one good jump, I tell myself, I could solve all my problems forever.

"You know, the horizontal bop. Hide the salami. The hot thing. The big O. Getting lucky. Going all the way. Hitting a home run. Scoring big-time. Laying pipe. Plowing a field. Stuffing the muff. Doing the big dirty," Adam says.

"Quit trying to fix your life. Deal with your one big issue," Adam says.

"Little brother," Adam says, "we need to get you laid."

9

The Creedish church district is twenty thousand, five hundred and sixty acres, almost the entire valley at the headlands of the Flemming River, west-northwest of Grand Island, Nebraska. From Grand Island, it's a four-hour car trip. Driving south from Sioux Falls, it's a nine-hour trip.

That much of what I know is true.

The way Adam explained everything else, I still wonder about. Adam said the first step most cultures take to making you a slave is to castrate you. Eunuchs, they're called. Just short of that, some cultures make it so you don't enjoy sex so much. They cut off parts. Parts of the clitoris, Adam calls it. Or the foreskin. Then the sensitive parts of you, the parts that you'd enjoy the most, you feel less and less with those parts.

That's the whole idea, Adam says.

We drive west the rest of the night, away from where the sun will come up, trying to outrace it, trying not to see what it's going to show us when we get home.

On the dashboard of the car is glued a six-inch plastic statue of a man in Creedish church costume, the baggy pants, the wool coat, the hat. His eyes are glow-in-the-dark plastic. His hands are together in prayer, raised so high and out so far in front he looks about to take a swan dive off the passenger side of the dashboard.

Fertility told Adam to look for a green late-model Chevy somewhere within two blocks of the truck stop outside Grand Island. She said the keys would be left in it, and the tank would be full of gas. After we left the Casa Castile, it took us about five minutes to find the car.

Looking at the dashboard statuette in front of him, Adam says, "What the hell is that supposed to be?"

It's supposed to be me.

"It doesn't look a thing like you."

It's supposed to look really pious.

"It looks like a devil," Adam says.

I drive.

Adam talks.

Adam says, the cultures that don't castrate you to make you a slave, they castrate your mind. They make sex so filthy and evil and dangerous that no matter how good you know it would feel to have sexual relations, you won't.

That's how most religions in the outside world do, Adam says. That's how the Creedish did it.

This isn't anything I want to hear, but when I go to turn on the radio, all the tuning buttons are preset to religious stations. Choir music. Gospel preachers telling me I'm bad and wrong. One station I come across is a familiar voice, the Tender Branson Radio Ministry. Here's one of a thousand canned radio shows I taped in a studio I don't remember where.

The abuse of the Creedish elders was unspeakable, I'm saying on the radio.

Adam says, "Do you remember what they did to you?"

From the radio I'm saying, The abuse was never-ending.

"When you were a kid, I mean," Adam says.

Outside, the sun was catching up, making shapes out of the total darkness.

On the radio, I'm saying, The complete way our minds were controlled we never had a chance. None of us in the outside world would ever want sex. We'd never betray the church. We'd spend our entire lives at work.

"And if you never have sex," Adam's saying, "you never gain a sense of power. You never gain a voice or an identity of your own. Sex is the act that separates us from our parents. Children from adults. It's by having sex that adolescents first rebel."

And if you never have sex, Adam tells me, you never grow beyond everything else your parents taught you. If you never break the rule against sex, you won't break any other rule.

On the radio, I say, It's hard for someone in the outside world to imagine how completely trained we were.

"The Vietnam War didn't cause the mess of the 1960s," Adam says. "Drugs didn't cause it. Well, only one drug did. It was the birth control pill. For the first time in history, everybody could have all the sex they wanted. Everybody could have that kind of power."

Throughout history the most powerful rulers have been sex maniacs. And he asks, does their sex appetite come from having power, or does their will for power come from their sex appetite?

"And if you don't crave sex," he says, "will you crave power?"

No, he says.

"And instead of electing decent, boring, sexually repressed offi-cials," he says, "maybe we should find the horniest candidates and maybe they can get some good work done."

A sign goes by saying, Tender Branson Sensitive Materials Sanitary Landfill, 10 miles.

Adam says, "Do you see what I'm getting at?"

Home is just ten minutes away.

Adam says, "You must remember what happened."

Nothing happened.

On the radio, I say, It's impossible to describe how terrible the abuse was.

More and more along the sides of the road are bits of smut mag-azines blown off uncovered trucks. Fading full-frontal nude shots of beautiful women wrap themselves around each tree trunk. Rain-soaked men with long purple erections hang limp in the branches. The black boxes of video movies lie in the gravel along the road. A punctured woman made of pink vinyl lies in the weeds with the wind waving her hair and hands after us as we drive past.

"Sex is not a fearsome and terrible thing," Adam says.

On the radio I say, It's best if I just put the past behind me and move on with my life.

Up ahead, there's a point where the trees lining the road stop, and there's nothing beyond them. The sun is up and overtaking us, and ahead in the distance is nothing but a wasteland.

A sign goes by saying, Welcome to the Tender Branson Sensitive Materials Sanitary Landfill.

And we're home.

Beyond the sign, the valley stretches out to the horizon, bare, lit-tered, and gray except for the bright yellow of a few bulldozers parked and silent because it's Sunday.

There's not a tree.

There's not a bird.

The only landmark is at the center of the valley, a towering concrete pylon, just a square gray column of concrete rises from the spot where the Creedish meetinghouse stood with everyone dead inside. Ten years ago. Spreading out on the ground all around us are pictures of men with women, women with women, men with men, men and women with animals and appliances.

Adam doesn't say a word.

From the radio I say, My life is full of joy and love now.

From the radio I say, I look forward to marrying the woman chosen for me as part of the Genesis Campaign.

From the radio I say, With the help of my followers I will stem the sex craving that has taken control of the world.

The road is long and rutted from the rim of the valley toward the concrete pylon at the center. Along both sides as we drive, dildos and magazines and latex vaginas and French ticklers cling together in smoldering heaps, and the smoke from those heaps drifts in a choking haze of dirty white across the road.

Up ahead, the pylon is larger and larger, sometimes lost behind the smoke of burning pornography, only to reappear, looming.

From the radio I say, My whole life is for sale at a bookstore near you.

From the radio I say, With God's help, I will turn the world away from ever wanting sex.

Adam turns off the radio.

Adam says, "I left the valley the night I found out what the elders did to you, to tenders and biddies."

The smoke settles over the road. It comes into the car and our lungs, acrid and burning our eyes.

With tears running down each cheek I say, They didn't do anything.

Adam coughs, "Admit it."

The pylon reappears, closer.

There's nothing to admit.

The smoke obscures everything.

Then Adam says it. Adam says, "They made you watch."

I can't see anything, but I just keep driving.

"The night my wife had our first child," Adam says with the smoke leaving his tears traced down his face in black, "the elders took all the tenders and biddies in the district and made them watch. My wife screamed just the way they told her. She screamed, and the elders preached and wailed how the wages of sex was death. She screamed, and they made childbirth as painful as they could. She screamed, and the baby died. Our child. She screamed and then she died."

The first two victims of the Deliverance.

It was that night Adam walked out of the Creedish church district and made his phone call.

"The elders made you watch every time anyone in the church district had a child," Adam says.

We're only going twenty or thirty miles an hour, but somewhere lost in the smoke just ahead is the giant concrete pylon of the church memorial.

I can't say anything, but I just keep breathing.

"So of course you'd never want sex. You'd never want sex because every time our mother had another child," Adam says, "they made you sit there and watch. Because sex to you is just pain and sin and your mother stretched out there screaming."

And then he's said it.

The smoke is so thick I can't even see Adam.

He says, "By now, sex must look like nothing but torture to you."

He just spits it out that way.

Truth, The Fragrance.

And at that instant the smoke clears.

And we crash head-on into the concrete wall.

8

In the beginning there's nothing but dust. A fine white talcum powder hangs in the car, mixed with smoke.

The dust and smoke swirl in the air.

The only sound is the car engine dripping something, oil, antifreeze, gasoline.

Until Adam starts screaming.

The dust is from the air bags protecting us at our moment of impact. The air bags are collapsed slack and empty back onto the dashboard now, and as the dust settles, Adam is screaming and clutching his face. The blood coming from between his fingers is black against the talcum white coating everything else. His one hand clutching his face, his other hand yanks the passenger door open and he stumbles out into the waste-land.

Then he's lost in the smoke around us, stumbling over naked bodies, layers of people caught fornicating forever, and I'm yelling after him.

I'm yelling his name.

What direction he's in I can't tell.

I yell his name.

Everywhere I step, the magazines offer Horny Dreamgirls.

Big Dick Lovers.

Lips, Tits, and Monster Clits.

The sobbing comes from all around me.

I yell, Adam Branson.

And all I see is All-Male Anal Adventures.

And Girls Who Love Girls.

And Bisexual Sex Parties.

And behind me, our crashed car explodes.

The concrete pylon, gray and towering over us, is all flames on one side, and in the light of its bonfire I see Adam, kneeling a few yards away, his hands clasped over his face, rocking forward and backward and sobbing.

His blood runs down from his hands, down his face, down the powdered white front of him, and when I go to pull his hands away, he screams, "Don't!"

Adam screams, "This is my punishment!"

His screams break into laughter, and Adam opens his hands to show me.

The tiny plastic feet of the Tender Branson dashboard statuette are sticking out of the mess of blood where his left eye used to be.

Adams half laughs, half screams, "This is my punishment!"

The rest of the statue is embedded, I don't know how far.

The trick, I say, is not to panic.

The way to handle this is we need a doctor.

The black smoke from our burning car rolls over us. Without a car, the twenty thousand acres around us are empty and vast.

Adam collapses to his side, then rolls onto his back, looking up at the sky, blind in his one eye from the statue and in his other eye from the blood. Adam says, "You can't leave me here."

I say I'm not going anywhere.

Adam says, "You can't let them arrest me for mass murder."

I say I'm not the one who delivered anybody to Heaven.

Breathing heavy and fast, Adam says, "You have to deliver me."

I'll go get help.

"You have to deliver me!"

I'll get him a doctor, I say. I'll get him a good lawyer. We'll plead insanity. He was trained in the church just as much as I was. He was only doing what he'd been trained his whole life to do.

"Do you know," Adam says and swallows, "do you know what happens to men in prison? You know what happens. Don't let that happen to me."

A magazine nearby says, Backdoor Gang Bang.

I'm not going to deliver him to Heaven.

"Then destroy how I look," Adam says. "Make me so monstrous no one will ever want me."

A magazine says, Anal Fixation.

And I ask, How?

"Find a rock," Adam says. "Under all this trash, find something solid. A rock. Dig."

Still on his back, with both his hands Adam is pulling at the plastic feet of the statuette, his breath catching as he twists and pulls.

With both my hands, I dig. Through people locked together crotch to crotch, face to face, crotch to face, crotch to ass, and ass to face, I dig a pit.

I've dug a hole as large as a grave before I hit soil, the Creedish churchyard, hallowed ground, and I lift out a rock the size of my fist.

In one hand, Adam holds the statuette smeared with blood, more of a devil now than ever.

With his other hand, Adam grabs at the ground beside him and drags an open magazine across his mutilated face. The magazine shows a man and woman copulating, and from under it Adam says, "When you find a rock. Bring it down on my face when I tell you."

I can't.

"I won't let you kill me," Adam says.

I don't trust him.

"You'll be giving me a better life. It's in your power," Adam says from under the magazine. "If you want to save my life, do this for me first."

Adam says, "If you don't, the minute you go for help, I'll crawl away and hide, and I'll die out here."

I weigh the rock in my hand.

I ask, will he tell me when to stop?

"I'll tell you when I've had enough."

Does he promise?

"I promise."

I lift the rock so its shadow falls across the people having sex on Adam's face.

And I bring it down.

The rock sinks in so far.

"Again!" Adam says. "Harder."

And I bring the rock down.

And the rock sinks in farther.

"Again!"

And I bring it down.

"Again!"

And I bring the rock down.

Blood soaks up through the pages, up to turn the fucking couple red and then purple.

"Again!" Adam says, his words distorted, his mouth and nose not the same shape anymore.

And I bring the rock down on the couple's arms and their legs and their faces.

"Again."

And I bring the rock down until the rock is sticky red with blood, until the magazine is collapsed in the center. Until my hands are sticky red.

Then I stop.

I ask, Adam?

I go to lift the magazine, but it tears. It's so sodden.

Adam's hand holding the statuette goes slack and the bloody statuette rolls into the grave I dug to find something solid.

I ask, Adam?

The wind carries smoke over us both.

A huge shadow is spreading toward us from the base of the pylon. One minute it's just touching Adam. The next minute, the shadow has him covered.

Ladies and gentlemen, here on Flight 2039, our third engine has just flamed out.

We have just one engine left before we begin our terminal descent.

7

The cold shadow of the Creedish church monument falls over me all morning as I bury Adam Branson. Under the layers of obscenity, under the Hungry Butt Holes, under the Ravishing She-Males, I dig with my hands into the churchyard dirt. Bigger stones carved with willows and skulls are buried all around me. The epitaphs on them are about what you'd imagine.

Gone but Not Forgotten.

In Heaven with their mistakes may they dwell.

Beloved Father.

Cherished Mother.

Confused Family.

May whatever God they find grant them forgiveness and peace.

Ineffectual Caseworker.

Obnoxious Agent.

Misguided Brother.

Maybe it's the Botox botulinum toxin injected into me or the drug interactions or the lack of sleep or the long-term effects of Attention Withdrawal Syndrome, but I don't feel a thing. The insides of my mouth taste bitter. I press my lymph nodes in my neck, but I only feel contempt.

Maybe after everybody dying around me, I've just developed a skill for losing people. A natural talent. A blessing.

The same as Fertility's being barren is the perfect job skill for her being a surrogate mother, maybe I've developed a useful lack of feeling.

The same way you might look at your leg cut off at the knee and not feel anything at first, maybe this is just shock.

But I hope not.

I don't want it to wear off.

I pray not to feel anything ever again.

Because if it wears off, this is all going to hurt so much. This is going to hurt for the rest of my life.

You won't learn this in any charm school, but to keep dogs from digging up something you've buried, sprinkle the grave with ammonia. To keep away ants, sprinkle borax.

For roaches, use alum.

Peppermint oil will keep away rats.

To bleach away bloodstains from under your fingernails, sink your fingertips into half a lemon and wiggle them around. Rinse them under warm water.

The wreck of the car is burned down to just the seats smoldering. Just this ribbon of black smoke flutters out across the valley.

When I go to lift Adam's body, the gun falls out of his jacket pocket. The only sound comes from a few flies buzzing around the rock still clutched with a print of my hand in blood.

What's left of Adam's face is still wrapped in the sticky red magazine, and as I lower first his feet and then his shoulders into the hole I've dug, a yellow taxi is bumping and crawling toward me from the horizon.

The hole is only big enough for Adam to fit curled on his side, and kneeling on the brim, I start pushing in the dirt.

When the clean dirt runs out, I push in faded pornography, obscene books with their spines broken, Traci Lords and John Holmes, Kayla Kleevage and Dick Rambone, vibrators with dead batteries, dog-eared playing cards, expired condoms, brittle and fragile but never used.

I know the feeling.

Condoms ribbed for extrasensitivity.

The last thing I need is sensitivity.

Here are condoms lined with a topical anesthetic for prolonged action. What a paradox. You don't feel a thing, but you can fuck for hours.

This seems to really miss the point.

I want my whole life lined with a topical anesthetic.

The yellow taxi humps across the potholes, getting closer. One person is driving. One person is in the backseat.

Who this is, I don't know, but I can imagine.

I pick up the gun and try to wedge it into my jacket pocket. The barrel tears the pocket lining, and then the whole thing is hidden. If there are bullets inside, I don't know.

The taxi rushes to a stop about shouting distance away.

Fertility gets out and waves. She leans down by the driver's window and the breeze carries her words to me, "Wait, please. This is going to take a minute."

Then she comes over with her arms raised out at her sides for balance and her face looking down at every step across the sliding, glossy layers of used magazines. Orgy Boys. Cum Cravers.

"I thought you could use some company about now," she calls over to me.

I look around for a tissue or a crotchless underwear to wipe the blood off my hands.

Looking up, Fertility says, "Wow, the way the shadow of that Creedish death monument thing is falling across Adam's grave is so symbolic."

The three hours I've been burying Adam is the longest I've ever been out of a job. Now Fertility Hollis is here to tell me what to do. My new job is following her.

Fertility turns to gaze around the horizon and says, "This is *so* totally The Valley of the Shadow of Death here." She says, "You sure picked the right place to smash in your brother's skull. It's so totally Cain and Abel I can't stand it."

I killed my brother.

I killed her brother.

Adam Branson.

Trevor Hollis.

You can't trust me around anybody's brother with a telephone or a rock.

Fertility puts a hand in her shoulder bag and says, "You want some Red Ropes licorice?"

I hold out my hands covered with dried blood.

She says, "I guess not."

She looks back over her shoulder at the taxi, idling, and she waves. An arm comes out the driver's window and waves back.

To me she says, "Let me put this in a nutshell. Adam and Trevor both pretty much killed themselves."

She tells me, Trevor killed himself because his life had no more surprises, no more adventure. He was terminally ill. He was dying of boredom. The only mystery left was death.

Adam wanted to die because he knew the way he'd been trained, he could never be anything but a Creedish. Adam killed off the surviving Creedish because he knew that an old culture of slaves couldn't found a new culture of free men. Like Moses leading the tribes of Israel around in the desert for a generation, Adam wanted me to survive, but not my slave mind-set.

Fertility says, "You didn't kill my brother."

Fertility says, "And you didn't kill your brother, either. What you did was more like what they call assisted suicide."

Out of her shoulder bag, she takes some flowers, real flowers, a little bunch of fresh roses and carnations. Red roses and white carnations all tied together. "Check it out," she says and crouches down to put them on the magazines where Adam is buried.

"Here's another big symbol," she says, still crouched and looking up at me. "These flowers will be rotten in a couple hours. Birds will crap on them. The smoke here will make them stink, and tomorrow a bulldozer will probably run over them, but for right now they are so beautiful."

She's such a thoughtful and endearing character.

"Yeah," she says, "I know."

Fertility gets to her feet and grabs me on a clean part of my arm, a part not crusted with dried blood, and she starts walking me toward the cab.

"We can be jaded and heartless later, when it's not costing me so much money," she says.

On our way back to the taxi, she says the whole nation is in an uproar over how I wrecked the Super Bowl. No way can we take a plane or bus anywhere. The newspapers are calling me the Antichrist. The Creedish mass murderer. The value of Tender Branson merchandise is through the roof, but for all the wrong reasons. All the world's major religions, the Catholics and Jews and Baptists and whatall, are saying, We told you so.

Before we get to the taxi, I hide my bloody hands in my pockets. The gun sticks to my trigger finger.

Fertility opens a back door of the taxi and gets me inside. Then she goes around and gets in the other side.

She smiles at the driver in the rearview mirror and says, "Back to Grand Island, I guess."

The taxi meter says seven hundred eighty dollars.

The driver looks at me in the rearview mirror and says, "Your mama throw out your favorite jerk-off magazine?" He says, "This place goes on forever. If you lose something, no way are you going to find it here."

Fertility whispers, "Don't let him get to you."

The driver is a chronic drunk, she whispers. She plans to pay with her charge card because he'll be dead two days from now in an accident. He'll never get the chance to send in the charge.

As the sun comes up to noon, the shadow of the concrete pylon is getting smaller by the minute.

I ask, How is my fish doing?

"Oh, geez," she says. "Your fish."

The taxi is bumping and rolling back toward the outside world.

Nothing should hurt by now, but I don't want to hear this.

"Your fish, I'm really sorry," Fertility says. "It just died."

Fish number six hundred and forty-one.

I ask, Did it feel any pain?

Fertility says, "I don't think so."

I ask, Did you forget to feed it?

"No."

I ask, Then what happened?

Fertility says, "I don't know. One day it was just dead."

There was no reason.

It didn't mean anything.

This wasn't any big political gesture.

It just died.

It was just a damn fucking fish is all but it's everything I had.

Beloved fish.

And after everything that's happened, this should be easy to hear.

Cherished fish.

But sitting there in the back of the cab, the gun in my hand, my hands in my pockets, I start to cry.

6

In Grand Island, we had a little son crippled with lupus so we could stay a couple days in the Ronald McDonald House there.

After that, we caught a ride in half a Parkwood Mansion headed west. This was nothing but four bedrooms, and we slept apart with two of them empty between us.

In Denver, we had a little girl with polio so we could stay at another Ronald McDonald House and eat and not feel the world going by underneath us while we slept at night. In Ronald McDonald's House, we had to share a room, but it would have two beds.

Out of Denver, we caught a Topsail Estate Manor headed for Cheyenne. We were just drifting. This wasn't costing us any money.

We caught half a Sutton Place Townhome headed for we didn't know where, and we ended up in Billings, Montana.

We started playing house roulette.

We didn't wander into the truck stop diners to ask around about which house was headed where. Fertility and me, we just cut our way inside and sealed the way shut behind us.

We rode three days and nights sealed in half a Flamingo Lodge and only woke up when they were setting it on a foundation in Hamilton, Montana. We stepped out the back door just as the happy family who bought it was coming in the front.

All we had with us was Fertility's tote bag and Adam's gun.

We were lost in the desert.

Out of Missoula, Montana, we caught one-third of a Craftsman Manor going west on Interstate 90.

A sign went by saying, Spokane 300 miles.

Past Spokane, a sign went by saying, Seattle 200 miles.

In Seattle, we had a little boy with a hole in his heart.

In Tacoma, we had a little girl with no feeling in her arms and legs.

We told people the doctors didn't know what was wrong.

People told us to expect a miracle.

People with their real kids dead or dying of cancer told us God was good and kind.

We lived together as if we were married, but we almost never talked.

Headed south on Interstate 5 through Portland, Oregon, we rode inside half a Holly Hills Estate.

Before we feel ready, we're home home, back in the city where we met, standing on a curb. Our last house is just pulling away and we let it.

I still haven't told Fertility that Adam's last wish was she and I would have sex together.

As if she doesn't already know.

She knows. All those night I was passed out, it was all Adam talked to Fertility about. She and I have to have sex. To set me free and give me power. To prove to Fertility that sex could be more than just a wealthy middle-aged marketing consultant squirting his DNA into her.

But now there isn't any place either of us live here, not anymore. Her apartment and my apartment have both been rented out to other people, Fertility knows that.

"I have a place we can stay tonight," she says, "but I have to call ahead."

In the pay phone booth is one of my stickers from a million years before.

Give Yourself, Your Life, Just One More Chance. Call Me for Help. Then my old phone number.

I call, and a recording tells me my number has been disconnected.

Right back at the recording, I say, No kidding.

Fertility calls the place she thinks we can crash. Into the phone she says, "My name is Fertility Hollis, and I was referred to you by Dr. Webster Ambrose."

It's her evil job.

It's the agent's closed loop of history. Fertility's being omniscient is looking pretty easy. Nothing new ever does happen.

"Yes, I have the address," she says. "I'm sorry about the short notice, but this is my first opening I've had. No," she says, "this is not tax-deductible. No," she says, "this is for all night, but there's a separate charge for each attempt. No," she says, "there's no cash discount."

She says, "We can work out the details in person."

Into the phone she says, "No, you don't have to tip me."

She snaps her fingers at me and mouths the word "pen." Then on the sticker for my crisis hotline she writes an address, repeating the number and street into the phone.

"Fine," she says. "Seven o'clock then. Goodbye."

In the sky overhead, it's the same sun watching us make the same mistakes over and over. It's the same blue sky after everything we've been through. Nothing new. No surprises here.

The place she's taking me is the house I used to clean. The couple she's breeding for tonight are my speakerphone employers.

5

The trip to Fertility's bed is lined with streaked windows and peeling paint. Mildewed tile and rust stains. Everywhere along the way are clogged drains and scuff marks. Sagging curtains and snagged upholstery. All the stations of the cross.

This is after the man and woman I worked for were upstairs with Fertility doing God knows what.

This is after I've crawled in through the basement window Fertility knew would be unlocked. This is after I hid out among the fake flowers in the backyard, each of them stolen from a grave, and after Fertility rang the doorbell at seven sharp.

Dust coats everything in the kitchen. China coated with microwave leftovers fills the sink. The inside of the microwave is crusted with exploded food.

Bred and trained and sold little slave that I am, I go right to work cleaning. Just ask me how to get baked crud out of a microwave.

No, really, go ahead.

Ask me.

The secret is boiling a cup of water in the microwave for a few minutes. This loosens the crud so you can wipe it off.

Ask me how to get bloodstains off your hands.

The trick is to forget how fast these things can happen. Suicides. Accidents. Crimes of passion.

Fertility upstairs doing her job.

Just concentrate on the stain until your memory is completely erased. Practice really does make perfect. If you could call it that.

Ignore how it feels when the only real talent you have is for hiding the truth. You have a God-given knack for committing a terrible sin. You have a natural gift for denial. A blessing.

If you could call it that.

All evening I clean, and still I feel dirty.

Fertility told me the procedure would be over before midnight. They'd leave her in the green bedroom with her feet propped up on pillows. After the couple were asleep in their own room it would be safe for me to sneak upstairs.

The microwave clock says eleven-thirty.

I take my chances, and the trip to Fertility's bed is lined with wilted houseplants and tarnished doorknobs, fly specks and fingerprint smudges of newspaper ink. Drink rings and cigarette burns mar all the furniture. Cobwebs drift in every corner.

It's dark inside the green bedroom and out of the shadows Fertility says, "Shouldn't we be having sex now."

I say, I guess.

She says, "I hope you don't mind sloppy seconds."

I don't. I mean, it's what Adam would've wanted.

She says, "Do you have any rubbers?"

I say, I thought she was barren.

"Sure, I'm sterile," she says, "but I've had unprotected sex with a million guys. I could have some terrible fatal disease."

I say that would only be a problem if I wanted to live a lot longer.

Fertility says, "That's how I feel about my giant credit card debt."

So we have sex.

If you could call it that.

After waiting all my life, I get myself in her just half an inch and it's all over.

"Well," Fertility says, and pushes me away, "I hope that was really empowering for you."

She doesn't give me a second shot at making love.

If you could call it that.

A long time after she falls asleep, I watch her and wonder about her dreaming, if she's dreaming up some terrible new murder or suicide or disaster. And if she's dreaming it about me.

4

The next morning, Fertility is whispering on the telephone to someone. I wake up, and she's dressed and
out of bed asking, "Do you have an eight a.m. flight to
Sydney?"

She's saying, "One-way, please. A window seat if you
have it. Do you take Visa?"

By the time she notices me watching her, she's hung up
and putting on her shoes. She starts to put her daily planner into her tote bag but puts it back down on the dresser.

I ask, where is she going?

"Sydney."

But why?

"No reason."

I say, Tell me.

By now she's started lugging the tote bag toward the bedroom door. "Because I got my surprise," she says. "I got the damn surprise I wanted, and damn it, I don't want it. I don't want this!"

What?

"I'm pregnant."

But how does she know?

"I know everything!" she screams at me. "Well, I knew everything. I didn't know this. I didn't know I was going to have to bring a child into this miserable, boring, terrible world. A child who would inherit my gift for seeing the future and living a life of crushing ennui. A child who would never be surprised. I didn't see this coming."

So now what?

"So I'm going to Sydney, Australia."

But why?

"My mother killed herself. My brother killed himself. You figure it out."

But why Australia?

She's out the bedroom door now and dragging her tote toward the top of the stairs. I'd follow her, but I'm naked.

"Think of this," she yells back at me, "as a very radical abortion procedure."

A man steps out of the master-bedroom doorway dressed in a blue suit I've pressed a thousand times. In a voice I've heard on a thousand speakerphone calls, he asks me, "Are you Dr. Ambrose?"

By the time I've jumped into my clothes, Fertility is down the stairs and out the front door. Through the bedroom window, I watch her cross the lawn to a taxi.

Back out in the hallway, a woman wearing a silk blouse I've hand-washed a thousand times steps up to the man in the blue suit. The two of them frozen in the doorway of the master bedroom, the woman I used to work for shouts, "That's him! Remember? He used to work for us! That's the Antichrist!"

I tuck Fertility's daily planner under my arm and make a run for it. Still running, out the front door, down the street toward the bus stop, it takes me another minute to find today's date in the book, and there's the answer.

At 1:25 this afternoon, Flight 2039, nonstop from here to Sydney, will be hijacked by a maniac and crash somewhere in the Australian outback.

Ladies and gentlemen, as the last person aboard Flight 2039, out here above the huge Australian outback, it's my duty to inform you that our last engine has just flamed out.

Please fasten your seat belts as we begin our terminal descent into oblivion.

3

The airport is full of FBI agents looking for Tender Branson, Mass Murderer. Tender Branson, False Prophet. Tender Branson, Super Bowl Despoiler. Tender Branson, who abandoned his lovely bride at the altar.

Tender Branson, Antichrist.

I catch up with Fertility at the airline ticket counter.

She's saying, "One, please. I have a reservation."

The black dye we used was weeks ago, and my blond roots are showing. The greasy road-trip food has me fat again. It's just a matter of the right armed security guard looking at me and pointing his gun.

My jacket pocket is empty when I check. Adam's gun is gone.

"If you're looking for your brother's gun, I've got it," Fertility ducks her head and tells me. "This plane is going to be hijacked even if I have to do it myself."

No bullets, I say. She knows that.

"Yes, there are," she says. "I was lying to you so you wouldn't worry."

So Adam could've shot me dead at any time.

Out of her tote bag, Fertility hefts a shining brass urn. To the ticket agent, Fertility says, "I'll be taking my brother's cremains in the flight. Will that be a problem?"

The ticket agent says, no, it's no problem. The urn can't be x-rayed at security, but they'll let her take it on board.

Fertility pays for the tickets and we start toward the gates. She hands me the tote bag and says, "I've been schlepping this for the last half hour. Make yourself useful."

Security is too worried about the urn to give me a second look. It's metal, and nobody wants to open it, much less put a hand inside.

Here and there along the way, the security people all seem to be in pairs, looking at us and talking into walkie-talkies. The urn rubs against my leg through the tote bag. Fertility looks at her ticket and at the signs for each gate we pass.

"Here," she says when we get to the gate. "Give me my bag and scoot out of here." Around us are people getting in line as the airline makes the first boarding call.

People holding tickets for rows fifty through seventy-five, please board now.

Which one of these people is a crazed terrorist hijacker, I don't know.

Down the concourse behind us, the pairs of security guards have come together into foursomes and sixsomes.

"Give me the bag," Fertility says. She grabs the handle next to my hand and tugs hard.

Her taking Trevor with her doesn't make any sense.

"I need my bag."

People holding tickets for rows thirty through forty-nine, please board now.

The security guards are moving in, trotting down the concourse, coming our way with every holster unsnapped, every gun with a hand on it.

And it hits me. Where Adam's gun is.

It's in the urn, I say, and try twisting the tote bag away from Fertility.

People holding tickets for rows ten through twenty-nine, please board now.

One handle of the tote bag breaks and the urn clunks to the carpeted floor with Fertility and me chasing it.

Fertility plans to hijack the plane.

"Someone has to," she's saying. "It's fate."

The urn's in both our hands.

People holding tickets for rows one through nine, please board now.

I say, Nobody has to die here.

This is the final boarding call for Flight 2039.

"That plane has to crash into Australia," Fertility says. "I'm never wrong."

A security guard shouts, "Freeze."

We repeat, this is the last boarding call for Flight 2039 to Sydney.

Security has us surrounded when the urn comes open. The mortal remains of Trevor Hollis going everywhere. Ashes to ashes. Into everybody's eyes. Dust to dust. Into their lungs. Trevor's ashes spread in a cloud around us. Adam's gun thuds on the carpet.

Before Fertility, before the security team, before the plane can leave the jetway, I grab the gun. I grab Fertility. Okay, okay, okay, okay, we'll do this her way, I say with the gun against her head.

I walk us backward toward the gate.

I yell, Nobody make a move.

I stop to let the ticket agent tear her ticket, then I nod toward the open urn and the mess of Trevor all over the carpet.

Could somebody maybe scoop that stuff up and hand it to this woman here, I say. It's her brother.

The security team is all crouched with their guns aimed at my forehead while a ticket agent gets most of Trevor back into the urn and hands it to Fertility.

"Thanks," Fertility says. "This is so embarrassing."

We're getting on this plane, I say, and we're taking off.

I walk us backward down the jetway, wondering who on board will be the real crazed hijacker.

When I ask Fertility, she laughs.

When I ask why, she says, "This is just too ironic. You'll guess soon enough who the hijacker is."

I say, Tell me.

People on the plane are all crowded into the back half of the plane, cowering with their heads down. Sobbing. In the aisle near the cockpit is a pile of everybody's wallets and watches and personal laptop computers, cellular phones, minicassette recorders, personal compact disc stereos, and wedding rings.

People are really trained.

As if this has anything to with them.

As if this has anything to do with money.

I tell the flight crew to secure the cabin doors. It's not as if I haven't been on a lot of planes going stadium to stadium. I say, Prepare the cabin for takeoff.

In the seats closest to us are a fat Pakistani-looking business-suit guy. A couple white college-looking guys. A Chinese-looking guy.

I ask Fertility, Which one? Who's the real hijacker?

She's kneeling next to the pile of offerings and picks through it, pocketing a nice woman's watch and a pearl necklace. "Figure it out yourself, Sherlock," she says.

She says, "I'm just an innocent hostage here," and she snaps a diamond tennis bracelet around her wrist.

I shout, Everybody, you should please stay calm, but you need to know that a dangerous killer terrorist is on board this flight and plans to crash it.

Somebody screams.

I say, Shut up. Please.

I tell everybody, Until I find out who's the terrorist, everybody just stay down.

Fertility takes a diamond solitaire out of the offerings and slips it on her finger.

I say, One of you is a hijacker. I don't know which one, but someone here is planning to crash this plane.

Fertility just keeps giggling.

There's the terrible feeling I'm missing some huge joke.

I say, Everybody just stay relaxed.

I tell the steward to go up front and talk to the captain. I don't want to hurt anybody, but I really need to get out of this country. We need to take off and then land somewhere safe, someplace between here and Australia. Then everybody is going to disembark.

To Fertility laughing next to me, I say even she's getting off.

We're going to complete this trip, I say, but just me and a single pilot. And as soon as we're airborne the second time, I say, I'll let that pilot parachute.

I ask, Is that clear?

And the steward with the gun pointed in his face says, Yes.

This plane is going to crash in Australia, I say, and only one person is going to die.

And it starts to dawn on me.

Maybe there is no other real hijacker.

Maybe I'm the hijacker.

Around us, people have started to whisper. They've recognized me. I'm the mass murderer on television. I'm the Antichrist.

I'm the hijacker.

And I start to laugh.

I ask Fertility, You set me up, didn't you?

And still laughing she says, "A little."

And still laughing I ask if she's really pregnant.

And still laughing she says, " 'Fraid so, but for honest I didn't see it coming. It's still a bona fide miracle."

The cabin doors whump shut, and the plane starts creeping backward from the terminal.

"Here," she says. "All your life, you've needed other people to tell you what to do, your family, your church, your bosses, your case-worker, the agent, your brother . . ."

She says, "Well, nobody can help you with this situation."

She says, "All I know is that you will find a way out of this mess. You'll find a way to leave your whole screwed-up life story behind. You'll be dead to the whole world."

The jet engines start their whine, and Fertility hands me a man's gold wedding band.

"And after you can tell your life story and walk away from it," Fertility says, "after that we'll start a new life together and live hap-pily ever after."

2

S omewhere en route to Port Vila in the New Hebrides, for my last meal I serve dinner the way I've always dreamed.

Anybody caught buttering their bread before breaking it, I promise to shoot them.

Anybody who drinks their beverage with food still in their mouth will also be shot.

Anybody caught spooning toward themselves will be shot.

Anybody caught without a napkin in their lap—

Anybody caught using their fingers to move their food—

Anybody who begins eating before everybody is served—

Anybody who blows on food to cool it—

Anybody who talks with food in their mouth—

Anybody who drinks white wine holding their glass by the bowl or drinks red wine holding their glass by the stem—

You will each of you get a bullet in the head.

We are 30,000 feet above the earth, going 455 miles per hour. We're at a pinnacle of human achievement, and we are going to eat this meal as civilized human beings.

1

And so here is my confession.

Testing, testing, one, two, three.

And according to Fertility, if I could only figure out how I could escape. I could escape being up here. I could escape the crash. I could escape being Tender Branson. I could escape the police. I could escape my past, my whole twisted, burning, miserable, snarled story of my life so far.

Fertility said, the trick was to just tell people the story of how I got to this point, and I'd figure a way out.

If I could just walk away and leave my old life story behind.

If I survived, she said, we could work on having better sex.

We could work on making a new life together.

We could take dance lessons.

She said to tell my life story right up to the moment the plane hit the ground. Then the world would think I was dead. She said to start from the end.

Testing, testing. One, two, three.

Testing, testing. One, two, three.

Maybe this is working. I don't know. If you can even hear me, I don't know.

But if you can hear me, listen. And if you're listening, then what you've found is the story of everything that went wrong. This is what you'd call the flight recorder of Flight 2039. The black box, people call it, even though it's orange, and on the inside is a loop of wire that's the permanent record of all that's left. What you've found is the story of what happened.

And go ahead.

You can heat this wire to white-hot, and it will still tell you the exact same story.

Testing, testing, one, two, three.

And if you're listening, you should know the passengers were put off the plane in Port Vila, in the Republic of Vanuatu, in exchange for a half-dozen parachutes and more tiny bottles of gin.

And after we were back in the air and headed for Australia, then the pilot parachuted to his freedom.

I'm going to keep saying it, but it's true. I'm not a murderer.

And I'm alone up here.

All four engines have flamed out, and I'm into my controlled descent, my nosedive into the ground. This is the *terminal phase* of my descent, where I'm going thirty-two feet per second straight at Australia, my *terminal velocity*.

Testing, testing, one, two, three.

One more time, you're listening to the flight recorder of Flight 2039.

And at this altitude, listen, and at this speed, with the plane empty, this is my story. And my story won't get bashed into a zillion bloody shreds and then burned with a thousand tons of burning jet. And after the plane wrecks, people will hunt down the flight recorder. And my story will survive.

And I will live on, forever.

And if I could figure out what Fertility meant, I could save myself, but I can't. I'm stupid.

Testing, testing, one, two, three.

So here is my confession.

Here is my prayer.

My story. My incantation.

Hear me. See me. Remember me.

Beloved Fuck-up.

Botched Messiah.

Would-be Lover. Delivered to God.

I'm trapped here, in a nosedive, in my life, in the cockpit of a jetliner with the flat yellow of the Australian outback coming up fast.

And there's so many things I want to change but can't.

It's all done. It's all just a story now.

Here's the life and death of Tender Branson, and I can just walk away from it.

And the sky is blue and righteous in every direction.

The sun is total and burning and just right there, and today is a beautiful day.

Testing, testing, one, two—

"Few contemporary writers mix the outrageous and the hilarious with greater zest." —Newsday

CHOKE

Victor Mancini, a dropout from medical school, has a problem. He needs to pay for elder care for his mother, who is suffering from Alzheimer's. His solution is an ingenious scam: he pretends to choke on pieces of food in upscale restaurants, allowing himself to be "saved" by fellow diners who, feeling responsible for Victor's life, go on to send checks to support him. After pulling this ruse in hundreds of restaurants, he develops a solid base of benefactors.

Actually, Victor has a number of problems. He cruises sexual addiction recovery workshops for action and spends his days working at Colonial Dunsboro, where his stoner colleagues are put in the stocks for any behavior, such as cursing or smoking, that doesn't fit the colonial theme. And he is desperate to find out the truth of his paternity, which his mother, in her addled state, suggests may be divine. An antihero for our deranged times, Victor finds that his whole existence is a struggle to wrest an identity from overwhelming forces. His creator, Chuck Palahniuk, is the visionary we need and the satirist we deserve.

Fiction/0-385-72092-0